1

What is the meaning of it, Watson?" said Holmes, solemnly, as he laid down the paper. "What object is served by this circle of misery and violence and fear? It must tend to some end, or else our universe is ruled by chance, which is unthinkable. But what end? There is the great standing perennial problem to which human reason is as far from an answer as ever."

From the Adventure of the Cardboard Box

"There is nothing in which deduction is as necessary as in religion," said he, leaning with his back against the shutters. "It can be built up as an exact science by the reasoner. Our highest assurance of the goodness of providence seems to me to rest in the flowers. All other things, our powers, our desires, our food, are really necessary for our existence in the first instance. But this rose is an extra. Its smell and its color are an embellishment of life, not a condition of it. It is only goodness which gives such extras, and so I say again that we have much to hope from the flowers."

From The Adventure of the Naval Treaty

"The greatest schemer of all time, the organizer of every deviltry, the controlling brain of the underworld, a brain which might have made or marred the destiny of nations – that's the man!"

"Barker beat his head with his clenched fist in his impotent anger. 'Do not tell me that we have to sit down under this? Do you say that no one can ever get level with this king devil?' 'No, I don't say that,' said Holmes, and his eyes seemed to be looking far into the future. 'I don't say that he can't be beat. But you must give me time – you must give me time.' We all sat in silence for some minutes while those fateful eyes still strained to pierce the veil."

From The Valley of Fear

The Confessions
of
Sherlock Holmes

The Theological Odyssey of the Great Detective

By

Thomas Mengert, Esq.

Volume 1

The Wager at Reichenbach Falls

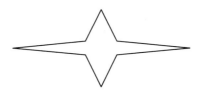

Preface

It has seemed to me that a few words of preface should precede all else, particularly since the following book will perhaps first be brought forward in an e-book format for a general audience. My initial intention was to bring the book forward in a limited edition to be sold directly by the author to the purchaser after an appropriate lecture by way of introduction to prepare the reader for the unique demands of its content and length (over 800,000 words and some 2,000 pages) to explain my intentions in writing the book at all. The function of the present brief preface is to turn aside those readers who may imagine that a novel featuring Sherlock Holmes must of necessity be merely a tale of amusement and diversion rather than one probing into the very depths of the character of the man himself and the deeper mysteries of life. These readers may be distressed and disappointed if they expect only a vapid adventure tale and may attribute failure to the author, expecting him to have undertaken what he never undertook to do at all, simply to amuse and not challenge the reader.

The ideal reader of the following volume will be one who is willing to enter upon an intellectual adventure of no mean magnitude and to suspend his disbelief to the degree that he will find the Sherlock Holmes contained herein to be deeper in character and more worthy of esteem than any accolades ever afforded to him by Dr. John H. Watson might justify and to find herein a solution to many mysteries left unresolved in the original canonical tales. Since the present work exceeds the length of the entire corpus of the original tales, its existence may be very good news indeed to that ideal reader who wishes to hear more of Sherlock Holmes and Dr. Watson.

I shall here revive an old 19th century custom by greeting you dear reader. I trust that you will find a great intellectual adventure in reading the text that lies before you. It is no easy matter for an author to entrust his creation, formerly visited only by the mind which conceived it, to those he hopes will prove to be an indulgent public. A few introductory words before you begin seem in order. You are about to read a mystery that returns to the origin of all mysteries in the Mystery Plays of England which attempted to explain the mysteries of the Christian religion by combining theology with popular entertainment and spectacle. The following story is told in two different fonts with two different narrators: Sherlock Holmes and Doctor Watson. There are no chapter divisions. Instead there is a prologue, epilogue, and sixteen books. The span of time covered is from 1891 – 1899 with some short selections from 1914 through 1917 when both narratives were assembled by Doctor Watson. Together the two manuscripts constitute what may be called a discursive or picaresque narrative where ideas may be fully explored and examined. This type of book was quite common in the Victorian era but is less so today though the need for such books is perhaps greater than ever before. I have long been concerned that with the decline of leisure, which is after all the basis of all that is most civilized within us, that we have forfeited as well the craft of the baroque prose of the 17th and succeeding centuries until the dawn of the contemporary literary scene. Even as late as the Victorian Age in England, some last vestiges of this sophistication and balance remained in the writings of men like Matthew Arnold and novelists such as Thackeray, Dickens, and Henry James. The work that you hold in your hand will I hope recall a vanished era, a more graceful period in the history of our common literature. Having made this brief apology for its ornate style I must move ahead to consider the extraordinary length of the complete book. Had this book been published in the 19th century, it would have been published in multiple volumes as was common for many of the books written by Charles Dickens and his friend Wilkie Collins, the originator of the modern detective story. I have often lamented the passing of that more discursive era when there was time and leisure to enter another world when reading a novel and to count on dwelling there for some time. I hope to have re-created something of that experience for the modern reader by writing this book in the fashion of an era, which I trust is not forever lost to us, when ideas might be fully explored to their furthest limits.

Any introduction should serve the purpose of explaining to the prospective reader the intentions of the author. It allows the author the liberty of an advance apologia, to deflect from the beginning any criticism for failing to achieve what was in fact never intended. Since the novel of ideas has become a rarity and since a didactic format has

8

become unfashionable, I have thought it best to admit quite frankly that this novel is meant to take its inspiration from models whose several excellences have inspired my own effort. That a novel may include elements of the essay and extensively explore ideas is common in the Russian novels of Tolstoy and Dostoyevsky. The French also allow for the scope necessary to explore ideas in the works of Victor Hugo. English Literature is also not without models to inspire an endeavor such as the one that lies before you in this work. The primary genre or rather mix of genres, since I have taken instruction from several sources, includes the picaresque novels of Tobias Smollett, the writings of Samuel Johnson particularly Rasselas, and such unique works as Tristram Shandy by Sterne and Vanity Fair by Thackeray. The novel of ideas has been best represented however by the German writers. I have a special affection for two great German contributions to the novel of ideas: Thomas Mann's, The Magic Mountain and Robert Musil's, The Man without Qualities.

To allow form to be flexible enough to allow for such content as I have intended here means to take liberties with the tradition of the novel of detection. Ordinarily the experience of the detective novel is considered to entail light entertainment or to be concentrated around adventure and romance. The appeal of Sherlock Holmes however exceeds both of these, for in the last analysis it is Holmes and Watson themselves who emerge from these narratives of Sir Arthur Conan Doyle as characters of such a unique and complete set of individual traits that the reader comes finally to have an affection for them far beyond perhaps any other protagonists in literature. It is for this reason that the focus of the present book is upon those very characters and the opinions and inner struggles that may have lain latent in the original tales, but that may now be explored in depth. Certain recent copyright issues have resulted in a need to steer clear of any direct use of character traits or circumstances peculiar to the stories gathered together in the last full book of Sherlock Holmes stories to be published. Since my own exploration so exceeds in depth and penetration any mere list of abstract traits of the major characters, I trust that I have not offended in any way nor usurped anything protected under the twilight canopy of the exclusive uses still protected by copyright of the last book, The Casebook of Sherlock Holmes.

The present book is an effort to account for many problems of improbability or inconsistency in the original narratives of Sherlock Holmes. There are many cases that Doctor Watson mentions in his narratives of the great detective which he might have included in the annals of Holmes but never did. I have long thought it time for someone to attempt a grand synthesis using some of the brief and fragmentary hints provided by the established Canon. Although Sherlock Holmes appears occasionally as the narrator of a story we do not possess a sustained narrative in the Master's own hand until now.

Many readers of the Holmes saga may have wondered as much about the haunting character of Holmes himself as they have been curious about his untold cases. To round out the character of the man I thought it time that someone probed those moral obsessions and that hunger for the deepest meanings of life that evidently possessed him. Drawing on hints in the original stories I have therefore pieced out a narrative that I hope will reveal Sherlock Holmes in a deeper light and to solve mysteries that no previous chronicler has attempted to probe.

In writing this book I hoped to explore how Sherlock Holmes might have grappled with that most elusive problem posed by philosophy and by the many religions of the world, viz. how to account for the human condition and to explain the problem of evil. I thought it only appropriate that the greatest detective the world has ever known be given a chance to resolve these matters to the best of his ability and I thought it likely that he would have done so. What better time for him to have made this effort than during his long hiatus from London between the years of 1891 and 1894?

I have no desire to add mystification to mystery. This book presumes a certain knowledge of the original tales just as a symphony by Vaughan Williams depends upon a certain acquaintance with English folk melodies and the chromatic scale. For devotees who have loved Sherlock Holmes for years yet detect a certain mendacity and improbability in some of the endings as hitherto received, this narrative may pose some valuable answers. My desire is with this narrative to create a new unity where chaos and contradiction have reigned. May I not be thought presumptuous to undertake this task and may it serve to bring to rest the shade of the great detective who has no doubt asked why no one has yet followed up the clues so liberally sprinkled through the familiar accounts of Dr. John H. Watson. I hope that these will show how deeply imbedded in the original narratives is my own text, which growing from this fertile soil, will attempt to be true to the spirit and flavor of the original narratives and in addition serve as a substantial addition to the Canonical tales which with hopefully little effort of imagination on the part of my readers might be ascribed to the original characters brought to life by Sir Arthur Conan Doyle. If I appear to take liberties with the genre of the detective story by dwelling at length on matters of philosophy, of history, and of theology, then pray allow me to defend myself here before the bar.

Originally the mystery genre, of which the detective story is only one late example, referred to the religious mystery plays of the middle ages. These plays had a decidedly didactic purpose. Wonders and surprises were meant to widen the horizons of the audience to entertain the possibility of the miraculous and the wonderful. Are not these the very emotions we feel when we see Sherlock Holmes solving seemingly impenetrable puzzles? But more than this, the detective story has as its theme the struggle between good and evil. Nowhere is this dualism clearer than in the struggle between Sherlock Holmes and Professor Moriarity. I have taken the opportunity offered by these two icons of the moral struggle between good and evil to write a book in the ancient tradition of Christian apologetics to probe the nature of good and evil and explore in detail the Christian account for the origin of this struggle. In doing so, I have taken the model of the book of confessions such as that most famous example, The Confessions of St. Augustine, as my model. These confessions are meant to be the reflections of Holmes as recorded in his journal during his long sojourn of several years between 1891 and 1894 and continued in 1896 and 1897. Along with this account of what Sherlock Holmes scholars have termed, "the great hiatus," I have woven a tale told in the traditional manner by Doctor Watson that takes place primarily in the years 1897 and 1898. Together these twin narratives may answer some of the most perplexing problems left within the Canon of the original tales of Sir Arthur Conan Doyle. I have long been a devotee of those masterful stories and have wished to fill in

11

certain lacunae that exist to complete the picture of Holmes' career. Sherlock Holmes is often spoken of as the most famous character in English fiction. The man who appears to wish to be thought of only as a scientific student of crime is fascinating because his own habits are so unusual. Does every detective study medieval music, ancient British charters, palimpsests, and do chemical research on coal-tar derivatives? Do they play the violin, attend concerts, and keep their tobacco in a Persian slipper? Are they beset with addictions, melancholia, and deep speculations upon the reason for human existence? Do they at once solve the crime and forgive the criminal in case after case? Do they enjoy the performing arts and masquerade? Do they have a sense of humor and enjoy teasing members of the upper crust? Do they enjoy horse-racing, fencing, single-stick, and boxing? If we eliminate these fascinating personal characteristics and the unique relationship with Dr. Watson, what would remain? Would the Master's immortal appeal be what it has been? Then why not, I asked myself, explore these ultimate questions of religious truth and ultimate meaning in a text written by the hand of Sherlock Holmes himself in the form of a journal accounting for the years spent on what has become known as the great hiatus, those years between 1891 and 1894, while not denying the pleasure of an old-fashioned Watson narrative at the same time in a parallel text occurring in 1897 and 1898? The result is the twin-narrative that now lies before you. It is my hope that the reader will find within this book not only a revival of the lost discipline of Christian apologetics but also that by meditating on the challenging thoughts and feelings of both Holmes and Watson this book may explore the deepest dimensions of human experience wrestling with the eternal problems. To use characters of fiction, well-known perhaps beyond all others, to enunciate and give form to life itself would surely be within the ambit of Sherlock Holmes, the greatest detective of all time. I also desired to explore the parameters of Holmes' relationships, the better to vindicate him from easy charges of vanity and if anything to make him more beloved when his unique personality is shown in greater clarity than ever before by revealing the hidden facts of his life, now hopefully revealed through the interlocked cases that lie before the reader in this long-suppressed account.

The reader will note that many ideas will throng these pages and it would be surprising if every reader agreed with the opinions that I have portrayed as existing in Holmes or in Dr. Watson. I have tried not to place opinions within them that would contradict what we already know of their established characters but I do admit to a didactic purpose in many of their discourses. This account may then be considered a fantasia of my own construction upon the essential themes provided by Sir Arthur Conan Doyle. That gentleman was known for the courage of his convictions that often led him to espouse extreme opinions in his own day and I claim similar latitude in exploring my own characterization of Holmes and Watson. It is the prerogative of the author to write his own book and to set before the reader only what the author possesses. If it be too much to hope that the graft will take in the original body of work, I shall be content if the indulgent reader will treat this account as a mere suggestion of what might have been and not what was. There will remain Sherlockian fundamentalists who will always look askance at the temerity of any additions to the Canon. For this reason all additions must be seen as what they are, an attempt to gratify the hunger of those who would wish for true immortality to descend upon the great detective so that there will always be another tale to read. May you enjoy reading this tale then as much as I have enjoyed writing it and hearing again, as if I were merely a channel for them, the old voices and feel again that sense of adventure known first to me in my youth when I feared to read the last Sherlock Holmes mystery and to know irrevocably that there would be no more.

Here again then, the curtain rises upon what I trust will reward the discerning reader of the old tales who has hungered for more, not merely of the stage props of Holmes and Watson in new and improbable adventures, but to find instead an answer and a completion in this addition to what has become the larger Holmes peripheral canon. May this contribution attempt an answer to the deeper mysteries posed by the original tales themselves. It is for the ideal reader who having read with a discerning eye the original tales and also for those specialists known as Sherlockians, but also for new readers, who will take this work as a useful hypothesis for what may have actually happened, that I have the pleasure to announce in that immortal phrase: the game is afoot!

[Editorial Note: I am aware that in the original tales that the Baron's name is spelled Maupertuis and not Maupertius. I have chosen the latter spelling because I found it easier to pronounce and trust that my readers shall also. If this should not prove to be the case the former spelling may be mentally restored].

Prologue

Letter of John H. Watson to His Solicitors in the Year 1917

Dear Sirs:

In the event of my death or incapacitation it is my desire that the manuscripts placed in your care should be eventually delivered to the British Museum. You will find accompanying them certain trust documents explaining my wishes as to their eventual publication. You will see that the trustees include Sherlock Holmes, Mycroft Holmes, and Irene Adler or their representatives. Due to the nature of their contents I have determined that these manuscripts, including the rather long narrative that accompanies this letter, be held secret until fifty years after my death at which time they may be accessed by such scholars as the trustees or their successors may approve for a period of fifteen years. After that time the trust will terminate and they shall be the property of the British Museum and as such they may be published at the discretion of the British Museum or its directors and be available to the general public.

You will see at once that the longest manuscript contains the journal of my friend Sherlock Holmes between the years 1891 and 1894. Interwoven with this journal is my own account of the years 1897 through 1899. Together these twin narratives, in which I have attempted to harmonize as far as possible two narrative threads, form a single work. This work was undertaken by me with the express desire that I might live up to the appellation of his Boswell, a title bestowed upon me by my friend and associate Sherlock Holmes. It has been my desire to err on the side of completeness and comprehensiveness rather than to titillate the reading public by providing a mere adventure tale. Perhaps I flatter myself in thinking that any curious public will remain that will care to read this account so many years in the future, but since I believe it contains the wisdom of my friend and his views on certain religious questions which must be of interest to anyone desiring to know something of the origins and purpose of our lives, I have composed what may be the most complete statement yet made of the actions and personality of Sherlock Holmes as my final opus.

In addition, the narrative illuminates the flow of the history of the last decade of the nineteenth century and may aid historians of the period with certain startling and perilous features of that era in which we were personally involved. For these reasons this manuscript may be of some interest at least to certain individuals. I ask that it be published in its entirety so that the reader may select those portions that are the most meaningful and in any case receive the sum total of the legacy of my friend's wisdom on various subjects. It may be that certain mysteries and misapprehensions may be cleared up at last. For that reason I have desired to provide a completeness and encyclopedic scope to this final work of my writing career.

In any case I shall soon be long past caring for public recognition or acclaim. My sole desire is to benefit future generations by discharging my duty as friend and biographer to the best and wisest man whom I have ever known.

Signed,

John H. Watson M.D.

To the Reader of this Manuscript:

The following narrative which may be the last that I shall ever live to record of the adventures that I have shared over a period of forty years with my friend Sherlock Holmes will I hope stand as a unique testament that should explain to all who imagine that reason must always be its own end that as Blaise Pascal once said, "the heart has reasons that reason knows not of."

In my efforts to at least partially comply with the wishes of Sherlock Holmes that any written account of his adventures might serve as a practical manual in the art of detection, I may have given at times to my readers the impression that Sherlock Holmes was a man without passions. Let me state here that no more faulty conclusion could be

16

reached as to his true nature. It was precisely because he was a man of deep passions, nay I will even go so far as to say obsessions, that he kept his own thoughts and feelings under such a close rein lest the wild steed of his true nature should break loose. He was a man haunted by the inscrutable world in which we live that very world which as our own mature experience bears witness resembles nothing less at times than a charnel house of disappointments and shattered dreams with the attendant failure of our aspirations towards the attainment of the good. To a man like Sherlock Holmes the questions of ultimate meaning could not remain mere idle fancies or speculations, but must assume a rigor and an insistence that demand a final answer.

In pursuit of this great goal he began, at the time of our association in the case entitled "The Sign of Four" with the facile atheism of Winwood Reade. That philosophy is explored in the latter's book entitled, "The Martyrdom of Man." but Holmes could not rest easy with Reade's contemptuous dismissal of theism. That man liberated from belief would automatically attain virtue on his own seemed an unjustified faith in human nature. The presence of evil in the world was all too evident to a man such as Holmes who had spent his entire professional life battling its various manifestations in the cases that came before him.

So it was at last that he set out upon what must be seen as his greatest adventure, an adventure at least partially recorded in his own hand in the form of a journal covering the years 1891-1897. In the case that I now propose to set before the reader Sherlock Holmes was both client and detective at the same time, serving at last his own needs and ends by seeking to resolve that most intractable of philosophical problems, the problem of the nature and existence of evil. In order to find an answer to this problem, he was forced at last to abandon the comforts of his secure domicile in Baker Street and to venture out upon the wider world.

His practice had already grown to include an international dimension, but beyond an occasional trip to his beloved France he still preferred the fogs of Baker Street and the familiar step of a new client upon the stairs. It took more than the usual case to disrupt so iron-clad a routine. That most unusual case is the one that I have already given to the public under the title of, "The Adventure of the Final Problem."

It now lies with me to correct certain inaccuracies in that text by presenting for the first time the true story, not only of that adventure, but of many others so intimately linked and related that they form a single if complex tale that will span the years of 1891 – 1899. These years include Holmes' journey to Tibet, to Persia, and to Africa as well as his chemical research in the south of France. They also include his, as yet unrecorded journey (with me again at his side) to America in the year of 1898. For the reader's convenience the following text will interweave the two narratives so that Holmes' reflections in his journal may supplement my own humble efforts to recount the events of our adventures together from the fall of 1897 through the spring of 1899.

I must apologize for the long delay in writing of these tumultuous events, but recent events in world history have convinced me that in the present moral vacuum that has led to the unprecedented slaughter of the great war that has just begun in 1914 and is even now still raging some general answer to the great questions of our lives must be attempted by even as ordinary a man as I claim to be.

The present century which opened with such grace and optimism seems to have now fragmented into an unprecedented chaos so that civilization itself seems to hang in the balance. It is a great sorrow to have one's old age coincide with disruptions and upheavals in history. One would wish to leave the world with an abiding sense that during his life the prospects for mankind had improved and that the savagery and blindness of other epochs have been at last put to flight by the better angels of our nature. Such good fortune is not mine. A cold and mechanized darkness seems to have now descended upon the European continent. A generation of young men may soon be needlessly sacrificed while their elders look on helpless to imagine the formula of a lasting peace to be arrived at between the striving empires. It seems that these are being uprooted by the war but there is still hope of an early American intervention to impose peace by siding with the allied powers against Germany. I believe that the tale

18

that I am about to tell may show that as early as the last years of the nineteenth century the bitter seeds of the present conflict were sown.

Just as my first tale of Sherlock Holmes began when I was a young doctor invalided home by a Jezail bullet in Afghanistan my last shall deal again with the scourge of war, a scourge which must bring tears to the eyes of an old doctor who has spent his life trying to heal the wounds of my patients. So it is that I take up my pen in this tumultuous and tragic year of 1914 and begin -

The Narrative of Dr. Watson Commences...

To Sherlock Holmes he was always the Napoleon of Crime. I had never heard him speak of Professor Moriarity by any other name. As a result I had, as his friend and biographer come gradually to conceive of this one man as the very embodiment of evil and of the struggle between Sherlock Holmes and James Moriarity as the apotheosis of my friend's career. I now realize that in this assumption I was mistaken. What I had long assumed to be the main event was but an example, an instance, that however important in itself was only illustrative of the true obsession of the life that I have hitherto attempted to record and celebrate in my accounts of his genius through the years that we spent in an association of which this present document must remain the final statement.

This obsession of his of which I speak was once summed up by Holmes himself when he asked me, "What is the purpose of it, Watson? What object is served by this circle of misery, violence, and fear?" I believe that my friend's entire life was devoted to solving the philosophical problem that is generally referred to by the term: the problem of evil. Behind his recurring sense of ennui, his experiments with cocaine, and his unique knowledge of every horror perpetrated in the century was this single dominant desire, to find a meaning in the cycle of events, the tides of empires, the suffering of the innocent, the purpose of pain and disappointment, and the final dissolution into the mystery of death. Various crimes were for him merely illustrative of the more general problem of evil itself.

He must have been tempted at times of darkness and despair to surrender the comfortable dualism of struggle and to assume that goodness and faith are so far the exceptions to our general experience that only evil exists, that this bitter world of age and suffering shows that truth itself is only the ultimate triumph of adversity, that no one man may attempt to successfully trace a brighter pattern in the web of time. It was at such times that my own resources, which are only those of a humble medical man, seemed inadequate to do more than to simply keep Holmes company until his own eager mind and grim determination to find the answers to all questions would reassert themselves and he would plunge again into the fray.

As a man who has seen much of life I realize that the greatest temptation of age is simply to acquiesce to the world as it is, to accept the way that we appear to be flies to the gods who kill us for their sport. Perhaps it is true as William Wordsworth once said:

"The world is too much with us late and soon. Getting and spending we lay waste our powers. Little we see in nature that is ours. We have given our life away, a sordid boon."

Perhaps Matthew Arnold was right when he said that:

"This world which seems to lie before us like a land of dreams so various, so beautiful, so new, has really neither love, nor light, nor certitude, nor peace, nor help for pain and we are here as on a darkling plain swept with confused alarms of struggle and flight where ignorant armies clash by night."

Ah, but perhaps these dark visions are wrong. There may be ground for hope that evil which seems so triumphant and even to be part and parcel of the bleak evolution of life itself on this cold and remote living cell in a dead universe may at last be left to its own place while a place is provided of light, happiness, and peace for those who struggle to find them. It was upon this great perhaps that Sherlock Holmes spent the efforts of his life.

It was in the period of the years of 1897 through 1899 that a most remarkable series of events occurred that collectively represented the very summit of the career of my friend Sherlock Holmes. It had long

20

been my custom to write up his cases, even if their publication might have to be indefinitely delayed. Still, I could not repress a desire to stimulate the curiosity of the public which was always clamoring for more tales of my friend, so I would often cite a few facts or circumstances in no particular order in the cases that did appear from time to time in The Strand Magazine as a hint of adventures to come. The fact that many of these cases were interrelated and involved perhaps the most dangerous and eventful years that we were ever to spend together had to be hidden from the public for there were circumstances of a most delicate nature that made it highly unlikely that the full truth could ever be brought before the general public's purview.

The great and extended case which I now intend to relate began in that very year of 1897, the year when I discovered that I had myself been misled by Sherlock Holmes, that certain conclusions that I had reached in some of the most central matters of his career were in fact unfounded.

That this realization came as a shock to me and an embarrassment of no small order, I am sure that my readers will understand. I have tried on the whole to be as accurate in my accounts as discretion would allow, but there have remained certain conflicting dates and other minute variations which, because they may have not seemed essential, I have had to misrepresent for reasons of confidence. In addition, an element of danger has always followed from my desire to explore the character and methods of my remarkable friend while he remained in active practice in London. Added to this was a sense of responsibility towards living persons and the confidence bred in me as a physician for the intimate revelations that were often made to Sherlock Holmes and to me by outside parties. These facts have often hampered me in my desire to give a complete and full account of events whenever I took my pen into my hand. It was with some relief therefore that I obtained from Holmes in 1897, the year when Sherlock Holmes appeared again to have disappeared from London and to have retired from his long pursuit of various malefactors, permission to write this narrative.

21

The years of 1897 through early1899 might be called the years of summation of all that had gone before. Indeed, the years that followed this period might best be described as an epilogue to the events of those most eventful years that closed the 19th century, the last years of the reign of Queen Victoria. At the time of which I speak we had both sought retreat in the Southwest of England. I had finally prevailed upon my friend to withdraw for a time from the poisonous atmosphere of London. After a consultation at my insistence with Dr. Moore Agar of Harley Street the noted lung specialist confirmed my own preliminary diagnosis that Holmes was suffering from renewed symptoms of consumption. It was imperative that he seek out at once the bracing air of the seaside and of the moors in the southwest of England and that he adopt for at least six months a quiet and disciplined routine of proper diet, exercise, and even partial abstention from his inveterate pipe and his vile tobacco.

Holmes had long entertained an idea (which was to me quite fanciful) that there were similarities between the ancient Cornish language and that of the ancient Chaldeans and that ancient Phoenician tin traders had once visited these shores. Taking this as a handy pretext for an enforced retreat I urged him to finally complete his long proposed and contemplated monograph upon the subject.

It was therefore in January of the year 1897, that he joined me in Cornwall to begin a convalescence period that was (unknown to both of us at the time) to initiate a chain of events that led to one of the greatest adventures of his career. He spent the spring of that year engaged in research of a philological nature into all things Cornish as well as into old English Charters. These involved archeological research, a pursuit using that capacity which he possessed to an unusual degree of immersing himself completely in all aspects of a problem. He was making excellent progress in his thesis, so much so in fact that he felt a need to continue his researches with actual archeological excavations into the ancient barrows of the early Britons in Devonshire. So it was that after first visiting me in Cornwall and undertaking the solution of a local mystery there during the first months of his enforced retreat, he decided to remain in the Southwest of England near to his friend Sir Henry Baskerville, whose estate borders the villages of Coombe Tracey and Grimpen.

22

(My previous readers will recall that it was on this very ground that we had both been involved in that most unique series of events involving the legendary Hound of the Baskervilles).

After settling in at his cottage there Holmes was making excellent progress in his field of research and his health had substantially improved when he summoned me in late September of 1897, ostensibly to hear of his progress in his researches, but in reality to be informed that he was about to engage in a most strenuous pursuit, that he was once again upon the scent for the game was afoot. Holmes had been as good as his word to Doctor Agar since March. His temporary retirement had been both safe and secure. He had left practice gradually, still acting by proxy in the occasional case when it interested him or when the importance was such that he could not in conscience refuse. He exercised his usual care and vigilance in hiding his present whereabouts and so he felt that he could walk without trepidation over the moors behind his house and on occasion to pay a welcome visit to his dear friend Sir Henry Baskerville at Baskerville Hall.

I must say here that I always found the scenery of Devonshire to be a bit too bleak for my taste. I was happy to be residing in nearby Cornwall though I often visited Holmes during the course of the year, since I still enjoyed the company of my friend. I had not re-married after my wife's death but spent my days with the fond memory of the woman who had consented to marry me after the case entitled, "The Sign of Four." I had learned since her death to value a solitude that had eluded me in my more active years. I enjoyed such social life as the nearby village provided and still maintained a limited local practice there to support my frugal needs. I would take the local train up to visit Holmes from time to time, traveling by coach from the station at Coombe Tracey to the village of Grimpen-on-Moor.

I had come to adjust myself over the years to Holmes' peremptory nature and to accept his surprises for the sake of the adventure that they offered. I recall that I had arrived the previous afternoon of a late summer day in answer to his urgent summons and that we were sitting together in the cozy drawing room of the cottage which he had purchased some years before when as he often did when he wished to spring some new surprise upon me he suddenly broke the silence by a startling announcement that had had no prelude in the topics of our previous conversation.

"I think perhaps that the truth may now be told," said Sherlock Holmes turning from the window where he had stood for the past fifteen minutes gazing out upon Dartmoor.

"What?" I said, looking up at the interruption from an excellent novel by Joseph Conrad.

"I say, I think the truth may now be told," said my companion fixing me with a humorous glint in his grey eyes. "I am referring of course to several of those cases which you have persisted in holding back from your faithful readers during the course of your chronicles of those exploits which may be referred to as my professional career."

"Well, if I have held them back it was for good reasons often because they touched upon matters of a most delicate nature," I protested.

"My dear fellow, you are always the soul of discretion but one must consider the virtue of completeness. After all, Boswell attempted to display the complete man in his biography of Dr. Johnson and how often have I taken you to task for that persistent air of romance that so often obscures the pure formula of detection. Certainly some of the cases that you have omitted show in the utmost clarity those techniques and methods of mine that you have made so celebrated."

"But it was in deference to your own desires..."

"Yes, I admit that my own reticence is partially to blame. I have had to deceive even you at times my dear Watson and through you your readers for I respected your own candor and that special relation of trust that you have maintained with your readers too much to ask you to concoct deliberate falsehoods. As to my methods...."

"Your cases and the methods you have devised are the most marvelous examples of ratiocination that the world has ever known!" I expostulated.

"So you say, and so have you long flattered my own occasional sense for the dramatic. But surely, a faithful chronicler should not withhold those cases without which the outline of my career must remain forever incomplete. Your tales have often been confined to the more humble and prosaic cases while omitting those the solution of which have had a most telling impact upon the world at large and I may even say played a significant role in history."

I was somewhat nettled at the entire tone of this discussion for I have always attempted to consider his wishes at all times and to honor, at his own request, the demands of the art of scientific detection and to deal with questions that best displayed his gifts. It was often as I have remarked that the smaller cases raised the most intriguing issues and best displayed his unique methods of reasoning. Still there were exceptions of note.

"There was the matter of your service to the King of Bohemia," I reminded him.

"A trifle."

"Or your discovery of the fate of the Bruce-Partington Plans!"

"A plaything."

"Well then, I can think of nothing in which I have been inaccurate."

"My dear fellow, I would be the last person to accuse you of duplicity. Indeed, it has always been your penchant to what I might call the inclusion of fulsome detail that exceeds the pure chain of cause and effect which alone must be the essence of any inquiry to a scientific investigator. Only the tendency to this melodrama has ever invited any criticism from me."

"Well, what was I to do since you have always insisted on keeping a leash upon me when it has come to the choice of your cases to be made public. You have always insisted upon the value of the commonplace and abjured those cases which you have solved for some of the greatest families of the Empire. What would my readership be if confined to a series of governesses and solitary cyclists? Romance was forced upon me if I hoped to retain my cadre of followers."

"There is a certain element of the social climber in you Watson. You would always insist when we would discuss the matter that the lives of the great and the wealthy are less predictable and mundane than that of the lower classes and hence that they make better subjects. I on the contrary have always maintained that all of the drama of life occurs on the level of the ordinary. What tiny hamlet but has its own Romeo and Juliette? How many dock-hands are a secret Othello jealous of their Desdemona? What can be more boring and predictable than the aspirations of the upper classes? What more foreseeable than their perennial pursuit of money and of more money? No, my dear fellow, if you would sound the depths of human nature you must enter the jungle of unfulfilled dreams and vain aspirations that are entertained by those who imagine that when their needs are ever completely fulfilled that they can then join the privileged classes. These struggling ones little suspect that the members of those classes which they envy struggle daily to bear the least inconvenience and finally come in their boredom to lament the human condition itself. All desire fades when it is easily satisfied. Passions are honed against the wet-stone of adversity. Therefore it is to the commonplace that the man must turn who is a connoisseur of crime."

"Very well," said I, "But beyond my manner of recounting your cases how have I disappointed you?"

"My dear friend you never disappoint me, it is merely that I regret the image of me that you have left with those lacking in imagination. Surely a proper Boswell must pierce the soul and not confine himself to a mere collection of eccentricities, tobacco in Persian slippers, correspondence affixed to the mantel, etc. Then you have assumed that my every passing fancy is to be believed as Gospel rather than as an effort to make of this passing Vanity Fair some sense and to discover some purpose to the cycle of anxiety and terror. My life like that of most men is a series of essays, preliminary attempts at a synthesis."

"Can you give me an example?" I inquired.

"Well to begin let us take your proposed theory, based upon an occasional remark of mine, that I plan to eventually retire to a bee farm in Sussex one day. When you, dear friend, with your usual foresight purchased your own small country retreat by Poldu Bay in Cornwall, I could hardly imagine living in distant Sussex when I retire. I must have my Boswell within call. When I actually do retire it shall probably be to my home here in Devonshire. But in any case I am growing restive. I have done my best to cooperate with the recommendations of my doctors this year. Indeed with the single exception of that matter of the Trevelyan family I have lived a most sedentary life during these last months of 1897, but the time has come for action as you shall soon hear, for the case before us is the opposite of commonplace. Indeed, it is not too much to say that it shall involve issues that will find their place in the history of the age and involve the destiny of nations."

His announcement came as such a shock that I found myself plunged into a sort of trance. The room seemed to whirl about me. I was alarmed to hear that he was about to end his period of rest and recuperation. We had discussed the matter of his temporary retirement and his remarkable restoration to his normal state of vigor upon my arrival in answer to his urgent summons. As I had ridden up in the train I had recalled the strange course of the recent two years. Holmes had spent the previous year of 1896 mostly abroad while I in turn occupied our old lodgings in Baker Street taking occasional trips to the cottage that I had purchased in Poldhu Bay near the hamlet Treddannick Wollas which is not far from the larger village of Cwry in Cornwall. I had done so for the sea air for my own health left something to be desired. I had retired in late 1895 at Holmes' request, selling my small Kensington practice to a young doctor named Verner. The young doctor later proved to be a distant relation of Holmes. It was Holmes who supplied the money for the purchase, secretly. He knew how the death of my wife had affected me, that my own dismal spirits had caused my practice to suffer, and how the strenuous life of my early military years now told upon me. Holmes' own practice had by now assumed an international dimension and his ties with his brother Mycroft were such that he received various assignments of a state nature the details of which he could not share even with me. Still, he pursued some few cases of the old sort, accounts of which I have continued to publish, and as always he maintained the humble London residence that had for so long been his only home.

As I sat that September morning by the side of a warm hearth in the stone tower-like structure that was now his home, I thought of the disadvantages of its location near the village of Grimpen, an obscure place but not too distant from the town of Tavistock. Grimpen lies on the southern border of Exmoor, east of Hartland Point and south of the port of Ilfracomb and of the village of Clovelly. The house had been expressly modified along a design that Holmes had shown me some years ago in our rooms at Baker Street.

"If I should ever retire, this is the design of the home in which I intend to live," he had proclaimed as he proudly spread his plans before me.

"But this is a veritable fortress," I had had said at the time when I first saw the embodiment of his retreat in Devonshire. On the present visit I raised the same point once again in relation to the isolation of his location and the sturdy walls of his dwelling with its high windows which could not be easily reached unaided from the ground. I asked if his preparations were not excessive.

"You must remember that I have many enemies Watson and it is well to be on my guard if I am to live alone in the countryside."

"But surely if you retired permanently to a bee farm in Sussex...," I said, for I could not rid myself of my image of his once stated intention to purchase an apiary there, "You will have more neighbors than you do here and could in consequence live a less sequestered existence. Besides, Sussex is not as far from London."

"My blushes Watson I shouldn't live out a week if I retired there! I'd be found on a footpath with my bees buzzing about my head."

"But you always said..."

My companion's eyes gleamed with amusement as he said, "Sussex hah! You never do get my little jokes Watson. This whole matter of Sussex and bees...I did hope that you would print it though and by doing so provide me with a measure of security. That story would at least show my scorn for my pursuers, just a tiny hint that I despise their fulminations and prognostications of my demise. But you must understand that it is to my place in Devon that I have long intended to return when I do retire. This place has character, and I prefer a western exposure to the dull and foggy channel ports. I prefer a good bracing Atlantic storm to that from the enclosed waters off the bleak chalk-faced Sussex Downs."

"But the closeness to London and the nearness to the channel ports to your beloved France," I remonstrated again.

"Well, Devon is hardly the moon, my dear fellow. Besides I hope to be able to afford always to keep my old rooms in London where I can put my feet up by our old fire. Baker Street is precious to me and has many memories..."

He left the window and returned to his place by the fire where he sat facing me.

"But this matter of your place of final retirement is but one example Holmes, surely you must produce more examples if you would accuse me of inaccuracy in my accounts." said I.

"Well then, what of that affair recounted in your story, "The Final Problem," in which you state that I brought about the death of Professor Moriarity? Should it not be revisited now and revised? For you see my dear fellow, Professor Moriarity is not dead," said my companion quietly.

"What?" I cried out.

"My dear Watson, have you not in all these years reflected upon the absurdity that the brilliant Professor, the very Napoleon of Crime, would act in the manner that you proposed in that story. That he would frontally attack a younger man on a narrow ledge by throwing his arms about him hoping to cause both of us to fall backward into a convenient waterfall; why the whole thing is absurd. Such behavior might be contemplated by a Limehouse thug if intoxicated but in cold wrath after trailing us for weeks across Europe? Surely the Professor would be more resourceful."

"Alive? Do you mean to say that my account of his death in the Final Problem was...?"

"Almost entirely erroneous, my dear fellow," he answered with a smile.

"But this is unworthy of you Holmes; you always led me to believe that Moriarity was dead."

"On the contrary, my dear fellow, I left you to draw your own conclusions and simply chose not to dispute them."

"But the note, the Alpenstock!" I cried.

"The bodies Watson," said Holmes quietly. "Did it never occur to you to seek for the bodies of the Professor and his victim?"

"Inspector Gregson advised against it. He said that immediate news of the death of Sherlock Holmes would have the most serious effects at home in England. Mycroft also said that your body should rest in the deep pool at the bottom of the falls. It was not until some time later that I shared the events with the public in my story 'The Adventure of the Final Problem.'"

"Quite so, my dear fellow, in any case, I assure you, it was for no whimsical reason that I allowed you to reach your erroneous conclusions, nor was it in any way to disparage the great service that you rendered me in that story, that I have so long refrained from correcting your misapprehensions. Pray allow me to explain. It is true that the Professor so forgot himself in the anger of the moment and his natural frustration at the ruin that I had brought upon him to charter a special train to pursue us to the English Channel and that he did follow us across Europe with ill-intent. One may not however countenance a man of the brilliant endowments that the Professor possesses rushing with open arms to grapple with a younger man above a seething waterfall. Surely this is the very acme of romance; but really, Watson, is such a tale believable? I assure you in any case that the Professor has always been quite myopic and has some retinal damage, thus his stooped and peering air and the habit of moving his head from side to side to bring an object into focus. Is it likely that such a man would attempt a frontal assault? Alas, too much study in youth is not a good thing and often results in a melancholy disposition as the great 17th century scholar Robert Burton has observed so wisely in his discourse on the miseries of scholars in his 'The Anatomy of Melancholy.' In addition it tends to incapacitate one for struggling by waterfalls later in life. So I say again, the Professor did not die at the Falls of Reichenbach. Still, your story was invaluable at the time and as I said, I believe that the true story can now be told at last."

I sat back in my chair in utter amazement. In all the years during which I had often been surprised by the revelations of my companion, this revelation was the most unbelievable.

"But Holmes, if as you say the Professor is alive what became of him after his supposed death at the Falls of Reichenbach? Surely there would have been word in the press during all these years of his unique brand of crime and you in turn would have been much occupied. I would have heard of it before now."

"Ah but you speak of the Professor as he was, my dear fellow, but you see, he has changed in answer to a wager that we made shortly after the incident at the falls for we did indeed meet there. Only the outcome was not as you supposed."

"Good heavens, are you saying that Moriarity has reformed?"

"Well, that is between the Professor and his conscience. Let us say that he has kept his part of the wager that we made and I like to suppose that some inner conviction reinforces that compliance."

"But Holmes, he is the Napoleon of crime!"

Holmes smiled and picked up his pipe from the mantle above the fire. "Even Napoleon had his Waterloo, Watson. One does not build empires of crime overnight. I left him with very little of his old life intact. It was surely time to switch allegiances. You see it was a particularity of Moriarity that he loved the power of crime and, yes, profited by its fruits but he never enjoyed the sheer sordidness that must accompany criminal activity. You would not find the Professor haunting opium dens as I have on occasion been forced to do. I will not say he is squeamish but rather that he is like an artist in his way. It is no accident that his seminal work describes the behavior of asteroids, dry barren bits of rock hurtling blindly through space and answering only to brute force in the form of various gravitational fields. It surely indicates a man with a rather barren temperament, unaware of the human dimension of his acts. Yet, he has a logical mind and an extraordinary reasoning ability. I simply took St. Thomas Aquinas at his word that the intellect can lead one to God and that virtue is above all rational."

"But Holmes, you yourself have always seemed to me an unbeliever. Why otherwise would you have commended to my attention Winwood Reade's book, 'The Martyrdom of Man?'"

"You will recall that I commended it to your reading, not necessarily to your assent. It is brilliant in its way, the effusions of a latter day stoic who found comfort in denying comfort's source. You see, Watson, there is a strange attraction for some minds to despair and a particular pride in asserting their own tiny flame of consciousness against an overwhelming black. No doubt you have read that grim poem 'The City of Dreadful Night.' Well that is their choice certainly but dare they deny comfort to the rest of humanity, particularly the children who every day enter upon eternity before they have even glimpsed this world and been able to reach a thought-out position towards existence? It is the responsibility of one who will adapt any such position that it be valid for others as well as for himself. What man has the right to opt for despair and desolation for all of humanity? Hope on the contrary is open-ended. It does not claim certitude but simply opens the mind and forestalls premature conclusions based on inadequate data. For the thinking man the table is always tilted towards further possibilities. The true scientist is always aware of the history of his field of endeavor. What is that history but a series of inadequate conclusions meant to explain the whole, nor does the man of passion yield easily to despair, for even if his passions incline to vice he must still desire to exist if only to continue the process of his own self-destruction. We cannot. We

32

cannot be indifferent to our own existence; I believe that we can assert this as a first postulate of all thought. The desire to continue to exist then already implicates us in a moral impulse, the impulse to survive. Yet we die. We know that we shall. So it is that we turn to the universe and ask why we should be frustrated in the deepest desire within us, to continue to exist so that we may pursue any and all other ends that we have in view. If the moral impulse arises only within ourselves with no answering voice from the universe, then our desire to continue to exist is a delusion, a vanity of man. But if even the desire to live is a delusion why then so is any other assertion we might make regarding God and our very attempt to deny the moral nature of things by opting for atheism as an exercise at proving by the mere assertion to God as a non-existent observer of our struggle as a species (for who else but God pays us any mind) is also delusory and we are simply forced as a collective species at last into silence. We might as well join the cows in the field and begin eating grass!"

"You made such an argument to Moriarity?" I asked in amazement.

"Well our discussions went on for some time. He is not an easy case as you know. One does not become the Napoleon of Crime without being quite rooted in evil. Still, I always had hopes for him. Where reason still exists unimpaired there remains a highway to God."

"But if he is still alive where is he? How is he?"

"Well like us all he is a little the worse for wear as you shall see. He will shortly call upon us this afternoon and you may ask him how he does. You see I have asked him to come over today since I required that you come down to assist me in a most important matter. I believe that between the two of us we can keep you amused over the next week or so and that you will care to add a final chapter to the annals of your friend, Sherlock Holmes. I have a startling series of tales to relate to you and you yourself may be present at one of the last chapters of events begun so long ago. We may in addition tie up some loose ends that may have perplexed your more astute readers for years. I am afraid that there appear to be some startling omissions in your published accounts of my cases and their complete portrayal of my values and concerns."

"But where has the Professor been living all this time? Why then was he not arrested long ago? You speak of him as though he were a harmless and congenial neighbor."

"He is, my dear fellow. He has an estate at Kings Pyland, the famous race-horse breeding farm, of venerable memory. The Professor still raises scions of the great horse Silver Blaze. It is well that he lives so close to me here. It allows me occasional contact and to reassure myself that he has not reverted to his former way of life. His interest in science and in higher mathematics still remains however and he still lectures occasionally under an assumed name at the University of Exeter."

"But how can all of this be and why have you delayed so long in informing me of such an essential state of affairs?" I asked in exasperation.

"Watson, you anticipate me. You really must let the magician unveil his tricks in due order. We really should await the arrival of the man himself. It is a tale that will require two narrators since even now there are points to which only the Professor himself is privy. I trust that you still carry your medical notebook? Excellent, you may wish to keep a few notes for the matter is somewhat complex."

"You will give me no hints then?" I replied as my curiosity overcame my wounded feelings.

"Beyond the assertion that it involves the period of my eclipse after my supposed death at the Falls of Reichenbach, that it involves the cooperation of the Professor in a most unusual wager, that it explains my presence on two continents between 1891 and 1894, that it involves the giant bamboo rats of China and Sumatra, and that the events of the next few days may save the Empire itself I can say nothing."

Holmes chuckled and rubbed his hands together as was his wont when displaying his choicest wares.

There was a sound outside of a carriage drawing up on the drive. "That must surely be the Professor. You may ask him directly any questions that remain which, will I am sure, my most dear fellow, reveal matters that even you, my Boswell and most trusted confidant, have yet to glimpse of the character and career of Mr. Sherlock Holmes."

Holmes left the drawing room and I heard his steps echoing on the flagstone passage as he went to the door. I was glad for the time to compose myself. After all it is no small matter to greet a man who has been literally raised from the grave, particularly a man whom the years had taught me to fear and to despise. Reformed indeed! I had seldom doubted the wisdom of my friend but I confess that I found myself wondering whether living in this isolated way upon the moors might have led his great mind to turn upon itself. Perhaps someone passing himself off as the Professor had convinced Holmes whose mind rebelled at stagnation that his old nemesis lived again. After all, the struggle with the man had consumed some of the best years of the great detective's life. Was it surprising then that deprived as it had been of its source for its usual exercise that his mind might have conjured up out of its own mists the ghost of his old enemy? I was about to search in his old desk for the revolver that was never far from his hand when the door opened and my companion returned. The huge oak door swung back to reveal a figure that even I recognized at once. Though stooped and bent like one of those trees upon the moor there could be no mistaking the gaunt, indeed cadaverous face of Professor Moriarity. Yet in the eyes there had been a change. All the intelligence and desperate purpose was present that I had seen from the train window so long ago. They were still there but where before there had been only a brutal evil combined with arrogance and pride now there was a composed manner and a glint that approached humor. He walked slowly into the room and bowed to me with an air of both gravity and humility.

"Come in Professor," said Holmes, "And try the settee. You are punctual as always which is well on such a day for it gives us time to relate such a tale as my friend Watson for all his abilities as a spinner of tales might find to pose a challenge. We will need to have our wits about us since I desire no detail to be omitted. It has been many years ago after all. Fortunately I have my journal to refer to which bears first-hand testimony to all that occurred even as the events unfolded.

You in turn, Professor, may supplement my narrative with matters of an interior nature that only you possess. But I must be a proper host. I have here a bottle of old Port from the cellars of my friend Sir Henry Baskerville which I am sure it is appropriate to open on such an occasion as this. It may soothe the tired vocal cords and awaken the mind to times gone by."

Holmes suited his actions to his words and taking out three excellent crystal goblets he poured three glasses with the tawny vintage. As he did so the Professor spoke for the first time. His voice though it was aged and weak revealed the clarity and force of his mind which remained active as ever.

"All this has no doubt some as a great shock to you, Doctor. Even now I perceive that your old habits as a military man have not deserted you. I assure you that you will not require a weapon from the wall or the desk to protect yourself or your friend. I of course go unarmed. Nor need you fear any of my old associates. It is true that some of my associates of old will not mourn at my funeral but such was my reputation that they still fear me and we need not fear reprisal at their hands, so you see I have no ill intent to Mr. Holmes or you on this bright September day."

Holmes walked over with the filled glasses. "And how are things over at Kings Pyland?" he inquired.

"Splendid! My horses are running well and I have a new yearling who promises to exceed the record of the great Silver Blaze. But I see that you are about to make a toast to our joint endeavor. Pray proceed."

My friend's eyes twinkled as he raised his glass. "Gentlemen, today we complete the circle. Friend Watson, you have made of my life something of a legend, so much so indeed that I am afraid that the public looks upon me through the somewhat romantic air of your own projections. How many readers have followed your hints and paired me with Irene Adler in some fancied latter-day romance merely because of a chance comment, made in a meditative mood, that I shall always regard her as, the woman, when I merely wished in saying so, to show respect for her resourcefulness and humor at my expense on a memorable occasion? Others, as I mentioned earlier imagine that I will spend my declining years pottering about bee hives and segregating queen bees. Others perhaps imagine that my old misanthropy will finally prevail and that I will take my seat with my brother Mycroft at the Diogenes Club. Nonsense! Even you my old friend have overlooked the true bent of my character. Would I pursue the course of aborted romance or bees or solitude or even crime when there are greater mysteries to be solved? What was I brooding upon during all those years in Baker Street? What vision was I seeking under the artificial stimulation of cocaine but the clarity and fulfillment that I was to glimpse at last in the snows above Llassa? What was I pursuing in my chemical researches in the south of France? And above all what strange sequence of events has led us to this moment when we three who have all shared lives of struggle can sit side by side in amity? This, my good Doctor is my true story, the last mystery of Sherlock Holmes, a mystery if I may say so that amounts to an answer to all the old questions of the fate of the soul of man. For you see though I took my passions from another source I was never a thinking machine. It was only when I saw in what strange ways my clients, even when seeking honor, brought instead the most untoward results upon themselves that I desired an explanation for the perversities of fate. I desired to answer the human riddle of why we exist at all. Oh, take no umbrage at my long silence on these topics my dear friend Watson. No one could have done better than you in revealing me to the public nor can I blame you for my own inscrutable nature, the causes of which you could not know, nor could you deduce where my aspirations might lead at last. But I cannot leave the matter as is and you yourself need to be disabused of any false notions you may still possess."

"But Holmes, surely this is a private matter and it is unworthy of you to go into it before the Professor." I expostulated for I had yet to trust the Professor.

"I assure you, Watson that the Professor has known a like purging of the spirit. Illusions are costly. They keep us laboring often for our entire lives seeking to fill a gap in our conception of ourselves. It is because of the strictness of your own temperament and your need to keep a certain formality in your fiction that you have maintained a certain professional medical distance in regard to even me. I have been saddled with a reputation for addictions and compulsions and if I may say a certain lack of humanity. I assure you I would not have been able to solve so many cases involving human passion if I had none myself. So now I release you my great biographer, from the strictures of my own retiring nature. The quest that I took during my long absence exceeds the grail quests of old as recorded in such tales as The White Company by your good friend, Dr. Arthur Conan Doyle. After I slipped away from you at Meiringen I began a journal that sits on the table before you. It will tell the tale even as it transpired and to it as you read either I or the Professor in the days to come, for I am afraid it is rather extensive, will append comments and clarifications. I commend it now to your earnest perusal. The Professor and I will meanwhile engage in a game of chess. Gentlemen, raise your glasses, a toast to the Great Hiatus and to success in our present venture!"

I arose and walked over to the table where the manuscript lay. I leather-bound book with gold-leaf embossed binding lay before me. On the cover in elegant chancery script was the appellation, "The Great Hiatus of Sherlock Holmes." I took up the volume before returning to my seat.

"I have a further word my dear fellow before you withdraw. Though I may have spoken disparagingly of the image of me that you have conveyed in your written accounts I want you to know that I have always considered you to be the very soul of propriety and that you represent what it truly is to be an English gentleman. It is not simply in your own heroic exploits in the field but in your innate honesty and courage that you have always distinguished yourself. If I have taken advantage at times of certain aspects of your character to convince the public it was out of sheer necessity, after all my very lodgings were known to my enemies. How many times have I left those lodgings never knowing when an assassin might be waiting for me? Our early days of obscurity did not last. I was therefore required to sketch a certain image which if not strictly accurate in all details was substantially true but with just sufficient shading to suit my deeper purposes. You were the artist of those shadings, Watson, but it was I myself who chose the character that you were to portray. I must for instance appear as somewhat unstable and possibly due to innate melancholia likely to give up my profession. Even in the cases that we chose to make public I chose those that presented obscure malefactors and unique incidents the better to lull my more customary adversaries into the illusion that I was not also following them. You see, my enemies had access to the same accounts in the Strand Magazine as the general public. I did allow some truth to emerge but only in an obscure manner and often hidden by dates that hid when the actual events occurred. Too much accuracy and I would not be here. Is that not so Professor?"

The Professor silently nodded.

"This is why we staged the little dramas that you have recounted in The Empty House and in The Final Problem for I assure you that both are fictions. By the way Professor, I trust that Colonel Sebastian Moran is doing well in on his island in the Straits of Malacca."

This was the second great shock of the evening.

"But Holmes, you can't mean that he escaped. Why he was the murderer of young Ronald Adair!"

"He was nothing of the sort. Young Adair it so happens had been found frolicking with a chambermaid and it was essential to his illustrious family that the matter should be hushed up. The Colonel was willing to oblige...for a price. There are families who desire to retain a sort of corporate dignity; the disgrace of one member is the disgrace of all. It was better that the young Adair be thought dead rather than that the disgrace be brought out. He repaired quietly to Canada. Suffice it to say that the Colonel's gambling records disappeared and that a sufficient sum remained for him to return to an island in the South China Sea where he maintains a tea plantation. Under his pseudonym of Colonel Upwood he had been fleecing some of the most eminent men of the city. He belonged to the exclusive card club, the Nonpareil Club in London. So exclusive was the club that the Colonel never needed to show that he had money to cover any losses. In any case, no losses of substance occurred. As his winning streak continued it was met first with wonder but finally with incredulity. Still, so subtle were his wiles that no actual cheating method could ever be brought home to him. The honor of the club was at stake and none of these men could afford to become the laughing stock of the country. It was agreed that if he would withdraw quietly no further inquiries would be made. Then there came the Ronald Adair episode and that of the airgun in Baker Street. It was time for Colonel Moran to depart. As India had once been too hot to hold him, now just so was England. So after his arrest he was taken by Inspector Lestrade to the East London docks where a ship took him away the very next day after the famous airgun episode recounted in your tale. The event was not without use as a cautionary example to other would-be assassins for if even the Colonel with his resourcefulness and reputation, famed as a big game hunter across two continents failed then further attempts upon my life would be vain indeed."

"But why did you never tell me," I asked in some chagrin.

"Because my dear Doctor other enemies remained as your reading of my account will reveal. It was imperative that you write your accounts with the appearance of absolute verisimilitude and mendacity is not one of your signal traits. Now gentlemen," Holmes said rising for a second time, "I think that it is well that Watson withdraw with the manuscript but before he does let me read from the dedication of my own book and I hope it may serve to make up to you, John Watson, for some of my slights and my obfuscations through the years for I know the sacrifices that they have entailed."

He took the manuscript copy from me and read as follows: This book is dedicated to my friend and biographer Dr. John H. Watson whose courage never failed, whose honor knows no equal, and without whose many efforts there would not be a Sherlock Holmes.

"A toast to you my very good fellow," said Holmes raising his glass to which the Professor added, "Hear, hear!"

Book One:

The Events Leading to the Falls of Reichenbach

From the Journal of Sherlock Holmes

April 24, 1891 London

I thought I should never take a pen into my hand to record my own adventures and I would hardly do so now were it not that I may require an adequate record to refer to in the future. Watson would no doubt wonder that my brain which he imagines can contain and keep separate every detail ready to be recalled at will requires a written record, but then, the good Doctor has always needed to believe that I am invincible and perhaps I have needed to believe so as well. Certainly no mere man would go up against the organization that the Professor has created least of all one such as I who prefers to retreat back into the domestic comforts of Baker Street while Lestrade, Gregson, or Hopkins see to all the sordid details. For me, it is the solution of the problem that matters; the arrest and punishment are mere epilogue. I never for instance go to trials. The idea of testifying is abhorrent to me. If it must be known, I hate the very smell of our temples of justice, the worn wooden benches, the stained and peeling varnish, the papers and parchments; all alike breathe a miasma of human degradation and despair. Then there is the absurd pomposity of the barristers and the judges, the whole self-serving arcane concepts of the legal mind which sift the data of human experience sorting into infinite categories acts which were probably impulsive in their conception and commission. The entire retrograde rationality of the law is a delusion. What have these distinctions and infinite gradations to do with the hearts and minds of actual people? The convolutions of criminal thought fall through the net that we weave to contain them. If I as a detective did not comprehend the bird in flight I would solve no cases. Once captured and shackled and helpless in the dock the diabolical becomes merely pitiable. Then does the forlorn character of existence most weigh in upon me and I begin to brood. Well, I am certainly not about to consult an alienist, nor am I prepared to return to the artificial stimulation of the demon drug cocaine which does indeed as Watson says bring the blackest reaction upon me. No, if futility does indeed sit like a great black dog or an incubus upon me then I must find an alternative solution. This was the state of mind that has led me to strip away the layers of protection that have hitherto guarded the Professor. He like me prefers to deal with the world dramatically, to keep outside himself the horror that dwells within his own breast, or I do not know the man. I have long been aware of him like a spider at the center of his web of crime, theft, blackmail, even murder. Oh there is money in it but surely by now the Professor has the means to retire. His life is most Spartan. Still he persists...why? Does he find a perverse, inverted meaning in crime itself? To understand the Professor and to be as successful as I think I have been in bringing about the destruction that will soon descend upon his organization, I have had to think from within the Professor's own mind as it were. The problem has been not to solve a crime after its commission because by then all traces leading back to the Professor have been obscured. No, I had to anticipate him, to have the authorities on hand at the very moment that the crime was committed and this I believe I have done. It will be the undoing of the work of years and I believe that the Professor knows it. The wheels are already in motion though and the Professor cannot now withdraw his hand. His very credibility in the underworld has always been that once he promises, he always performs. This central fact of his nature is as predictable and reliable as the laws of the behavior of asteroids in his famous monograph. He will not withdraw therefore he must convince me to do so and that I will never do. The moment prepared for years is at hand. Even now I can prove nothing but fortunately it is the Professor himself who will deliver the proof. This is his little slip and as I know him, he knows me. He will know that I have discovered his fatal flaw. The result is a foregone conclusion. This time I shall bag his confederates and their perhaps their head as well. The entire body lies supine before me. The events are in motion but shall I see their end? In a matter of days my case will be complete but will I be alive to witness the conclusion? Clearly, I must go abroad; today was the last straw. I was attacked in the very street! I went of course immediately to my brother Mycroft at the Diogenes Club.

He greeted me from the huge armchair by the great window that he usually occupies at the club looking out on Pall Mall. A cup of his usual heavy bodied Russian black tea was at the table by his side. The silent porter who led me to the great man withdrew and we were left alone. Speaking in the club precincts is of course forbidden since the membership are each and all united by a common misanthropy. Mycroft of course maintains his pride of place and has discovered in his solitary nook that he is beyond earshot of other members. He spoke from the depths of his chair.

"Well, have you done it?"

"Yes, the gears are in motion. Lestrade and Gregson are working together for once."

"Good. I will inform the Home Secretary. I trust that there have been no untoward consequences to your self."

"There have been a few attempts," I said quietly.

Mycroft stirred his huge bulk. "What? This will never do. How could you have allowed such a thing?"

"Well, I am not without faults and I needed to be close enough to the quarry to set my snares."

"But your disguises!"

"Ah, it is known that I use them so on this occasion I was forced to act in personem and without disguise. But it is only after the fact that my stratagems were discovered or I would not be sitting here now. It did put the Professor on alert though. In fact the man himself came to see me."

"Hmmph! That was indeed bold."

"He desired that I let go my hold. I refused of course."

"Then what are you going to do, Sherlock?" Mycroft asked with what was for him quite a display of concern and perturbation as he shifted in his chair.

"I think that a spell on the Continent would do me no harm," I said laconically.

"You aren't going alone!"

"No, I believe that Dr. Watson will accompany me. I will be going to see the good Doctor tonight."

"And will his wife be pleased that you will again be taking him from hearth and home and putting him again in harms' way?"

I smiled at this. "Your objection is well taken but then Watson is an old war horse and though he may wear the bit in his mouth he is far from broken. His loyalty to me is longstanding and straight as steel as I might add is yours my dear Mycroft. My escape from London will not be an easy one. I wonder if I might take the extraordinary liberty of asking you to assume the role of driver of a cab on the day of my escape for I fear that I trust no one else."

As those who are familiar with the annals of my life as recounted by Dr. Watson will recall my brother Mycroft is in his own person the clearinghouse for virtually all of the diplomatic and security data of the British Empire. To propose then that he be a cabbie for the day was indeed a liberty! My own particular sense of humor enjoys the charm of incongruity and the thought of Mycroft's bulky form balanced precariously atop a cab rather than seated securely in the armchair at his club amused me. His response however both surprised and touched me.

"Of course, Sherlock; I will be happy to do anything that I can."

"I have arranged for two other cabs to precede you in line. I will instruct Watson to take the third cab from Baker Street and disembarking will rush across the Lauder Arcade timing himself so as to rendezvous with you at a quarter past nine in the morning. You will be driving a small brougham. He will recognize you by your wearing of a great black cloak and... well yes, a touch of melodrama for Watson's future tale with a trim of red at the collar provided by this scarf which I am wearing now. You will then drive him to Waterloo Station where we will both embark on the boat-train for the Continent."

"That will do very well for Dr. Watson but my dear Sherlock how do you intend to get to the station unobserved from your lodgings in Baker Street?"

"I will not be returning to Baker Street. I have made other plans. After I have received his consent I will leave the good doctor's consulting room and repair to the Chapel of the Oratory in Lambeth. I will spend the night with the good fathers and borrow a clerical robe and berretta; I plan to assume the role of an old, Italian priest in which guise I will board the train and await Watson.

"Do you think that your ruse will succeed?"

"Ah, that depends upon the Professor. He will follow me of course."

"Then why not attend to him here and now in London where the entire police force can be at your aid? A single call from me and I can have a regiment of fusiliers at your disposal...why this nonsense of absconding to the Continent?"

I was silent for a bit because there were elements in my plan that I felt I could not yet reveal, even to Mycroft. At last I spoke up. "It is because I do not wish that the Professor be captured," I said quietly.

"What? I have always heard you speak of him as the most dangerous man in London and of course we both know his antecedents!"

"And so he is, but he is something more to me. He is the third most brilliant man in the country, if, that is, you and I may claim the first two positions. I cannot reconcile myself to the inevitability that under British justice he should be simply hanged."

"But he is evil Sherlock!"

"Yes. But what is evil but goodness corrupted and turned from the course that Grace would have intended. You see that I have read my Aquinas and my Newman. Are my wits then as blunt as the hounds of the law, the dull-witted authorities whose value is sufficient for Moriarity's minions but surely not for the man himself? No. I prefer to deal with him alone. After all, I have forgiven malefactions in the past by other criminals in order to pursue the greater good. You need only recall the affair of the Blue Carbuncle where I dismissed Mr. James Ryder to lead a more exemplary life."

"But how will you accomplish this?"

"I have my methods. To begin, I will play the stag to his hound and let him pursue me for a bit. I assure you that I will lead him a merry chase and when he thinks to have me at his mercy I will shake loose and turning bring him to bay at last. I shall cause him to question his life's work with all that it has meant. I will propose to him those ultimate ends which must cause us all to pause and in that pause I will propose another course to him. I have stripped him of his power over others as represented by his vast organization. I will end by getting him to surrender that false power that he seeks to exercise over himself."

"You begin to sound like the great apologists of the Church, my dear Sherlock. I had not thought that your practical nature indulged in the speculations of theology."

"It is the only practical course for the thinking man! May I recommend Mr. Kierkegaard's Concluding Unscientific Postscript to the Philosophical Fragments to your perusal? And if that be too abstruse then let this suffice. The most astonishing thing about the Divine is its marvelous patience. It may even seem to be acquiescence in the face of evil. But why does God act in this manner, is it not so that evil may finally be destroyed by transformation into its opposite. Evil in some inscrutable way aids God in the achievement of the Kingdom. In the celestial metaphysic the only true dialectic is reversal not synthesis. When dealing with absolutes no synthesis is possible, one or the other must yield. To triumph by appearing to yield is triumph indeed!"

Mycroft stood up. "Well you may be mad but I see glimmers of insight in your obscure assertions. I wonder though that you have abandoned what I always assumed to be your staunch agnosticism. You once recommended I recall that ardent work, The Martyrdom of Man, by the deist Winwood Reade to my perusal."

"Well that was in my callow youth. Youth often stretches its sinews on the rack of the arrogant denial of God. Winwood Reade did no less. The stoic's bitter brow is soon smoothed as one grows older by the marble of oblivion. We enter this world in tears and in tears we die reaching for life. We do not escape the burden of contingency though and as we age we moderate the demands that we make upon life. All pride must finally yield to the silence of our own clay."

"I should enjoy some account of the transformation of your own thinking."

"Well then, you may recall that in my efforts on behalf of the French government in the case of Hurat, the boulevard assassin, I found myself spending time in Narbonne and Nimes."

"Of course, you were then pursuing your chemical research."

"Ah but far more than that, you see, I spent some little time in the Cathedrals for I found the atmosphere conducive to thought. It was during that time that my net began to close upon Moriarity and I began to wonder how I should employ myself after he was gone. You cannot have failed to notice that many of the cases that Watson has recounted involve minor problems that however important to the people involved and however challenging they may have been to my professional acumen brought in very little business to the firm, as it were. The small pension of an army Doctor had kept Watson for many years in want of funds and with his marriage and the expense of setting up a practice it was only his writings of my cases that made his own life possible. I was left in Baker Street with only the occasional paying client to subsidize the many cases that I took simply for the artist's pleasure of the chase. It was my work in France that began to change things. It began with that matter of the boulevard assassin that had so engaged the imagination of the French public. By solving that case I acquired an international reputation, as you know. Only then did my own practice as a consulting detective begin to grow. Until then I was merely a pet of Scotland Yard, an organization that never had the imagination or the courtesy to put me on retainer. Watson had made me a household name in Britain of course with the result that I was beset by governesses with problems that they imagined after too many readings of Mrs. Radcliffe's romances. The French and Italians and the Spanish and Dutch cases were different. For the first time in my life I had some financial liberty and as I sat in the Cathedral I pondered the many problems and questions of a more metaphysical nature that must come to a man of thought and reason once the mere struggle for survival is assured. It occurred to me that soon the Professor would also be at liberty from the burden of running his organization of crime. His star was waning while mine was at its ascendant. I thought that I might be a bit gracious to the man whose infamous nature and activities had brought me so many cases through the years. I had long entertained thoughts of travel. What if now I might combine travel, speculation, and in so doing also bring about a more complete defeat of Moriarity than his mere end by a hangman's noose? I began to sense an inscrutable purpose in events. You will recall the great tale by that American author Melville of Captain Ahab and his White Whale, Moby Dick. Well, with a sort of reversal of roles I shall lead him to first chase me as I have pursued him. It is for that reason that I propose to draw him out of the country and from his usual pursuits to create what the Chinese so well describe as the opportunity provided by chaos. You see Mycroft, if evil is even a runner-up to good it is not sufficient. The complete defeat of evil requires more than the continuous struggle between equals posited by the Persian philosopher Zoroaster. Evil must be led to exhaust its own malice, to reveal its final impotence before the Good; that, you see, is the explanation for the patience of God who defers the end of history so that by and in our own efforts we may turn the tide of events. The function of the Church in Catholic thought is to embody that great effort of all humans under a common roof and with its indwelling Holy Spirit to be such an incarnation that each and all may participate in the Divine labor. I admit that this supreme elevation seems reserved to the Saints but then Grace is promised also to the Little Ones. I dare to hope for the rehabilitation of the great Church Father Origen who once dared to hope for universal salvation, rather than some sour Calvinist's dream of near universal damnation and I might add eager anticipation of the destruction of those who are not of the election. I may be wrong but I incline toward hope for the conversion of the wicked at last."

Mycroft shook his head sadly, "Who would believe that your speculations would have taken you into such matters? I for my part have adjusted my expectations to the world in which we actually live. Look about you at every level of social role and discourse and what do you see but what I call the valances of power. Power behaves much like electricity. Power has its own pressures and velocities of flow, its amps and volts, if you will. It makes no sense to discuss the world of power as being either good or evil; it merely is and that is all. The man of affairs must take up the currents of life and attempt so to direct them that a minimum of harm is inflicted. Look about you at these members of the Diogenes Club whose members include some of the most powerful men of London. Why do they come here? Is it society that they seek? No, it is to be among their own kind that they come here. Some of these men are like crocodiles sunning themselves on the Nile, others are leaders of social movements, still others are highly placed men of the cloth. Each knows the loneliness of the man who must do evil to obtain a modicum of good. Only the poets and the abstract theologians dream of a morally cohesive universe. I usually think of you living a myopic life around your little medieval manuscripts when you turn to research. I did not realize that you were a philosopher after all."

"Ah well Mycroft, who does not dream of a grand synthesis of all that he knows and of the vast experience of the many cultures of the world? To see the world in a grain of sand and eternity in an hour, if I may quote the poet, has long been my desire, Mycroft. Well the converse is also true. I hope in travel to test these little theories of mine by discussing them with some of the great representatives of other faiths and observing them in action."

Mycroft stood up. "Well all that is before you. As for the present you had best begin by arranging matters with Doctor Watson. He is a staid fellow and I entrust you to his care now as I have done in the past. I will act as your driver of course and I do hope that in your travels you will keep me informed of events. The British government and my own resources are at your disposal, Sherlock. You may find our mundane and quite ordinary powers of some use since you will no doubt be visiting some very unsettled regions. Farewell."

So we parted and I left him sitting in his great chair, no doubt puzzled by his mad brother. I am writing this in my small monk's cell at Our Lady of Lambeth Monastery. May all go well tomorrow! I pray for a safe and blessed journey. The game is afoot!"

April 25, 1891

Mycroft was as good as his word. Watson arrived at the station to find me in the guise of an old, Italian priest. I had arrived at Waterloo Station in the company of a band of garrulous fellow priests. Their noise and enthusiasm contrasted with my quiet manner and assumed infirmity. It is one of the paradoxes of stealth that it need not be quiet. By drawing attention to ourselves as a group, I, who wished to remain invisible, was in fact obscured. The men who were watching for me were drawn in strange directions all over London and even Moriarity who may have had the monastery watched may assume that I had remained there to receive reports from Inspector Lestrade quietly as events proceed. Such was my hope but as the morning events were to prove Moriarity was hot on my trail. What finally put him on to me was, I expect, an exercise of the imagination. The Professor no doubt followed my old dictum of putting himself in his opponent's shoes in order to discern his intentions. We each have come through the years to understand the inner workings of one another's minds. While differing in motive we share a common mental sphere. Fortunately the delay involved in his reading of my intent, unaccustomed as he was with the role of being the detective, allowed me to escape.

Watson arrived on schedule looking over his shoulder in the most suspicious manner possible and gawking like a bird-watcher looking for signs of me. I am afraid that I laughed most heartily. I might not have done so however if I knew how close Moriarity followed upon our traces. As the train was about to leave Watson climbed aboard with a resigned air and entered the only unoccupied compartment where I awaited him. He nodded politely me as he sat down and proceeded to read his newspaper. He had managed to obtain a copy of the Times on the platform before climbing aboard.

As the train was about to pull out I thought it safe to disclose my identity. I spoke up with the feeble voice of assumed age, "Praego Seniore..."

He looked over the top of his paper. "Yes, Father?"

"I was simply wondering why, my dear Watson, since you have so far inconvenienced yourself to arise at such an early hour which is not your habit and come away with me out of your stuffy rooms smelling of idaform that you have yet to greet me, though I did appreciate your acting as my interpreter with the conductor." Watson has always been the perfect audience for my little theatrics and he did not disappoint me now.

"Good heavens Holmes is it really you?" cried he.

I had turned to look out the window as the train gave its initial lurch. "Quiet, my dear fellow, full explanations will follow but first let us get well away, even now every precaution is necessary. Look! Do you see? There, the tall man, he is endeavoring to stop the train. Ah, he has failed. Thank heaven for the efficiency of the British rail system. Now my good friend I am at your disposal."

As the train began to move we were both able to discern above the crowd the great bald head of Moriarity himself. His efforts were vain though since he had the great sullen body of the London train passengers and stoic platform conductors with which to deal. They acted as a sort of treacle to slow his progress. Yet I was surprised that even with all of my elaborate preparations that we were followed so closely. I lay back against the cushions to catch my breath after the strain of our departure and to find the first moments of peace that I had known for days.

"You see Watson, that even with all of our preparations that we have still cut it rather fine," I said casting off the cassock and biretta that I had worn and stowing both in a voluminous portmanteau. I used my handkerchief and a tube of petroleum jelly to remove the greasepaint that had given my usual pale features their olive Italian hue, and the sallow look of age. I took out my pipe, stretched my legs and back and assumed that languishing air of confidence that Watson says I am wont to assume in moments of triumph.

I see that you have a copy of The Times. If you will open it to page three you will find an article that concerns us, I am afraid that they set fire to our old rooms in Baker Street last night.

"Really Holmes, this is intolerable! One would think that we were the criminals! Why did you not simply have Moriarity arrested?

"Because, my dear fellow that would have upset all of my carefully laid plans. Moriarity is the head of course but it is the body of his organization that accomplishes his ends. If I had had Moriarity arrested I would have the big fish but the small would dart left and right out of my net. No, we must wait until Monday when my case shall be complete and until then we must take our chances."

"We may seek refuge in London then and await events."

"Nothing of the kind"

"But why, surely we would be safer there with the London constabulary to assure our safety?"

"They are not without their limits as last night's events make clear. But that is not why we are fleeing to the Continent. You touch upon deep waters. I prefer, you see, to deal with Moriarity directly and in my own way. Call it my little revenge."

"You must know Holmes that it is not from a desire to escape danger but there are motives of prudence. Why deal with such a dangerous beast...?

"Ah but that is not what he is Watson; Colonel Sebastian Moran, perhaps, is the beast of the organization and even he...but the Professor? No. He is instead a great force, Watson, and like any force it may be acted upon by a contrary force. We shall now apply that force."

"But why not a frontal assault then?"

"Ah, Watson, you are still the old campaigner! You would no doubt have collared Moriarity there on the platform. Let me assure you that I have far more in store for the Professor than either you or he may yet have imagined. We shall meet but in due time."

"You intend to kill him!"

"No, not at all! If I have managed things properly that will not be necessary. He knows that if he stays in London, then Lestrade will apprehend him on the stated date. He feels the noose tightening about his throat and he will be forced therefore to the undignified necessity to bolt. That alone is a triumph for he is a man of settled habits and enjoys his position of respectability at the university. Since he must leave London in any case, I am leading the way the better to have him at my mercy when I turn upon him."

"Ingenious!"

"Tush! Elementary, my dear fellow."

"But Holmes, we have left him behind."

"Do you think so? What would I do in similar circumstances? He will hire a special and pursue us."

"He will catch up with us at Calais."

"He will not. We shall leave the train at Canterbury. I have a little present for the Dean of the Cathedral from the good fathers at the Oratory that sheltered me last night."

"But what if Moriarity divines our plans and alights at Canterbury also?"

"Ah that would indeed be a master coup but even Moriarity has his limits. Still, I trust that you have your old service revolver in hand in case his own dark passions should override all reason and he should rush upon us with murderous intent. Good. Shall I ring then for the porter? I believe that a plate of kippers and a banger sausage or two will fortify us for what lies ahead."

When we alighted at Canterbury we took shelter behind a pile of luggage. My expectations were not disappointed when a short time later we observed a special train come through the station drawing a single black carriage. We were able to catch a passing glimpse of the grim visage of my foe in the window as the train passed. He was indeed hot upon our scent but I knew he would not discover his error until he reached Dover. This would give us a few hours at least of respite. We left the station and walked the quiet streets of Canterbury, the old medieval city and the spiritual center of England. It was a lovely spring day and the green of the land and the freshness of the Kent winds brought the scent of the new hay in the nearby countryside. How I shall miss the green of England, the calling of the gulls, the moist air and morning mists! We came to the great cathedral which had been the site of the martyrdom of St. Thomas Beckett, a victim of the perennial struggle between the rights of the monarchy and of the Church. Inside we were wrapped about by the silence of the old stones and the peace and venerable history of the place. The Dean greeted us warmly and received the relic I offered him with a grateful smile.

"How nice of you to bring this to me in person," Mr. Holmes. "The French are generous to lend us such a precious relic or do we owe our thanks to your own intervention?"

"I have in recent years in pursuing my own ancestry spent a great deal of time in France and was of some service to the French government who requested the Monastery at Cluny to part with it. But it is the Oratory of Lambeth who lends it to you now, not I."

"You are too modest Mr. Holmes. Even in our retreat we have heard of your role in the arrest and prosecution of Hurat the French boulevard assassin. It is alas part of these unsettled times that the governments of the world are subject to the sudden threat of the anarchists."

"Perhaps the legitimate governments of the world will learn to so exercise their monopoly on force that desperate individuals will not be driven to such means of restoring to the world the justice of God."

"You are indeed tolerant Mr. Holmes!"

"No, it is only that I have come to realize how often we defend the present order not realizing the quiet violence of the status quo. Surely the care of God must be also for those who inhabit our colonies."

"But Hurat was a Frenchman!"

"From French Africa, my good sir. As such he considered himself to be a patriot and perhaps he was."

"Yet you aided the French government in apprehending him."

"He chose his targets at random in order to bring terror to the populace who are as powerless to change the order of events as he was himself. It had to end."

"You are to be awarded the Legion of Honor, I have read."

"Ah well, the honors of the world...all is passing away is that not so? But we really must not tarry, my friend Watson and I have affairs at hand this very day which carry some danger. You must forgive our not staying for lunch. If you will favor us with your blessing and your prayers we will depart."

The good Dean gave us his blessing and we found ourselves again on the streets of Canterbury. "Well, we have three choices, Watson. Shall it be Dieppe, Calais, or Ostende?"

Watson chose Belgium and so we departed. We had the pleasure of watching the special return and pass us on the other track as Moriarity retraced his steps. After a brief lunch in Dover served at an inn with a private upstairs dining room with a view of Dover castle, we pressed on. But as we sat over our claret and what will be my last English savory pork pie for some time, the landlord brought in a cable in answer to one that I had sent from Canterbury before leaving to advise Inspector Gregson of our intentions and

where we would proceed. It read: Shall keep to him like glue.
Advise London of destinations and progress – Gregson

Dr. Watson's Narrative Continues

After our toast I had repaired to one end of Holmes' sitting room with
the manuscript. I looked up from the manuscript that I had been
perusing with the greatest attention while Holmes and the Professor
were engaged in a game of chess at the other end of the room. I could
see at once that Holmes' account differed from that which I had given
to the public in my own story, The Final Problem. I had, for instance,
not mentioned the incident with the Dean of Canterbury nor of
Holmes' brief shelter with the fathers of Our Lady of Lambeth
Oratory. These omissions were made out of respect for the privacy of
these men of God. I had feared that the public if informed of all
particulars of our escape from London might have overwhelmed the
solitude necessary to their lives of prayer and reflection. It was a
revelation to even me though that in our headlong flight to the
continent that we were not alone as I had supposed but were followed
by the redoubtable Inspector Gregson who my readers may recall
from my first case with Holmes entitled, A Study in Scarlet.

Holmes noticed that I had stopped reading. His eyes twinkled. "You
have reached a snag in the narrative, Watson?"

"You always gave me to understand that we were quite alone and that
the official police were occupied with capturing Moriarty's gang in
London and perhaps Moriarity himself."

"Yes and it always surprised me that you were so ready to credit that
explanation. You habitually underestimated my willingness to use all
of the resources that I could summon.   It was essential that the
Professor be boxed in at both ends. He was pursuing us but at the
same time he was himself pursued. I did not hold the Professor's
resources in contempt and Gregson was to be at hand if needed. Also,
you and I Watson have no official legal standing and should an arrest
have been necessary, any actions that we might have taken against the
Professor might have had the most deplorable international
complications. Scotland Yard was only too willing to participate in

my little ruse to draw Moriarity forth from London. My doing so served the purpose of drawing the Professor forth at a critical juncture and provided an excuse to his associates for his precipitate withdrawal at their time of need. This protected the Professor from any revenge that they might have contemplated upon him for abandoning them since he was in pursuit of their nemesis in the person of myself. By arranging the drama at Reichenbach as events turned out and by simulating our mutual deaths we were both able to ensure that all further pursuit would cease. This created a certain community of interest in our mutual silence about what had actually transpired and it is only now that the truth is being revealed and first of all, my dear fellow, to you."

"But if, as your own efforts made certain, that the entire organization was captured; what had you to fear?"

"This is true but then not all were sure to be hanged and prison is not forever. There were many reasons that I had to be certain that the Professor was not captured as your further reading will reveal."

"So Gregson..."

"As he promised, he stuck to the Professor like glue."

"And you were not aware of it?" I asked turning to the Professor.

Professor Moriarity chose to ignore the rather stiff tone of my inquiry and the air of reserve that I had maintained since his entry. "I thought that I might be followed but I was unsure as to who might be doing so. Your little switchback at Canterbury did in fact deceive me. I assumed that you would rely on speed and take the short route from Dover to Calais and then proceed to Paris. I had not reached a firm plan of attack yet and I must admit that for the first time I was acting under the pressure of events, a position somewhat unique in my experience. I had not at first intended to leave London. I am a man of the most sedentary habits and did not relish leaving for what might be an extended leave without my books and papers. The loss of power is an extraordinary thing. I had come to assume that I was in a sense invisible. To be brought with a jolt into the glaring light of public scrutiny was abhorrent to me."

"You no doubt feared arrest and trial also," I said with some sarcasm to the Professor whose general manner I still did not trust.

"I knew that my name would emerge in a series of trials dealing with some of the greatest unsolved mysteries of the age and that was sufficient. It is true that my former occupation was no more but you must understand that crime was for me an adjunct to what I felt was my real life. It had become for me a mere intellectual game played against the authorities. I had persuaded myself that I was even advancing a peculiar social agenda by honing the knife of public indignation at the failure of the police to solve the problems that I posed. I must also say that crime had its rewards in the pecuniary sense and that I supplemented my scholar's salary by it. Unlike your friend, Mr. Holmes, I was not of the country gentry. It had only been by an extraordinary effort worthy of the great Dr. Samuel Johnson, himself that I had been able to rise in the world. At last I was able, after the publication of my treatise on The Dynamics of an Asteroid, to attain what for a mathematician was a European vogue. Having come so far I must say that I bore a certain degree of resentment toward Mr. Sherlock Holmes who had been so instrumental in my undoing. Like a knife into an oyster shell he had entered and daily his force pried open what had been closed for years. Still I was not without reputation and your own revelations of the eccentric nature of your friend flattered me that I would not be actually convicted even if I was tried. The public would simply assume that years of cocaine abuse had addled his brain at last to the extent that he was daring to accuse in a most public manner the august, Professor Moriarity."

Holmes rubbed his hands together as was his wont when delighted. "I think that you realize now Watson that these are deep waters indeed and why it was essential that the public receive a different version of events as recounted in your story, The Final Problem. "Caught up as I was in these revelations, I had not yet thought to question the full reasons why Holmes had so long hidden the truth even from me. I addressed the Professor again, "If then you did not fear arrest and conviction, why did you leave London at all and pursue us as you did?"

"Because, as your friend has stated, I had everything to fear from my own people. They had long trusted me to keep them from harm's way. A few had been captured over the years but a wholesale rounding up, never! One of these men or their confederates would surely have succeeded in my own destruction. Besides, I was intrigued. What was the purpose of this absurd flight across country? It wasn't like the Holmes that I knew who preferred his danger before him and not behind him. It of course never dawned upon me that I was being led a merry chase out of that strange sense of humor that your friend unfortunately possesses. I assure you Doctor that I am haunted still by that arduous week of brisk hikes over mountain gorges."

Holmes interrupted, "It was my little revenge. We must not forget that the Professor's activities had long frustrated my best efforts nor must we forget that his actions had caused much suffering. Though I was willing to spare the Professor arrest and conviction, I demanded at least some expiation for his career of crime. I knew that the Professor would prefer Paris to London and if he must be arrested then it must be in the grand manner of the French Prefect of Police. I enjoyed the humiliation in making him contemplate arrest by the Constable of a small Swiss village. The result was that I led him onto ground of my own choosing. I was never in the dark. Throughout our flight I was informed by reports from Inspector Gregson who followed close at his heals. But, it is time that you returned Watson to the reading of my manuscript as I perceive that the Professor is anxious to return to our game and I perceive that my Bishop is in danger."

I poured myself a glass of Port before resuming that reading, resolving to keep the many questions that crowded upon me in abeyance for the time being. I must say that for the first time I was placed in the position that my own readers had occupied as I awaited the revelation of this greatest mystery of Sherlock Holmes. I adjusted my glasses and began again to read from the volume of Holmes' journal. A single coal fell in the grate and a brisk wind came in off of the great Atlantic and howled about the cottage eves as I settled down to read.

From the Journal of Sherlock Holmes

April 26, 1891 Brussels

After leaving Dover we had a fair journey over the channel to the Belgian coast and Ostend where we spent the night. A short train journey the following day brought us to Brussels where we spent a restful day after the demanding days that I have spent recently. We had a delightful dinner of Grouse cooked in a Brandy sauce and repaired later to our comfortable suite of rooms at the Hotel Brussels. It was a relief to have a good night's sleep after the many weeks of preparing my case against the Moriarity organization. Upon descending to the dining room the following morning for breakfast I stopped at the front desk and found a telegram waiting for me from inspector Gregson. It read as follows: Professor on night boat to Calais/is delaying departure in case you arrive/ making rounds of hotels/inform me of further travel plans/Gregson.

I sent him a reply in care of his own Hotel that we would be departing today and that I would have a cable awaiting him in Paris and that he could reach me care of the British consulate in Paris or our next destination of Strasbourg. This route to Switzerland we shall maintain if all goes well.

I put the cable aside and turned to my toast and marmalade.

"Well Watson, what shall we see today?"

"You intend to tarry then?"

"And why not, since we have given Moriarity the slip? That was a cable from Gregson. The Professor is in Calais."

"Is he not more likely to retrace his steps to London when he does not find us?"

"No. I hardly think so. Having lost us he will make inquiries in Paris hoping to regain contact. He will know that I cannot pass Paris without at least a short stop, Francophile that I am. The trick right now is to leave just sufficient traces so that he can follow us but not overtake us."

"Why leave any clues at all if our desire is to escape him?"

"It is because he must remain in our sight Watson. Remember that we are leading him by the nose and for our own purposes."

"And what are those purposes?"

"Ah, there you must grant me some latitude my dear fellow. I have as the Americans say, something up my sleeve which events will reveal and I must say that my plans are not yet complete even in my own mind. I must beg your indulgence for the present."

"Well I hope that we shall move on at least. I have always found Brussels an ugly blackened city and I prefer the green fields leading to Paris."

"How poetic you are Watson. But anticipate me. We have a few days before the Professor will give up on Calais and proceed to seek traces of us in the other Channel Ports. Shall we stop over in Trier or Luxembourg?"

"Are you so casual then?"

"Well I would like you to enjoy the trip since you have been so good as to accompany me. I hope that your practice will not suffer."

"It is somewhat contracted of late and my partner can absorb the few patients I had scheduled. I hope of course that I will be able to keep my wife informed of our progress."

"That is the very means that I have had in view of keeping the Professor aware of our movements. He has no doubt bribed the telegram delivery boy to inform him of our whereabouts by just this means. I will let you know when we can afford to send a telegram. Let us first try the Professor's own means without our help. Let him blunder about a bit and feel what it is to act as the detective."

"Let us press on then, I can be packed and ready..."

"And miss the fine old government buildings of Brussels surely we can spend one more day here to leave a fresh scent for the Professor. You enjoyed our rooms last night."

"I will not stay in a country ruled by that swine King Leopold of Congo infamy."

"Well he is the rightful monarch of this country and our own queen Victoria has not escaped some of the burdens of empire. Morality is a luxury of the middle classes Watson. The ruler as Machiavelli noted must be above such matters."

"You don't believe that."

"No, I do not. Let us say merely that the order of human events seems tainted by power and its pursuit. Choice at such levels seems to me beyond the traditional either/or. Rather, a multitude of options exist and out of each option flows, like a river, both good and evil. It is a prime characteristic of power that as it increases so do the comforts of a good conscience decrease. For this reason the monks live in simplicity so that they may fine-tune their actions and aspirations to the will of God. But we must not tarry all day over these distinctions we are not at the academy nor at the Councils of statesmen but are mere British subjects on holiday. Finish your breakfast and we shall see if Brussels may redeem the impression you have of its monarch."

A short time later we emerged from the hotel. I desired to remain at least for one day so as not to lose the Professor completely. I must consider his age and infirmities so in the lift up I convinced Watson to tarry for one day the better to break the Professor in on our traces. I concluded that the Professor would go first to Dieppe to make inquiries and then proceed himself to Ostend. This will be the great test of his abilities. I shall keep him just out of reach. Watson and I are both armed and on our guard. There was also the chance that the professor would conclude that we had remained in England. In any case we must await his arrival for a day at least in Brussels until I am sure that he has caught the scent again. It is a delicate game that I am playing. I must stay just so far ahead of the Professor that we can avoid an actual confrontation but not so far that I lose him completely. This will of course seem absurd to Watson who will wonder why we do not keep a faster pace; after all one does not stroll about on the grand tour with such a man as Moriarity on one's very heels. On the other hand, I have seen little of my friend Watson in recent years due to his unfortunate predilection for marriage and the fair sex and I myself if my plans succeed may be absent from England and from Europe for some years. I intend then to cherish these halcyon spring days at Watson's side. Once I know that the Professor has caught the scent I shall proceed by the Strasbourg route to Switzerland.

The day was a peaceful one. We wandered the ancient streets and visited the impressive government buildings. We lunched on an excellent clam bouillabaisse. I could see at all times though that Watson was on his guard. We must soon move on if only to preserve his peace of mind. Ever since his days in Afghanistan Watson has been hyper-alert to any sign of physical danger. It has made him invaluable to me in any situations where action is demanded. His loyalty and courage know no bounds. He is the best of companions when the trail lies over rough ground. I do not wish to risk his life in this matter though and no doubt he wonders why I do not simply break free of Moriarity. He does not realize that this would risk all. I could never return to England for fear of his delayed vengeance. Still I cannot bring myself to Moriarity's actual death. It would be such a waste and then there is the challenge....

Later- After dinner and a visit to the grand opera house I was relieved to hear from Gregson again. The Professor has not left Calais. Evidently he is also dependent upon cables from at least one unknown source. He has taken up lodging in the best hotel in town and he sits silently in the dining room unaware the he is being observed by Gregson. He receives periodic cables where he sits alone in a corner of the room engaged in some manner of calculations. His great head is bent over a notebook perhaps figuring the odds of capturing his old foe, perhaps seeking refuge in some complex problem of celestial mechanics. Inspector Gregson meanwhile is posing as a London textile merchant and is entertaining a string of prospective customers who are actually members of the French police force in disguise. I have explained something of my own knowledge of the art of disguise to Gregson who has donned an enormous moustache for the occasion to prevent recognition. In matters of disguise less is often more. Well, I think that this will do for tonight. I am off to bed. After our day in Brussels laying the scent we should be off the day after tomorrow. We will proceed to Strasbourg by way of Luxembourg, Trier, and Paris unless events should force a more precipitate flight upon us.

April 28, 1891   Hotel Strasbourg, France

I have decided to follow a route via Strasbourg to Switzerland. Our last day in Brussels was a tense one. Moriarty, apparently satisfied that we did not return to England, has used his knowledge of probability plus his knowledge of me to effect. He took the 4:10 train to Brussels. I myself was at the station disguised as a porter when he arrived. He has if anything aged in appearance these last few days since he came to my rooms in London.   His usual sedentary habits do not adapt well to pursuing a wily foe across country. Then there is the change of foods from the simple but hearty English fare to Belgium's rich sauces. It is part of the curse of melancholic temperaments that they are so often dyspeptic. I watched him from one end of the platform where I was engaged in helping an elderly lady gather her hatboxes and trunks. I overheard the Professor name a hotel to his porter which is only a few blocks from our own. He will, no doubt, discover by morning where we are lodged.   I took the precaution of bringing our own luggage away myself by a back door to the station. Gregson had wired me of the Professor's departure from Calais having finally concluded that we had taken the boat to Ostend. It is unfortunate that we must leave since we had reserved seats at the opera again.   Instead, this evening we will be flying south through the Ardennes to Luxembourg.   There we will spend the night and then on to Strasbourg by the afternoon train. Watson has been watching at our hotel and will soon join me. These sudden departures are customary to an old campaigner and no doubt he feels that he is in the army again when breaking camp at a moment's notice was customary.

Later- Luxembourg has as always its air of the charm of fairy tales. Its solid burgerlich air has always reminded me of an overweight dowager. It was sad that we had to press on immediately but I am now assured that the Professor has sources of information about our whereabouts and I must, to be prudent, extend the lead. I must say that I was relieved as the train sped through Alsace and Lorraine after our short feint towards Germany by going to Luxembourg. To be flying south through the rich green fields was a joyful experience though I wish we had been able to stop at Paris for a few days or spend a week of repose at Cluny. These lands of Alsace and Lorraine must be our recompense for the necessity of haste in order to stay ahead of the Professor. They have been under German rule since 1870. The charming towns have never though surrendered the look of France. Perhaps a time will come when France will again embrace these rich pasture lands from which some of the world's finest cheeses are derived. I wondered as the train sped on how soon the Professor will pick up our trail and follow. I have left a few false trails so as not to be too obvious of my intent which should delay him for a day or two. He will wonder if we have proceeded to Aachen, Trier, or Koln. The motion of the train finally lulled me to sleep and it was only as we were passing through the outskirts and about to pull into the station at Strasbourg after dark that I was awakened by Watson who touched my arm to awaken me. We had an excellent pheasant dinner in the hotel dining room and then took a brisk after-dinner walk through the darkened streets past the immense cathedral.

"Holmes, I must ask, how long are we to proceed in this manner?"

"What manner is that," I inquired.

"By traveling as though we were simply on vacation and making the grand tour."

"Well we have shaken free of him for now."

"But what will he do? He can hardly return to London knowing that the trap is about to spring."

"No, he will follow us no doubt."

"Then the danger is not passed, will you not confide in me your intentions?"

"For now I can say nothing, so much depends you see on the Professor's actions. It is even possible that he will return to London in a last effort to keep the jaws of my trap from closing or at least to save some his more essential lieutenants."

"Why was not a mere warning to them sufficient?"

"Because, my dear Watson, his higher confederates are respected men in public life. They will hardly go scurrying for cover like so many dockside villains or wily Lascars. They will no doubt put my proofs to the test with some of the best barristers in England."

"Will they succeed do you think?"

"Ah, as to that I cannot say."

We walked on in silence. I have woven my net as closely as I might without giving the game away prematurely. So much of course depends upon salvaging records and getting the lesser fish to testify against the higher-ups. All of this is beyond my humble role as a consulting detective. My only answer to Watson must be that I hope that all will go well. I shall hear tomorrow from Gregson how the great series of arrests have proceeded. From then on it may be wise to confide my plans for the future to Watson. Since we are pursued, and who can say that it is the Professor alone who pursues us, I may advise Watson to return to London and proceed south alone. It may be weeks before I actually confront Professor Moriarity and I do not wish Watson to run unnecessary risks. Watson will refuse of course to leave me, being the man that he is. I may have to devise therefore a more careful stratagem to get him to return to London without me. Would the Professor go so far as to attempt a direct attack upon us? If so, Gregson who hangs close upon him would shoot him down. Gregson is as tenacious as a greyhound but he must keep his own distance from the Professor so as not to be spotted. The situation is indeed wearing and a crisis must come at last. We returned from our walk through the black and silent streets, chill even in this late spring. I write these notes in anticipation of the morrow before facing what may prove an uneasy sleep.

April 29, 1891 Basle, Switzerland

The telegram from London was delivered this morning at our hotel in Strasbourg. I palmed the second telegram from Gregson keeping me aware of the Professor's progress. If Watson will persist in accompanying me I shall at least spare him some of the anxiety of our position. I passed the London telegram to Watson who read it silently.

He looked up in concern, "I think that we should return to England at once."

"And ruin our holiday?" I smiled over my café au lait.

"Holmes, you must see the continuing threat. At least in London we should have the police at our disposal."

"But for how long? If the suspense of the last days has been trying for us both, what then would be a lifetime of waiting for the Professor or is aides to strike? No, I shall face the matter now and definitively and...alone. You must return to your wife."

"That I shall never countenance; I stay by your side."

"I may ask a great deal of you and certain matters must remain hidden, my dear friend, even from you if my larger plans are to mature in time."

He was silent for a time and his great noble face was troubled but at last he looked up and said, "I consent. What will you do now?"

"Well, speed is certainly the point at issue since I desire that he catch up with us while he remains in that dullness and perplexity of mind which is hardly his usual position. His mind may be inflexible enough to resist change while emotion dulls the force of reason. The wise course for him would be to return secretly to England and await a better day for his revenge but he is already well on the way and can hardly stop now."

"But he would be immediately arrested."

"Oh he might arrange to be smuggled in secrecy to some out of the way place. He is after all not without all resources. I did, however, read a most sinister purpose in his eyes when we met that day in our old rooms in Baker Street when he tried as a last measure to warn me off. No, he will soon act for better or for worse. We will therefore force his hand by slowing our pace. He will conclude that we feel that we have given him the slip. We will of course remain on guard. We shall proceed then, Watson, to enjoy as we may this excursion to the lovely valley of the Rhone while awaiting events. Keep your revolver ready though and your wits about you for there lie before us adventurous days, such days as we have never yet met in our career.

April 30, 1891 Meiringen, Switzerland

We arrived at Meiringen late yesterday after a majestic trip through the towering peaks and plunging gorges of the Alps. The entire country seems to consist of small valleys floored by pale green meadows followed by the pastoral cities such as Lucerne and the greater metropolis of Zurich. The Swiss are a stern and silent people such as befits their unique sense of independence and the struggle for existence in this harsh and challenging landscape. They rely on their animals to an extraordinary extent and seem to have learned their own patience from the cows, goats, and sheep that graze their fields. The stolid character of the Swiss is further seen in their sensible use of space in their remarkably clean and ordered cities. I must say that I was completely charmed by Lucerne. I sat gazing upon the lake and debated with Watson whether we might remain for some days but the pressure of keeping up an optimum distance from the Professor remained. The lovely views and the quiet of the town would have been ideal under other circumstances but I could not lose sight of my deeper purpose. No, I must find a place of isolation to draw the Professor finally out of hiding and to force that confrontation that I have both dreaded and anticipated. Our present retreat is the little village of Meiringen which lies in a shallow valley below the snow-line that in melting is withdrawing to the higher peaks. Meiringen is surrounded by bare slopes littered with the debris of landslides formed when the rushing waters of the melting snow carves out both rocks and boulders. The visibility is clear in all directions so that I feel that I have picked an ideal spot to avoid sudden death by ambush. This is the ground on which to meet my foe. The one advantage of the stag pursued by the hunter is that it may turn where and when it will there to stand at bay and confront its pursuer. So shall I.

I had already picked my ground in Lucerne and cabled our destination in care of the Staatspolizei in Strasbourg, Freiburg, and Basle. The Professor must pass through one of these towns. I calculate that the Professor is one or two days behind us at present but must also allow for days spent making inquiry after us. Gregson is proving his mettle by remaining unobserved, as I hope, while riding the same train as Professor Moriarity. He is able as an officer of the London police to requisition destinations from the local train authorities but he must also look to the fact that the Professor may anticipate that he is followed and leave the train before his assigned station should he suspect that he is pursued. Fortunately, the Professor has yielded to a desire for comfort by riding express which has reduced the number of stations where the train will stop. Otherwise he would have long since exhausted the Inspector who must finally sleep. He has shortened the leash as the chase is reaching its climax. Formerly, he could remain a day behind the Professor relying instead upon the rail authorities to advise him of the Professor's progress and on customs agents when crossings of national borders occurred. There are definite advantages to holding an official position that the gifted amateur if I may so style myself does not possess. Without Gregson and the cooperation of the international authorities the resources of Watson and myself should have been exhausted and the entire project that I have in mind been jeopardized. Even as it is there is a great element of suspense and uncertainty. How will the Professor mount his attack? Will he be alone or does he have other resources purchased or purloined that may yet cause me to fail? Has he not already been made suspicious by my own conduct in leaving so open a trail after my original rather simple ruse of early disembarkation at Canterbury? Has his great mind failed to realize that I may have learned certain principles of our role reversal from him? Now it is I who am acting as the spider in the center of its web and using my own associates and network the better to entrap my adversary. Perhaps he is relying on the impression conveyed by the stories of my career published by Doctor Watson that indicates that I always prefer to act alone and independently. Can it be that he is the true romantic after all and imagines that this duel is to be without seconds or observers? No, it is absurd! The Professor cannot be alone. He must have at least one trusted confederate at his side or within call and this no doubt an active man who might have some hope of overcoming me in a physical struggle should such occur. In that case the Professor is coming finally as a witness to my ruin and not as its agent. My death may come at the hands of another...ah well, we must await events....

It was a lovely spring day when we alighted at the station in Meiringen and were taken by carriage to the Englisher Hof. Watson was pleased with our rooms on the second floor overlooking the round drive before the hotel and with the Jaegerraum below where we will be well fed during our stay. Watson felt for perhaps the first time that we were indeed free. His own expansive nature came to the fore and he insisted upon throwing wide the shutters the better to breathe the invigorating mountain air while looking down at the drive, the terrace, and the small flower decked courtyard below. We changed into Swiss attire the better to blend in with our surroundings and took the old carved stairway down to the terrace where we were served and excellent lunch of Bockwurst dotted with parsley, a krautsalat, and some excellent browned potatoes served with bacon. The beer served was an excellent lager, pale and crisp as the mountain snows that surrounded us and the entire meal was enlivened by the running commentary of the proprietor of the Englisher Hof, one Peter Steiler, who came over to wish us welcome and to point out the advantages of our present location.

You must Meine Herren see the great falls of Reichenbach while you are here. They are truly as you English say magnificent, that is the word, a magnificent sight. It is surrounded by high cliffs and the walk alone is wunderbar, sehr wunderbar!"

"How long does it take to get up to them," Watson inquired?

"Ach, nur ein halbe tag, a half-day, as you say. I will for you a lunch-pack make. In the afternoon you will return for the nights are still cold."

"The path is in open country?" I inquired, still ruminating on the risks surrounding us.

"Ja, you can in all directions the hills over see," the proprietor answered. "As you climb you can the entire valley see."

He went on to say that after a walk of three or four kilometers we would come to the falls. He described a short ledge going out that allowed the best view of the falls. From the ledge one might gaze far down to the thunderous pools below. He warned us that there was no railing and that the track was muddy at this time of the year and we must take great care. He was willing, he said, to provide an experienced guide to enhance our safety and enjoyment.

Watson looked over at me. "Shall we try the ascent tomorrow?" he asked.

The landlord suddenly expostulated, "Ach nein, better the next day. Tonight and tomorrow these days are unglucklich, unlucky. Tonight is Walpurgis Nacht which lasts until sunset tomorrow. On this night the witches gather on the Brocken Peak in Germany, but wherever there are good folk, Frau Perchta, the Queen of all the witches, leads her hoelle hunt throughout the skies."

I am afraid that I looked up, amused by this sudden speech, surprised as I was that a stern Protestant land yet retained the old superstitions of centuries ago. We immediately assured him that this short delay would work no hardship upon us since we planned a stay of at least a week in his comfortable hotel. He showed immediate relief and pleasure at this assurance on our part and momently withdrew. He returned a short time later bringing us a complementary Apfelstruedel and two short glasses filled to the brim with fiery plum liquor imported from the region of Styria in Austria. He then withdrew with a bow.

71

We ate slowly looking up at the surrounding slopes and began at last to enjoy a welcome respite from our flight across Europe. It was good to see Watson enjoying the hearty Swiss fare. He had already disposed of a bowl of Swiss stew and was now savoring the flakey butter-crust of his dessert. Perhaps he has concluded that we have shaken the Professor at last and can begin a real holiday. If so I shall not disturb his confidence in that supposition. The dear old fellow has never disappointed me and no doubt my own confidence and willingness to run these extraordinary risks are due to having the old Afghan campaigner at my side. The proposed sojourn to the falls may well fall in with my plans. If the countryside is indeed as open as described, then the Professor must follow if he is on the scene, scenting his opportunity at last. But his approach may be observed by one who is on his guard. We shall be armed of course and perhaps Gregson will also be at hand to lend any aid that may be needed. I am afraid that the Professor's days are numbered if he insists upon playing his hand right down upon the table. Will he be so crude though as simply to mount an open assassination attempt upon us at this final hour? Where would he be then if were as alone as I without him to test my mettle? Could he ever return to a quiet life of mathematics without the power and excitement provided by his life of crime or will he attempt to rebuild his shattered organization should he succeed in killing me? What would I do in his circumstances? My imagination has always been my guide in matters of detection. Can the past be resumed, the lost trail of expectation of our projected futures ever be found again? We begin life with such a clear and unobstructed vision before events overwhelm us and the mere accident of encounters fills our days with unsought loyalties, often to projects unworthy of our deeper selves. At my time of life one looks back and finds that his life has been for the most part an accident. Somewhere the true way has been lost as Dante said so well in the opening passage of his Divine Comedy. It is then that the short time left becomes a mockery. There is little time even to continue what has been well begun let alone to retrace ones steps and begin to forge an alternate history. If I feel this way, I who have met some success in my profession and been of some use, then how bound must the Professor feel who has been evil and has only his sole self left as the repository of his wasted days. It is my hope though that the

Professor will discover that he has stumbled upon far richer ground even at this late hour for his great mind to pursue. No more back alley toughs, extortion, and murder. It is time for a wider sphere and I would invoke the great poet Robert Browning who said that "Man's reach must exceed his grasp else what's a heaven for." Beyond the tiny realm in which most of us live our lives thrashing out our meager loves and hates and enduring the thousand slights that flesh is heir to, there is the great international arena, the great mechanized whole, the huge beast that determines the lives of millions in pursuit of policies often more crude and simplistic then any fool would adopt to guide his private live. It is there that the entire experiment of civilization rests. It is there that men and soon women too will gather and in exchanging views in quiet rooms determine the future. Will peace come at last or will the young still bleed upon the perennial battlefields of the world? How many will taste death while the sweet sense of spring lies upon their young leaves of green? How many buds will close before their petals taste the dew of morn? To play a role in history and turn it from what so often seems its predetermined course: surely that is the only worthy task for a mind of the first order to pursue. This is why I must go to Asia. I must see how this great landmass, this bone of contention for empires will find itself and in doing so perhaps determine the destiny of the human race.

May 1, 1891 May Day in Meiringen

May Day dawned with that peculiar freshness and clarity that is found only in the mountains. As a weary city dweller accustomed to sticky fogs and blinding, coal dust fueled precipitations I must say that I welcome the days that lie before me as a certain re-birth. One cannot live within the strange fabric of empire without feeling its underlying complexity. The dynamic of power casts a pall over everything. I have found myself wondering, yes even I who once admired Chinese Gordon of Khartoum and traced the letters VR for Victoria Regina upon the walls of my rooms in Baker Street, whether the extension of power, even if pursued with the intent to share the benefits of British civilization with the world, is worth the cost. Have the benefits of this extension of our colonial presence been shared with even the people who lie at the center of our empire, the British, Scottish, and Irish? Does not a horrible

73

inequality beset us at home? Surely with the resources of the world at our disposal one would suppose that the problems of hunger, poverty, and ignorance among the masses at home would be more alleviated then they are. But the carrot of national security is ever held before us and the future painted in the brightest of colors and intricate design the better to distract the people from their present want. There is little sense of community except in the rural districts. The commons seems to have become a foreign concept. Instead each man's hand is raised against another and our lives are mortgaged and our time is not our own. Those who have mastered the great game are furnished with superfluity while those remaining are granted only so much as will keep rebellion in check! Such being the case, who can blame entirely those who share Moriarty's cynicism and pursue a policy of revenge against the quiet duplicity of government by making manifest the greed and violence which masks itself as public policy, pursuing his own independent course? In his open predation he has become a sort of hero to his underlings. What difference is there between him and the respectable members of our Parliament who hide their rapacity and betrayal of the public under the guise of Adam Smith, David Ricardo, and the lingua franca of free trade?

Ah well, there is no time for such speculations at present. While writing this I have sat at the window enjoying the perspective. Watson must soon awaken and we must set the day in motion. We must flush the wild boar Moriarity from hiding. I have hired a local guide, Hans, who will show us the region and act as a second pair of eyes in the village. I have described the Professor to him and also met with the local constable who has likewise promised assistance as needed and who has promised to make inquiries for unusual visitors in the vicinity. Is the Professor already upon the scene? I hope to hear from Inspector Gregson today. Ah, I hear stirrings in Watson's room. I must set this journal aside for now.

Evening-

I have heard from Gregson. He has lost Moriarity. The event was of course foreseeable. I have no monopoly on the technique of railway switches. As near as Gregson can make out the Professor went north again to Munich. Has the Professor given up the chase?

I can hardly turn and pursue him. I had thought to leave sufficient clues to keep Moriarity on the track without being too obvious and awakening his suspicions. I have wired Gregson not to pursue the Professor in hopes that his turn north was to escape Gregson who has been following him perhaps too obviously. The turn north may have also been simply a preemptive evasive maneuver to throw off any anonymous pursuit even if Gregson in his own person has not been observed. My first desire therefore is to set aside any anxiety that the Professor has. He must feel in control of unfolding events. Now begins a time of waiting and a war of nerves. Since a second observation of Gregson would be fatal to my plans Gregson must draw back. I must reconcile myself to the possibility that the Professor will lie just out of reach to await a time to strike. I in turn must feign confidence and provide for him just that vulnerable moment. I must appear to be utterly alone and yet have a hidden means of defense. In such open country I can think of no means to draw the Professor out unless I also can draw Watson from my side. Will the Professor dare then to appear similarly alone and out of hiding at last, here so far from London? What form will the duel between us take? Will the retired stoop-shouldered scholar attempt to attack me, the lean hound whom the habit of the chase has made spry? Bah, of course not, romantic and absurd! But still, if there is no place of concealment how can he fail to launch some form of frontal attack? Having come so far the Professor clearly has some specific intent but has emotion so overpowered reason that the Professor's revenge will brook no delay and take a physical form? Well, I must await events since I have no basis for a conclusion without data.

Watson at least is enjoying our present location but I have noted how he glances up at balconies as we walk through the streets for the muzzle of a firearm. My own efforts to enjoy the charm of our surroundings also cannot hide from him my own taut nerves. Having turned at bay we must marshal our resources as best we can. Still withal we have tried to amuse ourselves today. There was a festival in the village today with local folkdances. We enjoyed the knockwurst and the great steins of golden beer and the general air of celebration of spring. The country people have flocked in from the surrounding farms. The church bells rang in the morning and masses were held to honor the Virgin Mary whose feast day this is.

The evening closed with a quiet blue dusk and an amber glow over the mountains. Having written these lines I shall retire to rest for tomorrow may be active indeed.

May 2, 1891 Meiringen

Again the sun was shining upon the peaks this morning as we breakfasted on the excellent bread rolls and rich coffee with ample portions of schnitzel to fortify us for whatever the day will bring. I must say that the clear dry air has awoken in me a sense of purpose such as I have not felt in years. How often have I not lamented to Watson the dullness of London life? Who can endure the mere passage of time leading to inevitable age without a mission and driving purpose to lend significance to our days? For so many years Moriarity provided that sense of mission for me. Though he is not alone in infamy he had the advantage of being an inverse mirror image of my own nature. Without the Moriarity gang to provide the truly challenging crimes I have been haunted by the prospect of governesses who will consult me to discover the source of noises in the attic or heiresses beset by unwelcome suitors seeking an answer whom to marry. How often have Watson's accounts featured just such cases of domestic trauma? It is true that they often provide features of interest but what harm avoided in the larger scheme of life? The truly great crimes are seldom punished since they are often committed by heads of state and chief ministries. When faced by the daily massacre of the innocent through an engineered policy of scarcity of resources in order that the wealthy and powerful and their order may be preserved with all of its vanities, how can the expert in crime wonder if his talents have been wasted pursuing the wrong people? Even the recent and appalling attacks of Jack the Ripper upon denizens of the demimonde must pale before the systemic evils of beatings and gin that prematurely end so many young lives yet are part of normal life in the east end. The really successful murderers are the manufacturers of arms and the ministers of war who hide themselves and their hunger for blood in the guise of patriotism and the inevitability of conflict between nations. How ready we are to submerge our identities in these abstract groupings and in the arbitrary borders of the nation-state. If I indeed seek my future in Asia will I find in the oriental warlords and potentates any greater savagery than that which slumbers in the bosom of many a member of our own House of Lords?

Later-

Still no word from Gregson. If Moriarity has reversed his direction and come south he may be already upon the scene. I must provide an opportunity to draw him out so today I propose an expedition over the Gemmi Pass toward Interlaken and Leuk. We shall walk by the bleak and rocky shores of the Daubensee. If we need to seek sudden shelter there are always crevasses and deep ravines. The entire landscape is reminiscent of a poem by Percy Shelley in which vast forms seem to have been flung to earth by titans rather than being the fruit of successive glaciations. I wonder, is it the hidden dramatist lodged in my own bosom or is it fate that has decreed such a landscape for what may be my final encounter with my arch-foe? I trust that I have not become prey to a literary competition with my friend Watson to provide in my own narrative a continental adventure to keep any future readers of this manuscript amused and sell a few extra copies of the Strand Magazine! I do of course have a sense for the dramatic and the artistic effect, which no doubt stems from my French antecedents, which must be appeased. How often have I in my own way been tempted to treat life itself as an art form with myself as the artist or author of events. I have even wondered if Moriarity himself might have been in a way my own creation. Does the one who is pursued owe his existence to his pursuer? Might I even go so far as to suggest that Moriarity might long since have abandoned crime if it were not for the pleasure of thwarting my own efforts to solve his crimes? Is he also a victim of the stodgy confidence of the British Empire and the general boredom of the age? If I did not exist would not the Professor have turned to the heavens, if not to search for God, then perhaps to find in his cold theorems and abstruse speculations a material substitute? I have often felt that the Professor's talents were wasted. I have said as much to Mycroft on many an occasion. In fact, Mycroft himself with his connections to power might have seemed my more logical foe. But then perhaps the Professor is indeed vicious and his cold mind may seek recompense in the sheer physicality of evil and of bloodshed to feel as it were the soft fur of his victim yielding before his fangs. Here again we have the question of the recurrent atavism of man. Have we ever really left the jungle? Is Aristotle's pity and fear simply the exaltation of those who have managed to escape fang and claw in gazing on the bloody corpse of the slain as the hunter drags it away to be devoured? Perhaps it is true that evil like good admits not merely of degree but of type. Certainly the Saints, in their clear realization and intimate contact with God, seem of a different order of men and women from the generality of mankind. At least it must appear so to those of us who have so long pursued a rational belief in a supernatural destiny for humankind. If there is not God, then our destiny is confined to a mere lifetime which must always be inadequate to the ambitions of the artist and the saint. But the shortness of the number of our days is but one of the many evils that flesh is heir to. Ever since Zoroaster man has tried to confront the strangeness that God's omnipotence tolerates evil. The only answer must be that evil is so twisted that it resists direct extirpation. To grapple with evil directly may be to become evil oneself! No, evil must be as it were seduced backward into truth if it is to be conquered; such has become my credo. If mankind is the origin of its own ills then it must seek a remedy beyond itself, thus the doctrine of Divine Grace. Ah well, I am a detective and not a theologian, still my mind has often dwelled upon these matters and it is from those reflections that my policy towards the fate of the Professor is emerging.

Evening- Ah a strange day it was indeed! Was an attempt made upon our lives today? We took the road after breakfast, Alpenstocks in hand and climbed the steep slopes of the Gemmi Pass to view the Daubensee. The bleak and open snowfields drew back from the grey of the waters below us. The mountains pressed in from every side so that Watson and I felt something of the awe and grandeur of the place, similar emotions to those of the great poet Wordsworth recorded in his admirable poem The Prelude. It was essential to keep our eyes firmly on the treacherous path before us so that neither of us observed the instant when a great boulder came loose and fell, just missing us, to plunge into the lake waters far below. It thundered by just in front of us followed by a brief landslide of smaller debris. I climbed immediately to the ridge above but could detect no human origin for the event. Still, the incident seemed to confirm all of our anxieties. I gave Watson a significant look and we proceeded in silence. Are our nerves beginning to tell upon us I wonder? We both of us feel the need for some immediate action. May the event soon materialize as neither Watson nor I are accustomed to such rigors of suspense. Was it then the spirit of the place that pursued us? Where is the Professor at this very hour?

May 3, 1891 - Interlaken

There is still no word on Moriarity. I have asked that Inspector Gregson join us in Meiringen on the fifth and we will continue our journey southward to Italy. I must assume though that Moriarity is in the vicinity. Perhaps he has chartered a chalet since the village is too small to conceal his presence. If I am to draw him out it must be on open ground. I have heard from our landlord that the Falls of Reichenbach are an excellent local attraction. The walk there will take us through open country and perhaps I may glimpse the Professor at last. I do not know the outcome but I have the prospect of a few last days of joy and if I must die then let it be in these glorious surroundings of ice, snow, and crystalline skies.

Later- He is here! Today we returned to Meiringen from a night's stay in Interlaken. I took the precaution of hiring a Swiss version of The Baker Street Irregulars, my police force of local urchins, to spy out the whereabouts of Professor Moriarity. In this I was aided by Peter Steiler, the Innkeeper, who knows the local lads. This morning they came to me with the information that I sought. The Professor arrived by sleigh over the pass and is installed at a farmer's chalet along the very route that I propose to travel today. His prescience is remarkable as ever. Now I must decide upon a course of action. Inspector Gregson will not arrive until tomorrow and I hesitate to expose Watson to so certain a danger. He will of course refuse to leave my side. I have therefore arranged a ruse. Our landlord will send word of an emergency requiring a physician's aid. He will send a messenger to announce a sudden lung hemorrhage of an English woman at the Inn. This cannot fail to draw Watson whose natural chivalry and sense of professional duty will not allow him to leave a Countrywoman in distress. I shall proceed with the climb alone and promise to rendezvous later with Watson. I pray that this ruse will both protect Watson and draw the beast from cover and that Moriarity will make his play. I am armed of course, but so must the Professor be. Will he be alone I wonder? This may be my last entry in this journal. Should it be found after my death let me say only, my dear Watson, (since it will be your eyes that first peruse this final journal with its last entry) that I am sorry, dear friend, that my ruse drew you from my side, but I am not without affection for you, and must in any case spare my Boswell so that he can explain to what lengths I was forced to go to rid the world of Moriarity. Be assured, as always, John Hamish Watson, of my respect, of my gratitude, and of my undying esteem.

Sherlock Holmes

May 4, 1891 -Evening

I am writing this in a little inn some five miles from the Reichenbach Falls. I write it alone since Watson has no doubt by now returned to our lodgings alone and is now convinced of my death. I am deeply oppressed by the pain that I must be causing him but as my narrative of today's events will show, I had no other choice. The strange proposal of the professor in answer to my own challenge was dispositive and neither emotion nor my natural loyalty to Watson could prevent me from accepting. Can the Professor be trusted? No, of course not, in the ordinary course of affairs, but in this, where his self interest is so implicated feel that I may do so. The Professor's own mind, the workings of which I alone have fathomed, demands it. When I first read The Dynamics of an Asteroid I began to comprehend how to solve the multi-dimensional facets posed by the problem of Moriarty. To seek regularity in the irregular, that was the key. The dynamics of an asteroid, if I might summarize the Professor's theory as I understand it, are governed by multi-determination variables. Each object along the path of the asteroid exerts its own gravitational influence as the asteroid passes. The path of the asteroid is, therefore, neither spherical nor elliptical but rather consists of a series of irregular, interconnected arcs. An outside observer would perceive the path of the asteroid then as a series of "jumps." These "jumps" appear to be as if spontaneous and alive but are in reality segments separated only for the convenience of description, while the actual path of the asteroid is sustained by an ongoing momentum. No individual segment along the path is predictable or measureable while the overall movement is. The sum total of observations then would yield a single dynamic. Such local observations would lose themselves in endless permutations if every force in the universe were to be calculated. It takes arbitrary selection in order to describe the universe as a whole. A trillion equations could not solve or describe the entirety of events even if restricted to a single instant of time. But merely restrict one's scope to the momentary deflection a few particles and simplicity emerges which can then be generalized to explain the whole. Such is the course of scientific endeavor. The questions to be answered in science are then always dependent upon the level of approach. What is deterministic at one level may appear as pure spontaneity at another level. The great question of freedom vs. determinism lies in the level of inquiry of events that is chosen. The professor, in essence, writes that by spot checks of position and momentum the movement of the asteroid could be frozen in time and its next movement might then be predicted along a probability axis but that at the micro-level certain spontaneity seems to emerge. Complete certainty is impossible whenever one is dealing with infinities whether infinitely small or infinitely large. Science is confined to the intermediate sphere where generalities may be said to exist.

I believe that I can make an analogy between the physical and the moral spheres. What I hope to do with Moriarty is to create a phase change within the soul of Moriarty, a conversion of heart in the whole by probing the results that may flow from the individual moral decision. Character is the result of action rather than existing prior to action.

What appears to us as evil may be, from the perspective of God, the working out of the salvation of all of creation. In each moment we, in a sense, define our character for good or for evil; but the long parabola of our lives lies within the mercy of God who can do all things. Is conversion of heart then to be seen as the function of a moment or must the phase-change of conversion be the gradual product of years of moral actions that only gradually show within the individual the redemptive action of grace upon the will? That is the great question. My attempt will be to translate into the moral sphere Moriarty's own theory of the dynamics of objects in space.

There, in a nutshell, is my own approach to the actions and dynamics of the criminal mind. If I apply this theory to Moriarty specifically I will have the ultimate test of my general approach, a unified field-theory of human actions when the soul has gone awry! My method will be to increase general virtue by minor actions taken in a good direction so as to increase the chance of a phase change to a permanent habit of sanctity just as to sin in minor matters is to increase the odds of a major fall from grace seen from the perspective of the life as a whole of a given individual. Sometimes though, the process reverses itself and there comes such a momentous conversion that the soul changes first, a phase-change such as that in nature from solid to liquid or from liquid to gas and then the acts of virtue follow in due course but such is not the ordinary moral path. It is my hope that the conversion of Moriarity follows the latter course but I am prepared to use my influence to alter him by slow gradations. It may surprise my reader, if this manuscript journal should ever reach that audience claimed by my friend Watson's works, that I choose this moment when, a short time since, death was staring me in the face, to discuss the Professor's abstruse thesis of astral bodies, but all will come clear presently, for I used this insight into the professor's mind to guide me as I looked into the barrel of the professor's revolver.

The day was somewhat overcast as Watson and I began our journey to the falls. I must say that a deep sorrow lay upon me. I could not predict whether my attempt to draw the tiger would succeed nor could I know in advance if my trap would succeed. I knew only that I was running a great risk since I myself was to be the bait. My design was to appear utterly alone. Since I could not imagine that the Professor would imagine me to be so careless, I could only hope that his eagerness to come to grips with his opponent matched my own and would overcome his suspicions. Of course to appear defenseless would not work unless in fact I was so. There must be no cover where Gregson or some other source of support might spring to my aid and arrest Moriarity. I must also appear unaware or unconcerned that Moriarity was on the scene and I must provide a perverse cover so that he might approach. I found what I wanted on the narrow path to the falls. How long I would have to wait after Watson's departure in answer to my ruse to take him from my side I could not then have said. I was prepared to await events. How surprising it was therefore when I had scarcely accustomed myself to the thunderous roar of the falling waters when I should find that the Professor had appeared like a wraith a few feet from where I stood gazing into the abyss! Clearly he had so far anticipated me that my approach had been observed and he could see that I was indeed alone. I was armed of course but as I did not expect the Professor to shoot me down from cover like an assassin without warning my weapon was neither drawn nor pointed. This may have been foolish but my entire scheme depended upon my being able to challenge the professor to undertake the proposal I had elaborated in my mind before ever leaving London. I turned to the Professor with a smile therefore and addressed him.

"Ah my dear Professor Moriarty, you are a bit late but here you are at last, and alone I see. Our position is roughly the same as it was when we had our little discussion in my rooms at Baker Street."

The Professor glowered at me. "Yes, when you recall that I promised to bring destruction upon you if your pursuit of my organization was successful and you brought about my destruction."

"That was the very point that I wished to raise with you at the time. Evidently you are still of the view that your organization had a future and you still labor under the idea that your own identity is coextensive with that organization. You see I have long been aware that you were becoming bored with the entire enterprise. Would the Professor Moriarty of old have made that "little slip" that we spoke of in Baker Street? Of course not, this entire business was engineered by you to provide an opportunity for a little London housecleaning of men who were becoming as dangerous to you as for me. In fact, I should be a bit resentful at being used as a means for your own change of career. I knew as early as the incident told by my friend Watson in his tale, The Valley of Fear, that you were becoming weary with the whole thing. I stated at the time that the entire motive of the crime was for you to sustain the illusion of invincibility among your subordinates. I began to realize how near you were to your own destruction by the very forces you had gathered about you. It is my belief that any organization becomes unbalanced when it reaches a certain point of growth. Your organization was becoming a victim of its own success. It came as no surprise to me then when you acted so carelessly in betraying your entire organization into my hands."

"And myself along with it, because you can for the first time trace certain matters to me. I am exposed!"

"Nonsense, Professor Moriarity. All that I know and can prove is that a certain gravitational field exists which explains the behavior of your subordinates, but that you are that gravitational field would require a leap across empty space. It is a particularity of our legal system that it requires a chain of evidence. The law makes no leaps! I could never succeed in bringing you to justice in court and I believe that you know it. It is time that we lay our cards upon the table."

The Professor had followed me closely. "Then why am I here, Mr. Holmes?"

"Indeed Professor, why are you here? Shall I tell you? You are here for the same reason that I am here. You are awaiting news that your organization is neatly wrapped into a bundle by Scotland Yard."

The Professor smiled grimly, "You were quite clever to see that. What I mean though is why am I standing with you on a cold summit of the Alps?"

"A generous gesture since I'm sure you would have preferred Paris or better still London. You are here my dear Professor, because you are wondering why I am here. Since I posed no immediate threat to you, my flight across country and this pretense on your part of seeking revenge by my death becomes absurd. No, you are here for the same reason that a chess-master watches his opponent, to see first hand what I will do next. It is only the amateur criminal who fears the detective. The true master of the game does not let the detective pursue him; rather, he pursues the detective. You see Professor I have always known that you were in crime not for the rewards but for the game itself as am I. If I thought you relished blood or money, I assure you, you would also be in the London dock

84

with the other cutthroats. I cannot tell how often I have told Watson that his emotional little tales have ruined what should have been as clean and simple a telling as a quadratic equation. My first insight as regards you was that you took a precisely similar view. It was never the crime itself that you relished but its inscrutability. And that is why you may as well put your gun away, my dear Professor. Theatrics are beneath you. Kill me and you lose the only man capable of appreciating your art and your science!"

The Professor was still for a moment before putting his gun away. For the first time he smiled. It was not an expression to which his face was accustomed and it had a most uncanny effect. "Then why are you here, Mr. Holmes?"

"To protect myself until your subordinates are in the dock and to provide my friend Watson's romantic mind with a convincing story for my death."

"You are quite certain then that you will not die today?"

"No more will you, Professor."

"Then what do you have in mind?"

"Capital you come to the very point. Well first we will have to leave some clues which will indicate that a death struggle has taken place between us with the result that both of us will appear to have plunged into the abyss below. I am counting on Watson trying to apply my methods and having reached an erroneous conclusion to omit the one essential thing."

"And what is that?"

"Oh come now Professor the bodies of course. Only one with a romantic turn of mind will be convinced that there is no need to search for the corpses. Watson I am afraid will see the falls as the perfect sepulcher for the great detective. The thunderous chasm, the echoing cry of the opponents locked in each other arms. These will exert an overwhelming appeal to the poet within him but I trust that you are not such a fool as to wrestle with a man younger than yourself who is strong enough to straighten out bent fireplace pokers. Nor am I likely to allow you to come to grips with me when I am armed. All of this will be lost on Watson of course and I am counting on that."

"Very well, we are both dead.....what then?"

"Ah that brings me to a proposal that will require some little time and effort on your part, but we can discuss terms tomorrow if necessary after we see the results of today's little drama. I have arranged for two rooms in an inn some five miles distant under an assumed name for each of us."

"And I am to trust you, I suppose?"

"Well at least until we can jointly arrive at a future course for our relations such as they are. I am sorry but we really must make haste. Watson is undoubtedly even now hurrying to my aid with rescuers having discovered that my ruse that an English woman was in need of urgent medical attention from an English doctor was a sheer fabrication."

"This shows a certain cruelty on your part to your friend if I may say so Mr. Sherlock Holmes."

"See it rather as an effort to resolve an old issue between Watson and myself. He has long desired to copy my methods, alone, and without my aid. I am leaving him a clear ground to do so. If he solves the puzzle, well then Professor, you and I must still part ways until you give me the means to apprehend and to convict you in a court of law, and you in turn may know that I will still pursue you as of old. But, if Watson cannot solve this puzzle, well then, you and I are at liberty to play a game for even higher stakes, a more challenging game than I trust even you my dear Professor have ever imagined."

As I spoke I looked down into the valley and saw a small group of black figures struggling up by the way that Watson and I had ascended earlier. I bid the Professor to stand back against the sheer cliff wall that bordered the narrow path on which we stood. The path was quite muddy and where we stood I had paced the ground into a mire while talking with the Professor. I saw at once what must be done. There must be two sets of footsteps going to the edge, signs of a brief struggle, and then none returning. Fortunately the ground was wet and would not take a clear impression. This allowed me to be in effect both sets of footprints. First I walked to the edge of the cliff with my usual stride, turned about several times, dug in a bit with my toes, made some sliding impressions, and then walked slowly backward from the scene with a shorter stride. The effect was of two people walking to the edge of the cliff with none returning. This had the advantage of making the Professor's supposed footprints those of my own retreat. An observer seeing two sets of footprints and an imaginary struggle could only conclude that neither man returned. Once back on the more trodden area where the Professor awaited me, footprints became irrelevant. I walked back and keeping the Professor slightly in advance of me, we took the trail at the fork and continued over the summit to the valley beyond. After that a five mile hike took us to the inn where I am writing this. The Professor had arranged for his luggage to be forwarded to the train station in the same town before the day began as whatever was to be the fruit of our encounter he did not wish to be found in the neighborhood. I alas was not similarly placed but a few hundred Swiss Franks soon remedied my deficiencies. My ultimate destination after parting from the Professor is to be Florence.

I am happy to say that the Professor agreed to fall in with my plans rather than to face Inspector Gregson. As we walked the Professor had to take frequent breaks to catch his breath. When we did so, he took the opportunity to speak and to show me that I have read his intentions correctly and that his thoughts are parallel to my own.

"Is it true Mr. Holmes that you have escaped the malaise so well chronicled in that book of your exploits, 'The Sign of Four?' I must say that after reading it I was tempted to make you an offer of employment in my organization. You had come to esteem the illusion of clarity of mind granted by drugs for the joys of the chase. Indeed, I am not sure that the depredations of what you so crudely call the Moriarity Gang went a great way to saving your life and sanity at the time. Where would you ever have been without me?"

"Or you without me, Professor, what author writes but for the rare critic who can appreciate the great work? What composer composes without the music connoisseur to appreciate the intricacies of the score? But we are both rather in the same dire straits now are we not? Thus my proposal..."

"Before you speak further Mr. Holmes has your proposal anything to do with your former devotion to the philosopher Winwood Reade and his most extraordinary work, The Martyrdom of Man?"

"You surprise me, Professor. Watson would be gratified that you have perused his works so thoroughly."

The Professor was referring to a work that I recommended to Watson at the time of 'The Sign of Four.' Winwood Reade, a forward-looking young philosopher who died young, who looked at the great religious works of mankind and concluded that they all manifested a common desire for a transcendent meaning to existence that spoiled the life of man and stifled that creativity that might create a meaning from within itself to fill the great vacuum of life upon this earth. This rather grim, stoic position was reinforced by a most startling familiarity with the great religious cultures. After reading it I had long entertained the ambition to see for myself some of the lands that played host to the great world religions and to speak to those present avatars of those faiths in order to allay the doubts which had so long beset me. Did the Professor then apprehend that this was now the course that I proposed in the years that lay before me, that I intended to put the views of Mr. Reade to the test?

To test this hypothesis, I spoke up, "I intend to be absent from England for a time now that I can rest assured that your life of crime is at an end."

"Well Holmes but what if I should take to a new course in crime, what course will you take then?"

"I hardly think that likely. You see after you arrived at your dynamic theory of the asteroids little remains for you in astronomy and after once being the Napoleon of crime what remains for you in the field of criminal activity? You are sir between engagements as it were."

"Applications, Mr. Holmes, applications. No theory is of use until it is used in the real world to achieve some end. Perhaps my greatest labor is still before me. The energy of the atom for instance....."

"Well in any case I hope you are not anticipating becoming a mere tradesman, Professor?" I chided him.

"Hardly that, Holmes; my sense of the practical may surprise you. I intend to show mankind what may be achieved if mankind will rid itself of guilt and fear and build a better world without God. Nothing so inhibits the mind of man from attaining its proper ends as these archaic legal codes and rituals meant to please and placate some obscure deity hiding behind the scenes. Religion in any form is no more than a short-cut for the intellectually lazy. Its final function is to infuse some sort or patience and order into the great unruly masses of mankind by promising them that they are part of a larger whole which gives the nothingness of the individual some hope of ultimate meaning. Religions are trinkets for the more ape-like among us. These hold them up and watch them turning in the vagrant airs catching the sparkle of the sun on their many facets. Even some minds of the highest caliber have been bewitched by questions of religious doctrine and have attempted to reconcile various theological conundrums so as to be able to face the terror of existing in a universe which though intelligible is not itself intelligent. I assure you Holmes that we are quite alone here. The vast spaces of the universe are as mindless and bare as any asteroid. The evolution of mind on this one planet is merely the result of the chance that given an infinite number of throws of the dice, all combinations will sooner or later occur. Mind itself is the great absurdity. There is neither purpose nor end in our being here or in our being at all. It is this fact that creates terror in the heart of man and gives birth to religions."

"But if that is so Professor, then why do anything at all? Why do you for instance pose your various astrophysical conundrums? Why did you ever seek to stand out as an individual by becoming the very Napoleon of Crime?"

"Oh, I suppose it is mere whimsy on my part. I meddle with the world of men and women for the same reason that boys cut worms in two to watch the two halves squirm. You have become quite boring to me Sherlock Holmes, even more so when I hear statements that imply in you an interest in religious questions. Perhaps you intend someday to visit Palestine, that site of the people who of all peoples have most saddled mankind with the absurd notion of sin. No more life defeating notion has ever afflicted the mind of man. I assure you that there is no absolute moral magnetic pole to guide us. We are the sole arbiters of moral conduct and the strong may impose whatever moral standards they wish upon the weak while granting themselves immunity to act as they please. I can dispose of Judaism here in sixty seconds yet it has taken three thousand years and humankind is still burdened with the absurd pretentions of this 'chosen people.' The fundamental error of the Jews is so simple that it is hardly worth refutation. They are simply a group that insists on reading metaphysical significance into events from what is in reality an obscene level of national pride. What is Judaism in a nutshell but that at some endlessly deferred date the Jews will rule the world and why, because they have been chosen by some tribal deity carried about in scrolls that supposedly manifest His will. The Jewish laws are conspicuous for only one thing, their total uselessness. It is the genius of the Jewish people to have saddled the world with their own speculations from Moses to Marx. Always this hope for a lasting salvation, for a millennial paradise! The Jewish mind refuses to accept the meaningless and purely arbitrary struggle for existence, and why, because God demands it or history demands it in the case of Marx. In reality there is no demand made upon man by his existence, not even to continue to be. The universe would be no poorer for our extinction. Indeed, it might be a vast improvement for mankind distorts the world by his every action. What are we but the apex predators in the vast jungles of being distorting the world by our arts and artifices into an image of ourselves apotheosized at last into gods? The supposed sin of idolatry condemns the very project of definition and image creation that is always the point of origin of theology itself as indeed of all technology and art! I am surprised that the Jewish god does not condemn language as well if language were not necessary to carry

90

on the Jews' preposterous assertions and claims so that new generations are burdened in turn with the nonsense of sin and redemption."

He paused, "Or let us take Christianity: what is Christianity but bastardized Judaism as Islam is a bastardized version of them both? Christianity takes a historical tragedy, the death of a pious delusionary, and makes it incumbent upon mankind to embrace suffering and death so as to walk in His footsteps. And who is the Christ after all? Who can sort Him out from the fragmentary accounts that speak of him? Is Jesus not the creation of Saul of Tarsus later named St. Paul? Out of his own life's disappointments as an embittered Pharisee Saul of Tarsus embroidered a brief and unfortunate element of history with a cosmic significance out of all proportion to its source. He created certain cell communities who out of historical desperation shared his desire for a solution but these never quite managed to live up to the exalted conduct that he demanded from them. Nor could they ever really comprehend his vision of one man as the beginning and end of all things. Is Jesus the carpenter and teacher of Nazareth or is he some emanation by whatever inscrutable means from God, an emanation mind you that is incomplete since God must remain one or what becomes of the great Jewish innovation of monotheism? Then there is the preposterous idea that God would in some obscure manner clothe his very magnificence by assuming our human nature. Metaphysical contradictions and linguistic mush! Its very absurdity is the source of its attraction! Life is disappointing Mr. Holmes and defeat of all of our aspirations is inevitable. Only the man who despairs at once can really contribute anything to the world without fostering illusions in lesser minds. Theology of all sorts has retarded the progress of mankind by centuries. It is time to put these questions at last to rest. But let us leave this subject since you indicate that even you are willing to be self-condemned to wish to spend years on such a fatal pursuit; I at least shall not stand in your way."

"And what are your own intentions then Professor, if I may be so bold as to inquire now that you are bored with me?" I asked.

"Well I was considering testing my wits against Mycroft Holmes. Now there is something I can do from the quiet leisure of my armchair to his. We were never well-matched in some ways Mr. Sherlock Holmes. You like to be on the scene and I as far from it as possible. I desire a respite from your attentions and certain suggestions of your words have told me how I may obtain that respite. You are familiar of course with Pascal's wager, viz. that though we may not be certain of the existence of God we may as well place our bet in favor of his existence because the wages of that bet are infinite if we win and if God should not exist we are out nothing for we must die in any case. The human condition of course is always weighted in favor of the inscrutable idea of a God who has put us in the position where the dice must be thrown whether we will or no. It is this fact that makes the recourse to religious explanations so convenient to those who are willing to short-circuit the thought process by seeking a premature certitude. Pascal's wager merely proves that God will not condescend to step from behind the curtain where he hides and meet the mind of man just as we are meeting today in equality on a barren mountainside with one or the other of us about to be cast into the abyss."

I was appalled to say the least at the presumption of the Professor but I proceeded to prod the wild beast that stood before me.

"My blushes, I had no idea that you had ever entertained thoughts along the lines of these metaphysical matters!"

"And why did you think that? What scientist can avoid the question of origins; but since ultimate origins are hidden within the mists of a supposed divine intent, I choose to turn and flow with the current of time which moves only in a single direction and to pursue the future. What is the past to me? Since we cannot un-break the egg and piece the shell together, let alone decide what caused it to fall from the shelf, I suggest that it is time to make the omelet and eat it the better to get about with the business of the day. My own business of course has been to take the path of least resistance to pad my pockets with the fruits of crime the better to ensure my leisure to pursue greater goals?"

"Your tenure at the university was insufficient?"

"Pooh, my salary would hardly pay for the lenses of my optical instruments at the observatory let alone my other little enterprises. A Professor's salary is small while the pursuit of Physics is not cheap. But I have as you have said grown weary of mere crime. I now have something else in mind and to grapple with another Holmes brother whose talents of mind and scope of activity exceeds yours appeals to me."

"What do you intend?"

"To pose a problem that will set the British Empire on its ear."

"Mycroft is aware of the threats posed to British interests in every region. You will find in him a most formidable foe. But we have matters before us of more immediate urgency have we not, Professor? I suggest that each of us has reached that point in life where time is the commodity that we both desire. Our little war of wits makes demands upon that commodity which, since the number of our days is beyond our control, threatens certain projects dear to each of our hearts. If you desire a respite from me, then I must confess that for once your desires match my own. You have your work in mathematics and astronomy and I desire to devote time to travel and to pursue my chemical research. Can you not then suggest some common measure that may grant each of us a period of freedom to pursue our separate ends now that you have retired from the field of criminal enterprises... at least temporarily?"

"Very well, my proposal is simply this, and your revelation of your own sentiments merely reinforces it. I propose that each of us take his separate course for a time as you hint. We may each test the theory of Mr. Reade at the same time. We will see if mankind may be freed at once and forever from the prison of the metaphysical. We shall see if the idea of man may survive the death of this great observer of our actions. We will see if human consciousness may be grounded in nothing but itself. At the same time I will also pursue certain geo-political ends as a challenge to your brother Mycroft while you may pursue whatever transcendental ends you have in view. Your transcendental researches may of course have geo-political consequences and my pursuit of what I call geo-politics may yield a sort of moral justice, but by means of crime. We will see by lets say 1897 whose methods yield the better results in terms of ultimate realized good or evil in the pragmatic sense. As I have said, the application of theory is everything. Reason is nothing until it produces results. If religions in spite of their pretentions yield a sorry world, then perhaps it is the devil which is the ultimate benefactor of mankind after all."

"Well I would dispute your criteria for good and evil. You must remember that the Christian religion at least withholds judgment until all the data are in. The general resurrection lies still before us and not behind."

"Yes, how very convenient this infinite deferral is."

"You imply that this deferral is infinite while I insist that it is merely indefinite as to the time of its occurrence. You may yet be surprised Professor. As to man's capacity to create his own version of paradise in the meantime: if the most sophisticated science and technology yields but the moral destruction and diminishment of the stature of man where are we then with mere materialism as our only comfort? What if man will finally be a victim of his own unconscious guilt and desire for oblivion? What if man uses his technical progress only to further enslave not merely the weaker members of the human species but the stronger as well?"

"Well we may discuss these matters when you return, Holmes...if you return. Time presses, do you agree to my terms?"

"You have yet to make them clear. Shall I really leave you so at liberty? Really Professor! I fear that the results may prove irreparable if I should do so."

"Not so, for I shall simply weave the web of my plans but defer the execution of them. I shall prepare the entire series of events I have in view, but keep the trigger to their initiation in my hands alone. How I will do so is of course my modest art. It is the ultimate test of virtue (if you will have it that virtue exists) to have the means for evil at one's disposal but to refrain from its exercise. Come back to me with your transcendent rationale for the universe Mr. Sherlock Holmes and I will disable my own creation, even at its moment of its imminent fulfillment which I tell you in advance will be the destruction of the British Empire."

"Very well Professor, I will accept your wager. We go our separate ways to pursue the good of mankind by opposite means but to a common end. But it is getting cold. I do not believe that either of us cares to face a night upon these barren slopes. Let us press on to the inn."

I cast one last glance back to where my friend Watson was no doubt even then reaching his erroneous conclusions. It was with a heavy heart that I turned away to resume our passage through the deep snows. We proceeded to cover the last mile to the inn with its most welcome fire and food.

Later at the Inn-

I met the professor for a late supper at the inn. Our conversation did not alter our wager but it may be as well to jot down certain key points of our conversation as they indicate a starting point for the great contest that lies before us. The Professor began the discourse as we sat on opposite sides of a great oaken table before the fire sipping an herbal liqueur unique to the region.

"As I grow older I find that the minor comforts of life become more precious to me. I much prefer philosophy in a warm room. You on the other hand seem convinced that truth is more likely to manifest itself in the heat and cold of desert regions."

"Well history seems to support that taste at least when it comes to transcendent thought. Moses, Zoroaster, Mohammed, Jesus, all sought ultimate meaning in desert regions."

"This entire question of ultimate truth and final purposes for what we see about us is simply a veil for our ignorance Holmes. What is called revelation is always a post hoc pronouncement to justify the assertions of a priestly group. Its revealed character is merely a veil for its absurdity and obscurity. Its mystery is simply the measure of its violation of the rules of reason and probability. A true revelation is one that corresponds to our own perceptions but sharpens them.

Or are we to believe that God creates the laws of nature only to violate them when he pleases to do so. Once one dispenses with the miraculous the world emerges in all of its naked brutality. If in spite of this a god exists then He is by that very fact responsible in the court of man for all foreseeable acts of his own initial creation. Instead, the so-called revelations shift the burden of an imperfect world to man forgetting that every condition that might impose itself upon human freedom must have already been foreseen by God and could have been deflected in time before any harm was done. In order to escape from this quandary Calvinism has set up its monstrous version of predestination and attempted to vindicate God by denying human freedom. Catholicism retains that freedom but only by denying the fact that grace seems so seldom efficacious. The Calvinists assume that the majority of men and women go to hell and can do nothing to alter their fate while the Catholics assume that one may avoid hell by timely repentance, but both systems fail to account for the remarkable inability, based on what we observe, for most men and women to rise above the standard of intelligent apes. Would it not be more honest simply to assume as I do that we live in a jungle of conflicting aspirations, that ideals only serve to hide our true motivations, and that the honest villain usually does less harm that the reformers of the world? I fear my dear Holmes that you are entering upon a fool's errand in undertaking your proposed universal pilgrimage. Absurd in its beginnings, religion remains so in all of its permutations and variations. But worse still, these very purposes and ends proposed for human actions are meant to veil the fact that religion always involves a power struggle. There is usually a hidden sword beneath the holy vestments. If I were to believe in any religion at all I would look for one that does not benefit in a quite worldly manner its priests and adherents. It appears to me that most people believe because they fear the consequences of non-belief. When perceived as a structural whole a religion, particularly Judaism, Christianity, and Islam depend upon the will and, if I may say so, the willfulness of a fierce and fearful being, one who appears, based upon the historical accounts, to enjoy terrorizing his creation or at least parts of it. Do you wish for an example? Very well, let us simply turn to Exodus: Why should the Egyptians not have pursued this runaway people who had been fed, clothed, and employed for years by the

Egyptians? For that matter why should the innocent first born of Egypt die as a mere sign to benefit a so-called chosen people? Would a just god entertain such preferences of one people over another? The Egyptians had one of the greatest civilizations that ever existed. Why should a god prefer an absurd and quarrelsome set of tribes marching about with a tent and evicting people such as the Hittites and Amorites from their own lands? Is it likely that a God who created all men and women would show such arbitrary preferences? Is the Jewish Torah with its many prescriptions and proscriptions a sufficient basis for such a preference? Why would God be concerned with such minute matters? No, the entire affair was merely a case of rationalized slaughter of the indigenous tribes of Palestine by an invading people. All the rest is simply a case of seeking a post hoc purpose in history just as Hegel has now done with far more sophistication if less poetry than the Bible. But let us not stop here with the Jews; the entire plot does not get interesting until an obscure teacher from Nazareth makes the mistake of attributing certain affirmations in the Psalms and Prophets to himself personally and imagines that he is the Messiah. Under this delusory belief he manages to get himself crucified by systematically tearing down the very fabric of Judaism and substituting his own person for God and by doing so taking the ultimate Transcendent and dragging it down to his own singular body. Can anyone be surprised that the High Priests of Israel took umbrage? What had Rome to do with such petty quarrels among a subject people? If it happened today Pilate would be playing golf that very afternoon! Yet upon this admittedly tragic execution Christianity has erected its own religion with a pretense to universality across all of the diverse cultures of the world. If it was not for the collapse of the Roman Empire which left an immense void to be filled, Christianity would long since have died out along with most of the other mystery cults of the same period. The success of Christianity is due solely to historical accident and a rather unique organizational design: Popes, Monasteries, and an alliance with the most powerful dynasties across the European ages through the institution of anointed kings and queens. One need only look at the magnificent tombs and Cathedrals of Christianity to know that any pretense of the Christian faith to sell what it possesses and give to the poor ceased among the very men entrusted with the Christian message from the very beginning, when despite the expectations of the early cell communities Christ did not return. What is termed revelation is really the mere elaboration of theology; itself a mere series of contradictory statements such as that Christ is both fully human and fully divine. What is the doctrine of the hypostatic union but a mere political settlement meant to dispose of the Arian faction within the body of the Church. It is not a metaphysical mystery; it is politics! But let us not belabor the point; let us move on instead to Islam. Not willing to let a good thing die, Mohammed made one last effort to put the God of Israel, now called Allah, back in His heaven but with a properly restored dignity and without assuming the baggage of a human nature as in Christianity. The result was the Koran, a hodge-podge book of recitations which, whatever its merit as poetry, deserves no more reverence than the Iliad of the Greeks or the epic of the Roman poet Virgil. Again we have the sword as the means of promulgation. Believe or die! The result of course was the rapid spread of Islam across those areas whose martial spirit, no longer infused by early enthusiasm, was not finally able to respond to the assault of the alien Moslem creed. There you have it Holmes; there you may perceive the course of your revealed religions. My sole desire you see is to spare you unnecessary travel, if you wish though you may pursue your researches further into the non-revealed religions of Buddhism, Confucianism, or Shinto. There you may at least find some cultural usefulness for though they are no less mythic in their way, they at least make sense of this world to primitive peoples and aid their followers by imposing some sort of viable meaning upon the world as they find it for those without the benefits of science. They are not predicated upon a world beyond the one that we see. No Holmes, you would do better to simply betake yourself to Oxford and consult an oriental scholar rather than purchasing steam ship tickets to the orient."

I spoke up at last. "Nevertheless Professor, I intend to go."

"You admit my points then."

"Not at all; I fear that your entire argument begs the question, Professor. Revealed religion is not defeated by merely posing an alternative explanation for its origins and survival seen in purely worldly terms, nor is a religion defeated by the failure of its followers to adhere to its most exalted precepts. The question of the transcendent remains an open one in spite of your maledictions. In fact I would go so far to say that the very existence of evil is our best indication that another world exists."

"You are a hard case Holmes. Your first error of course is in confusing metaphysics and ethics. I would have no quarrel with you if you would merely stick to forces without endowing them with personality and purpose. If there is a God worthy of worship He is certainly not one who wastes His efforts in meddling with the affairs of men and women. Why should God concentrate His attention upon one tiny corner of the cosmos for even an instant? Are we to believe that God dilutes his own essence by mingling it with human concerns? What would you think of me if I were to assume as a man the guise of a beetle and crawl about with pincers mingling with insects and arachnids? If man is made in the image of God, then something has surely been lost in the translation process. My atheism is confined to the doctrine of an ethical god for such a concept defiles the very Being whose existence I would be attempting to prove."

"That is why revelation is necessary," I answered. "Unaided reason cannot bring us to the Holy. The most that the philosopher may prove is that there exists an uncaused cause."

"Ah even that may not be proven. Shall I demonstrate? Very well: if such a creator god existed then he would always have existed. This means that infinite time lies not merely before us but behind us as well. But if time lying behind us is infinite then any intention must be indefinitely delayed and creation would never have taken place, in which case we would not be sitting here debating the existence of God." The Professor smiled.

"But we are here," I objected. "Why could not God simply act in freedom at any point of infinite time which (for God at least who is outside of time as its originator) is equally accessible? All of time would be experienced by God as eternally present. Time and space are for God merely self-imposed restrictions on His complete freedom to define the characteristics of all things. We know that

God is free for surely God cannot be imagined to lack freedom since freedom is a perfection and God is by definition the one absolutely perfect being?"

"So your image of God is one who stands outside of time and space Holmes, but about such a god nothing can be affirmed or disaffirmed for our very language is conditioned by the categories of our own experiences among which time must surely be the most fundamental. A god outside of time becomes so distant from his creation that He becomes incomprehensible. Such a god cannot even be affirmed to have set up any laws for creation or to have created anything at all! Or if he did then this world of ours becomes a mere puppet show staged by god to amuse himself at our expense? If God is not constrained in some fashion by the laws of matter and energy, then we must convict God of a certain duplicity towards us as intelligent beings in that we are asked to abide by laws and live within the parameters of laws that He ordains will apply only for us while He is allowed to invert or bypass them at will. If that were so, could God invert good and evil at will? Even if I granted you that such a metaphysical god is the outside cause of all that is, then I would be forced to abandon the idea that such a god is even ethical let alone loving, because he must then be the ultimate cause of evil as well as good. He might better have made nothing at all and continued to exist in whatever perfection His divine state may suggest that he possesses. Surely the shortest route to so laborious a journey as redemption is never to have ventured upon the entire divine escapade or are we a product of a divine boredom with his unique state of perfection so that the advent of evil came to Him as a relief? To the metaphysical question of why there is something rather than nothing I have only this answer: 'Why indeed!'"

"So you despair of an answer?" I asked.

"I have simply followed the path of all men of true wisdom and have dismissed the question of God's nature and existence as meaningless from within our present frame of reference in space and time," the Professor answered sipping from his glass.

"Then what motive can there be for any human action?" I inquired.

100

"There you have it Holmes; human freedom is the true uncaused cause. We act or fail to act according to our own conceptions and must take whatever consequences these actions entail. We each make of the world a version of our own image. If you choose to people your world with gods and angels I can not stop you, but neither need I share your delusions," he replied calmly.

"Nor certainly need I share yours, Professor," I answered coldly.

"No, but the burden of proof is surely yours since you ask that I abstract outwards into infinity and beyond to posit a God," he replied. "So we begin at stalemate, Holmes. Shall we begin a new game?"

"This is not a game with me, Professor," I stated flatly.

"You would say that of course, for you were always beset by earnestness even as a lad is that not so? It is the romantic in you. Ah well, pursue your phantoms if you must. I merely desired to spare you a long journey," said he shaking his head in mock pity.

"It is my little effort to lessen the evil in the world," I said quietly.

"You mean me of course; you will still persist in viewing me as evil," smiled the Professor.

"Are you not Professor?" I queried.

"I should have said that I am merely a man humble enough to accept this world as it truly is and then to conform my conduct to the standard of everyday experience," stated the Professor.

"Ah but that is the question is it not, Professor? Is this world of experience that we know the one intended by God or is it the result of some primeval aberration of created being?"

"So we are back to the old crutch of original sin Holmes?" asked the Professor with a mocking smile. "You pile one absurd demand for belief upon another. First you ask that I imagine a perfect being called God and then you insist that he is a victim in a game where he has made all of the rules. What then becomes of divine omnipotence?"

"I would consider original sin to be the one undeniable fact to be observed each day in the world about us," said I. "Since it is you who claim to be the great empiricist, can you deny that this world is flawed?"

"If it is so, then why has it not been restored to its former state by God? But in any case by what standard is it flawed Mr. Holmes? You must assume then that there were other options and that God simply chose one model out of many? What then becomes of a standard for truth or is truth really legion like the devil is said to be? Or if evil originates not in God but in creation, why should God allow man to spoil His great work having once chosen a best version out of multiple alternative universes in which to place us? I take a more humble position in my metaphysics. Why after all should I assume that the nature of things must be convenient to me? Am I God?" asked the Professor with raised eyebrows.

"No Professor Moriarity" I answered, "Nor am I; but it is my faith as a Christian that God has taken on human nature in the person of Jesus the Christ and that by His cross and resurrection He has indeed set all things aright out of love for us. The world that we know is finally a redeemed world."

"Well if it is, it shows precious little evidence of the fact as you just so cogently observed..." he answered.

"Oh very well Holmes, pursue your original sin if you must. I have done my best to spare you a futile effort. I shall return to England and will enjoy the life of a country squire in Devon. Meanwhile you my dear fellow may rest assured that I will keep to the terms of our wager and shall even supply you with an escort to see that you shall come to no harm during your travels, for I look forward to seeing you again Mr. Sherlock Holmes."

With that we parted. I did not attempt at the time to counter every point of the Professor since I desired no preliminary skirmish prior to the main event. Besides it is late and but I cannot rest until I do something for my conscience as regards Watson. He is truly the most faithful and valiant of friends but he has one key weakness; he is absolutely incapable of duplicity. So much is this so that even as regards his "public" he feels an obligation to render his accounts with utter veracity when I allow him to do so. The result is that many cases have had to be withheld from publication to spare innocent persons and to avoid scandal. I have more than once suggested that just as in mathematics the principle could be demonstrated without the particular detail the same is true in regard to detection, but Watson's bulldog stubbornness would not have it so. No he must delve into motivations. Yet how many of his heroes speak with the same earnest voice? How many of the women in his tales show the same fiery spirit? The reason for these regularities is that Watson is essentially giving the reader his own romantic vision of life through the medium of my cases. He must have human interest and drama above all else. The very need to construct a story around my death of Wagnerian proportions will bias his judgment and obscure the truth. It will cause him to neglect what might so easily set his mind at rest, that I am still alive. The entire matter of course is to be read in the footprints since they are both made by my shoes coming and going. To look at the evidence without preconceptions, that is always the key to the truth. If he merely considers objectively the supposed joint death, he must stumble upon the truth. Is Moriarity such an idiot or so enamored of my embrace that he would throw his arms about me and drag us both to perdition in the falls? Why would he act thus, because his gang is no more? But to get rid of the gang was the entire purpose of all of the Professor's actions in recent years. Even evil evolves. What then does the Professor desire? The answer is freedom of course but freedom to what end? That is the very question that I have asked myself in those long evenings of my brooding. Then one day a chance comment of Mycroft gave me the answer. I have always said that Mycroft is the British government. His mind is the clearing house for policy. So when Mycroft mentioned what he termed, the problem of the east, I saw that Moriarity having exhausted the criminal possibilities of Europe must turn also to the question of Asia and the Americas. The entire civilization of Europe totters upon the various superannuated thrones where the offspring of Queen Victoria repose. A conflagration must come. When it comes it will leave Europe in ruins and the tide of history will move to the east and to the west. The man who will understand the future of the world must understand Asia. So it is that I propose to visit the cultures and the nations where repose the vast majority of humankind. It will be an effort that may occupy, dare I say, years, but could I in conscience leave the Napoleon of Crime to do his worst at home while I went about my great hiatus? Unthinkable! So what must be done, I asked myself. I must take my clue from that quote from the Gospels that God sends his rain upon both the just and the unjust alike. I must leave the Professor a free hand in exchange for his promise to allow me a degree of similar latitude. I hoped for a truce in our eternal struggle. I shall head east and the Professor back to his English armchair where at least Mycroft may keep him under surveillance. As to Watson, well, he has always written my history through his own eyes. I can see no other way to bring him to what I shall call the objective position other than to show him upon my return that fantasy always leads to folly in the end. I shall give him his head and let him run for a bit since that is his wish. How strange that my worst enemy and my dearest friend must share a common policy, that of allowing each to pursue his freedom and to define the world as he chooses! In doing so I am acting, I feel, with that strange tolerance that is perhaps the greatest paradox in the divine dealings with humankind, that God leaves us alone in the garden, with tree of the knowledge of good and evil standing beckoningly before us.

May 6, 1891 - Florence, Italy

The Professor and I parted on the morning of the fifth. Already news has appeared in the Swiss papers of the death of the two Englishmen at Meiringen. It was as I had supposed; Watson came to the very erroneous conclusion that my traces and clues suggested. I must speak to the man who trained him in the art of detection! The Professor indicated every desire to depart as soon as possible for Zurich and the North. I told him to take care that my message to Mycroft be allowed to precede his arrival in London. In it I will explain all. Gregson and the Yard must remain of course in the dark. The Professor had wound up his affairs with the university prior to his present expedition. His plan, insofar, as he was willing to share it with me is to take up residence in

Devonshire. From there he will begin, as he said, to spin his web of political intrigue. If so, he will have few natural advantages for he must access the world through the meager means granted one whose nearest urban connection is Exeter or Plymouth. I on the other hand have the world at my disposal. But then the Professor is my elder by some years and I deserve a handicap advantage in the race. Besides the challenge was his in this duel of wits, so to me goes the choice of weapons. There shall be travel to the ends of the earth where I shall pursue on their own grounds many of the sources of what transcendence there may be on earth. The great world religions have anchored every civilization. It was not only Constantine, when he accepted Christianity, who found a stable base for his Empire. No, every civilization rests upon more than power and the force of arms and trade. There must be an idea, a great centralizing force to draw the devotions of men and women. What greater ideas exist than that of the nature of God with its associated concepts of human destiny, and moral values?

I wish to stress here that even if this unique opportunity to confront Moriarity in the realms of pure thought had not presented itself, I needed to cast myself adrift for a time. The meager comfort provided to me by solving the little human problems that have come to me through the years in Baker Street no longer have the power to anchor my restless spirit. To say that I rebel at stagnation is inadequate to express the profound unease that envelops me when I am not operating at my full capacity. I am one of those haunted by time's passage. I cannot while away this short hour of frost and sun gazing as the sun creeps across the sundial in the garden. I must seek those centers of energy that are ever emerging and as quickly dissipating in the vast stream of events. Only at these unique pressure points may a man exert his force to alter history. I drank ambition at my Father's knee in the vast library which his own researches threw open to me. My youth was somewhat sickly as was that of Robert Louis Stevenson. I was left largely to my own resources while my brothers were kept to a more stringent schedule by our tutor. I was the last to leave for public school much to my mother's dismay. But her own illness was growing upon her and my father did not wish me to witness the painful last stages of consumption. Thus swiftly was my childhood at an end and I was deprived forever except for the all too brief long vacations of the

105

Holmes estate at Sigerside. I am in many ways but a continuation of the dreams of my sires.

So it is that I begin this quest in Florence, home of the great Medici family. Take families from history and there is no history. The individual must exist in a context of affection and of property. The short span of life is all too little to amass anything proof against the sands of time. Things grow and are preserved through the artificial means of succession. Who would build the pyramids anew with every birth? Who would re-invent the wheel? No, we build upon what was in order that the world may advance. Even today as I stood upon the Ponte Vecchio and looked at the Duomo I was struck by the preciousness of the past. What would a sterile present consist of were it not nourished by these antiquities? Just as the artistry of my forebears has turned in my blood to sculpting these little strings of probabilities into a case's solution, so does Mycroft sift the tremor of this varied world to find that prudent path that guides an Empire. It is in the blood. Shall I then write my own Nibelungenleid amidst the strange Gods of the east? Or will I find that it is our domestic deity of Israel to whom I must look in His various guises for the truth of all things. I have booked passage from the nearby port of Genoa for the east. I shall sail around Africa en route to India and then on to Tibet under the improbable name of Sigerson, a Norwegian explorer! The Norwegians were exploring America years before the Spanish expedition of that benighted colonialist, Columbus who thought he had discovered the Indies. In honor of my Nordic forebears I shall sail from Genoa on my own expedition.

May 10, 1891 - Genoa

Has it taken me so long to find this place of blue seas? Truly the Italian Riviera is a paradise. What better place from which to seek a newer world! The entire world of thought seems divided between those who would restore a golden age and those who would create new worlds out of their dreams. I wonder which of these am I? How small were my initial hopes as a student of chemistry when I first met Watson? It seemed then a wonderful thing merely to develop a test for bloodstains. What drew me then to crime with its horrors, surely not the atrocities themselves, no certainly not? It was that the criminal desires to cover his offenses, sometimes so perfectly that no offense may be said to have occurred. Crime always has its roots in the desire to maintain an illusion. It is the innocence of the criminal that hides the greatest evils, just as I once remarked to Watson that the loveliness of the countryside may hide the greatest nightmares and atrocities born of the human heart. We depend upon our common sense of sin as a corrective to private judgment. Who does not acquit himself while holding others to the impossible standards of his own highest vision? Is this why I am determined to grant to Moriarity a chance of reform, he who of all men perhaps least deserves it? If as the scholastic fathers say, the best when corrupted is the worst; then may not the converse be even truer, that the worst may through conversion yield the best within mankind? There is after all a limit to my own imagination when it comes to the inscrutable workings of criminal intentions. Perhaps it is here that Moriarity may be invaluable to me. In the retrospection of his own foul motives and devices, a tool may be found to solve the mystery of the dark times that lie ahead. But to bring him over, by what means, ah there is the question? If each man has a major weakness, pride, greed, lust, duplicity, inability to feel another's pain, what is his? The answer lies before me.

I stood today upon the shore where rocks seem to yield instantly to the waves, thinking of these matters. My ship is due to leave tomorrow. I have already managed to grow a slight beard to fit my character as Sigerson, the Norwegian. I have prepared a fictitious curriculum vitae of my many past journeys. It shall be a test of my acting abilities. If I can convince my fellow passengers that the armchair dreamer of London whose furthest journeys heretofore have been about our own British Isles and some few journeys to the continent, mostly France, is a true explorer, and that I have been recuperating in England from a jungle fever caught along the black, muddy regions of Surinam, I will be able to account for my thinness and pallor.

Why the east though, I can hear my prospective reader exclaiming? I realize that the Americas are growing every day in importance, and who can say, may someday create an American empire to succeed us, if our preposterous European squabbles continue? But Asia, that great connected landmass that truly cannot be ignored, surely it is there that the future of humanity will be decided. There the great ideas and unifying religions will be tested. Every form of extremism will rear its ugly head. Besides it is in Asia that every genetic strain and race is represented. How appropriate that the entire human race in all its permutations should be there allowed to exchange and combine both their genius and their malice towards a common end of development! For truly that is the question. If humans today are genetically the same as their ancestors from the past 100,000 years, then where shall we locate the source of that great efflorescence of culture, religion, and morals that created the Bible, the Greek dramatists, and the successors to Socrates and Heraclitus? It is in Asia where the masses have co-mingled to create the human race as we know it today? Then there is the whole phenomenon of atavism, the ape in man. Are we evolving as a species or returning to our origins? What shall be the end of man? Is man as we know him but a prototype of the superman? Will the outrageous practices of eugenics someday breed the savage out of our blood?

If I examine my thoughts at this juncture it is simply to provide a base to measure my thoughts as my journey progresses. If these pages are ever published, my readers may lament the romantic spirit of my friend Watson who by now would have introduced at least one ardent suitor and a languishing lady of high color and spirit whose love has been spurned, while I have only ideas to offer the reader. I can only hope that the higher stakes of this, my present performance will make-up for the lack of the more violent colors upon the palette of friend Watson. But then who can be sure that I will not find my own share of color and adventure as I proceed? But for now, to sleep as it will hardly do to embark without a good night of sleep that is the best respite for the troubled soul of man.

Dr. Watson's Narrative Continues

I put down the manuscript that had so consumed my interest during the last two hours. It had created something of a revolution in my mind. I assure the readers of my former account of the death of Sherlock Holmes that this narrative were as accurate as I could make

108

it, granted the knowledge that I possessed at the time. Having read the true account in the papers before me, I felt gullible indeed. How could I have imagined that the Professor out of sheer despair would attack a younger man by throwing his arms about him? Besides, since the Professor, according to my own prior account, brought aid with him in the person of Colonel Sebastian Moran, why should not both men have attacked Holmes, thus sparing the Professor's life, unless the Colonel was on the scene, unbeknownst to both the Professor and Holmes, and tracking him with the intention of killing both men and assuming Moriarity's former place as head of the London underworld. Why did I not long since glimpse the truth and question my own account? But I now had Holmes' word that even this man Moran, the great tiger hunter, was not what I had thought. He had not murdered young Ronald Adair as I had supposed in The Adventure of the Empty House. This meant that both this latter story, The Adventure of the Empty House and the one I entitled, The Adventure of the Final Problem, were alike absolute fabrications necessitated by the need of Sherlock Holmes to secure space and time to pursue a series of investigations into remote regions as the Norwegian Explorer Sigerson, and to allow Holmes' own archenemy, Professor Moriarity, an equal latitude to do battle head-on-head with Mycroft Holmes in the realm of foreign affairs. Finally, if the above revelations were not enough, I had been called down to the coast of Devonshire on this windy late summer evening to be part of some adventure, the nature of which had yet to be disclosed by my companion. Many questions assailed me: what was the nature of these transcendental researches that had led Holmes first to Llassa and then to the Moslem lands of Persia, Arabia, and the Sudan? What were these researches into coal tar derivatives in Montpellier? Or were even these former statements of Holmes fabrications also? I doubted that they were. Knowing my companion as I did and his love of sleight-of-hand magician's tricks I suspected that while drawing the reader's attention elsewhere, he yet left enough clues for the discerning to find the path to truth. If I had any complaint it was that the game he was playing was a dangerous one. For this reason I knew that his account of his travels now laid before me would be true in every detail. Though I might resent his cavalier treatment of my feelings I could now see the necessity that the London world should assume that he was dead. The extent of Moriarity's contacts was such that any suspicion that Holmes was still alive might have led to further attempts to discover his whereabouts, thus, also the fictional identity as Sigerson. Holmes had not mentioned it but that very knowledge or suspicion that he had survived would have placed me in continual danger of being kidnapped so that I could be forced to reveal his whereabouts. No, it was essential that I, even I, should think that Sherlock Holmes was dead. It was the guarantee of my own safety. Yet what danger was a mere army doctor without the genius of Holmes beside me? I had always known my position in this regard, but I had not resented it. As Holmes has so often said to me, some men without the power of genius themselves have the remarkable power of stimulating it in others. I knew that Holmes valued my aid where sheer bravery or resource was required. My medical knowledge had also been of some use time and again. But my real value to Holmes was as an audience to stimulate those elegant proofs that his own geometric mind required. The resistance that my common sense approach to life provided served to stimulate his fancy and to create those artistic flourishes that appear in the many cases I have narrated. I wondered if the present case would demonstrate anew those remarkable faculties which the passage of time had only enhanced. There had been few sounds from the other end of the room while I had been reading but I was surprised suddenly to find Holmes standing behind me.

I had as I have said lain the manuscript aside. I cannot describe what a unique experience it was proving to be to read Holmes' account of events that I had thought I had understood completely. How strange it was for me to step inside the consciousness of the man who had so often mystified me as he sat in his armchair, his chin sunk upon his breast, while his dreamy eyes seemed to lose themselves in speculation. I have often remarked in my narratives how pronounced was the difference between the man of action engaged in the chase as opposed to the melancholic and lethargic victim of those extreme reactions that seemed to plague him after his exertions. Now at last I was being given a glimpse of the moral obsessions and doubts that had long plagued him. His pursuit of crime, I now saw, was an attempt to restore or perhaps even to create order in a chaotic moral realm. I had often wondered why he had abandoned the class of country gentry into which he was born to inhabit a modest suite of rooms in

Baker Street. Until later in his career he often refused cases that might have brought him both money and fame in order to pursue an answer to problems brought to him by valets and clerks. I had often advised a more commercial policy only to be reproved for my philistine attitude. "The artist must have his models, Watson," he remarked. "Great art must seek the wider world." In reading now his account of his widest perambulations I had no doubt that both the inner and the outer man would find what he had so futilely sought in the phantasms of drug induced euphoria.

I stood up and stretched. I thought to stimulate my faculties with a cup of tea. The chess game was over. Moriarity sat in silence before the fire whose red coals lit his characteristic features, the grey ice-like eyes of the Professor and the piercing dark eyes of Holmes as he stood at my side. Outside the wind still continued to buffet the sturdy cottage. "Join us, Watson," said Holmes. "It is well that we have our plans in order if we are to intercept our foe."

I moved eagerly to rejoin them. I had long ago learned to let Holmes unfold events in his own order which was never accidental. He had the capacity to separate himself from concerns not of the moment and only to summon forth his full force and intensity when the hour for action was upon him. Was such an hour upon us now? I took my place on the old settee and gave Holmes my full attention.

"You have no doubt wondered why I called you up from your home. It is because I have greater need for you now Watson than I have for years."

"I am entirely at your disposal."

"I am sorry to interrupt your reading, but I think it is time for us to have a council of war."

"You are not interrupting me at all," I answered. "I had just left off with your stay in Genoa."

"Ah, an appropriate time for a pause, it was there that I first began to glimpse the outline of what lay before me. The challenge posed by

111

history is different for each generation. But then I can go into all of that after the Professor departs."

He was silent for a moment organizing his thoughts. The wind still boomed in the chimney and I could not doubt that a wild storm might not beset us for some days to come. The Professor was smoking a thin black cigar and had nodded at my approach. Holmes now sat in the chair that he had formerly occupied of old in our rooms at Baker Street. He put his finger tips together as was his habit when in a discursive mood and began.

"Your reading has no doubt revealed that the Professor was quite alone when meeting with me at the Falls of Reichenbach. Hence the story that I gave of the falling rock set in motion by Colonel Sebastian Moran from the cliff above the ledge where I had sought shelter in order to observe your investigation was a complete fabrication. I did observe you but from the cliff itself. Also, I must confess that the air gun episode where the Colonel supposedly tried to assassinate me was a complete fabrication also. It was done so that the Colonel could be spirited out of the country after the Non-Pareil Club card scandal. You will recall that your own account of the incident in The Adventure of the Empty House did not speak of the outcome of the trial."

"That is because there was no trial," I remarked.

"Exactly, a more discerning reader might have asked himself why you so coyly ended the narrative without satisfying the reader that the potential assassin was convicted and was even then paying the price of his crimes."

"But, you instructed me at the time...."

"Quite right, I told you, I believe, that the prosecution had been prevented due to the fact that Colonel Sebastian Moran had left the country."

"I assumed that he had escaped."

"Have I not repeatedly warned you about assumptions, Watson? The Colonel was not prosecuted because he was spirited from the country under orders from the Prime Minister himself at my request."

"Good Heavens why?" I asked.

"Because it was in payment of an old debt; in order for you to understand these matters, let me review my account of the life and accomplishments of the Colonel to refresh your memory. His father, Sir Augustus Moran, C.B., was once British Minister to Persia. Indeed the Colonel spent much of his boyhood in that fabled land and spoke fluent Farsi. His knowledge of the Pashtun tribes of Afghanistan and their language was also extensive. You will recall that he was educated at Eton and Oxford and later, after taking up a military career, distinguished himself in the Jowaki Campaign, the Afghan Campaign, in Sherpur, Charasiab, and Cabul. His knowledge of the Himalaya region was unequaled among Englishmen. His knowledge of the jungles of the Indonesian Isles of Borneo and Sumatra was no less excellent. Now having heard this can you perhaps draw some conclusions?"

I thought for some time before answering, "I confess that I cannot."

"Nonsense, apply my methods, Watson. Are not these points indicative of something? A certain parallel?"

"Well, I can only think of your account in The Adventure of the Empty House of the explorations of Sigerson. You said there that your journey took you to Lhassa in the Himalayas and to Persia, Mecca, Khartoum, and Montpellier in France."

"Capital Watson! You excel yourself. Now since you have just read of the duel of sorts set up between the Professor and myself whereby he returned to England where his every move would presumably be watched by Gregson or Lestrade who would report to my Brother Mycroft, would the Professor have no similar delegate to watch me?"

"But to what purpose?"

"Say as a control factor for our mutual experiment in human nature. The experimental method always demands that a control be present. Well, Colonel Sebastian Moran was my control. It was he who met me in Genoa and who took a separate stateroom on our vessel as it set forth to round the coast of Africa en route to the Persian Gulf. We chose this route to set at naught any mutual pursuers. They could easily be discovered aboard the vessel and at close quarters the Colonel is a tiger and I am myself a force that must be weighed carefully before attempting violence."

My head swam. Could it really be that the explorations of Sigerson had been undertaken with Colonel Sebastian Moran as his guide, the very man who I had assumed had twice pursued my friend with murderous intent? This meant that not only had the Colonel not tried to kill Holmes in Switzerland nor in London when Holmes returned, it meant that he was something of an ally. All of my former views had been directly upended and it took me some time to accustom myself to the revolution in my former conclusions.

"But, Holmes," I protested. "If this is all as you say and this elaborate charade has been played not simply upon me but upon the British reading public who have come to trust my accounts then what was the purpose of it all?"

"Good old Watson! You are ever to the very point of the matter. All of these as you say elaborate charades were in anticipation of what shall face us in the next few days. I assure you that even now forces are gathering that will place the British Empire, and yes, perhaps even key men in the Vatican itself in peril!"

"Then what are we doing in this remote corner of England," I asked. "Surely we cannot be of use so far from the great population centers, the centers of these respective governments?"

"Be calm my dear fellow. I do nothing by accident. We are here because it is here that our enemy will strike first."

"But how will they do so?" I asked.

114

"By means of the German freighter, Friesland, that is enroute from Sumatra to Cardiff, at least according to an advance warning made to Her Majesty's government by Colonel Moran some days ago. It must round Hartland Point some time in the next few days unless it has been delayed by storms. We shall in turn board a small armed vessel sailing out of the Exmoor Port of Ilfracomb. We shall attempt to intercept the vessel and destroy it with its hated cargo. It must be destroyed utterly because should its cargo land the population of these isles will be reduced within a year by half."

"Great Scott," I cried. "But what is the source of this extraordinary danger?"

Here the Professor spoke up at last. "Disease, Dr. Watson, but it is in the means by which it may be spread that the true horror lies. The ship carries a host of potential disease vectors. It carries a number of the great rats of Indochina who carry a most virulent bacillus! It is this rat alone among mammals that is immune to the disease and may therefore spread it far and wide among the local rodent populations that will carry the disease further still."

"What disease does it carry?" I gasped. For I was somewhat acquainted with tropical diseases from my time in the army.

"It carries," said Holmes quietly, "The disease that a decade ago left entire Indonesian islands devoid of all human life. It is the Black Formosa Corruption!"

Here I must pause in order to allow my readers to fully imagine the horror which those words conveyed to my very heart and soul, for I saw at once that a most fatal and nefarious plot was afoot.

"But if we should not succeed?" I asked Holmes, who had stood up and walked to the window which was being lashed by the fury of the storm. He turned to us both before answering.

"Why then Watson, any account of the matter will prove superfluous for there shall for many years be few to read it in the chaos which will ensue in this isle."

115

I poured myself a glass of port and had soon recovered myself from the shock of Holmes' words regarding the Black Formosa Corruption.

Holmes had looked concerned for me but was reassured at my recovery. "Good old Watson, the old campaigner still lives within you. But let me lay before you what may be required before you give too precipitous an assent to aid us in this endeavor of ours; the Professor has already signed on, you see."

"Then I can do no less," I replied with some asperity.

"But you must humor me by allowing me to stress that not only are we going up against a crew whose very fear of this horrible disease is exceeded by their fear of the man behind it all but we risk contagion ourselves if we are called upon to board the vessel."

"Nevertheless I am your man," I replied without hesitation.

Holmes reached out and grasped my arms in his own hearty clasp.

"Good old Watson, you stand up to every test of fidelity and courage."

Holmes nodded and a grim expression was on his face as he said, "I choose my words carefully, Watson. Not only is this disease of a horrific nature, but secrecy is required surrounding the entire topic. The reason for this is that I am more certain that the threat posed to England exceeds one ship's cargo. There will undoubtedly be further attempts."

I was gripped by a chilling apprehension at his words.

"It is a plague Watson of a most virulent nature, a plague that would spread throughout these isles in a matter of months. Economic chaos of the most appalling nature would ensue, all of it engineered in Amsterdam by Baron Maupertius, a most infamous foe.

"But to what purpose?" I gasped.

"Why to obtain a dominance of the finance of three continents!" Holmes leaned forward and his piercing eyes added to the earnestness of his voice. "Baron Maupertius is the owner of The Great

Netherlands-Sumatra Company and the President of the East Indies Mercantile Bank. His plantations provide spices, rubber, jute, and hemp to half of the world. He is immensely wealthy. His concerns reach across the entire spectrum of industry and finance. He is active even in this country through the East Indies Mercantile Bank managed by a man named James Tweed. In the Indies his vast plantations were once run by a Mr. Culverton-Smith of infamous memory. You will recall Watson that he attempted to bring about my death in the case that you have recorded as the Adventure of the Dying Detective. Fortunately he failed and we were able to obtain a confession of his murder of his nephew. He has since departed from this world but he did leave one legacy, his knowledge and cultivation of this rare but hideous disease. The plans of Baron Maupertius took root in that great jungle where for many years a most hideous plague has been known among the Chinese laborers called, the Black Formosa Corruption. It is carried by only one known vector that is itself immune to the illness, a giant rat. This rat is notorious for its ability to gnaw through bamboo forests. Its teeth grow at a prodigious rate. The beast must gnaw continually. It is a most cunning and aggressive creature. Its fierceness makes it easily able to subdue other rodents and to quickly dominate any biological space into which it is introduced. It breeds at a remarkable rate and once introduced into these isles it would spread rapidly. The disease I spoke of is carried in by mites that the rats acquire in nature by avian contacts but a deliberate injection will do as well. Once exposed to these mites or fleas that can be carried on any bird or rodent the disease may migrate beyond its initial host. The disease cannot be transmitted to birds but lives only so long as the mites and their immediate progeny infest them, but wherever the birds may carry the mites, so far will the disease spread. The agent of contagion slumbers in the blood of these large and aggressive rats to be passed on to their progeny. From them the disease may spread through other rodent vectors and be transmitted to humans. It is a most distinctive disease and virtually custom-made to serve the purpose of destruction for which it is destined."

"But how can that lead to any advantage. From what you have said, I can only suppose that the Baron intends to use this agent of death to instill terror and destruction but on a large scale?"

Holmes leaned back with a sigh. "Perhaps you would care to take the story from here, Professor."

The Professor sat in shadow but his clear and distinctive voice seemed to emanate from a source of great force. His age had done little to dim the fires of his nature. "You come upon these events as they are about to spring forth, Dr. Watson. I assure you they have been long in preparation. The philosophy of our century has long looked to a decisive event. Our age is not content with the slow cycles of time. It has looked to a manifestation of the will. Read your Schopenhauer! Read your Nietzsche or Marx! While Mr. Sherlock Holmes was traveling in the east, I turned as I promised to geo-politics. I had become convinced in the study of my asteroids that to study substances was pointless. This universe is determined by forces not substances. What we call substance is a mere mental category for observed phenomena. What are nations, states, laws, diplomacy, even wars? They are the play of forces. The man who purchases, say a share of common stock thinks that he owns a thing. What he owns is an entity whose behavior may raise or lower his fortunes, but it is the behavior and its field of expectations that determines the reality. I had come to see everything as a field for action between conflicting forces prior to your friend's return from his travels."

"But what action," I interrupted.

"The quality of the action is irrelevant just as to an asteroid there is no up or down. Until you specify the field coordinates there is no direction, no progress, no criterion for progress or evaluation."

"But that is nihilism!" I cried.

"Quite. The universe displays little that we as humans would call virtue. If we would find the human we must posit the human. We must look within and trust the echo of God that we find there...this latter insight of course I owe to Mr. Holmes. His journey was in pursuit of the ground for the human, for unless we posit a common origin and destiny, then we are at sea in a play of blind forces. But I shall leave this discovery for you to find in due course in the narrative you have been reading. Suffice it to say for the present that Baron

Maupertius is not troubled by the problem of living a coherent existence. His desire is power and profit."

"But by releasing a terrible plague he will only spread destruction!" I cried.

"Yes, but by causing fear, fear which will shake values, he will cause the values of assets to decline and then he may purchase them for a fraction of their real value. His plan is to cause a financial panic and to then monopolize the economy of the British Empire. The entire economic world is in a sense one great organism. It survives by means of trade and payments. Should trade cease or payments become frozen, then the organism is threatened with death. Even in war-time there must be a flow of goods and services to serve the logistics of death. It may astonish you, Doctor, because your training has been to save each life as an individual event to realize that there are people who view human deaths as merely one more cost of doing business. For them the tides of mortality are as predictable and as inconsequential as the carnage of the tidal pool to one who gazes into the Piscean world and sees the viscous appetite of tentacle and jaw. Baron Maupertius is one of these men. He uses his riches as a great reservoir of force, withholding its use until he can leverage it to greatest advantage. He will wait while the plague spreads and the terror spreads with it until the great industrial wheels of production falter and stop. The resulting financial panic will cause a collapse in asset values. It is then that the Baron will move into the equity markets, posing as a great benefactor. He will soon monopolize key industrial and financial sectors. These too will then be used to anchor further transactions until at last the man has his thumb on the very carotid artery that feeds the brain of this nation. All of it legal of course except for the importation of the organism. Who will prosecute his main allies, a virulent disease agent, a poultry mite, and a huge rodent? Yet together they form an alliance of death greater than any coalition of powers that has ever menaced Britain."

"But how does he plan to bring this animal to England?" I asked, turning from the Professor to Holmes.

"By boat, a specific boat, the Dutch freighter, Friesland, that is even now nearing its critical port of destination, that, my dear Watson is

119

why you and I and the Professor are here. It shall be our task to intercept that vessel and destroy it. To that end, her Majesty's government has entrusted us with a fast steam launch, the Albert John that even now awaits us in Ilfracombe Harbor. It is manned with a crew of a dozen men, all heavily armed. Its Commander is placed entirely at our disposal and will act on our orders even to raining fire upon the decks of the vessel for we will not arrest her. Any direct contact with the vessel and its cargo of death would be our own deaths as well! No, the vessel will be sunk with all hands and its vicious cargo sent to the bottom of the sea."

"But that would be an act of piracy. The laws of war...."

"Watson, this vessel is in its totality a missile of offense. We cannot alas parse the actors from the force that they embody. In any case I have Mycroft's assurance that the very highest authorities of our government have approved the action and that our part in the affair will be one of the great secrets of history."

I was stunned by the magnitude of these revelations and their grave import. Certainly no ambush that I had ever participated in with Sherlock Holmes held such deadly peril. No greater stakes had ever yet existed should we fail in our appointed mission.

"But Holmes, how do you know the position of this vessel and the nature of its cargo?" I asked.

"Its exact position is unknown to me but I have a lookout in the Bay of Biscay and at Hartland Point. As to the nature of its cargo, well, this event has been long in the planning and to that question, my dear fellow. I must refer you back to the manuscript that you have been reading. These events are but the final act of a drama that began years ago on my Asian journey. This current vessel is not the first attempt to land its nefarious cargo. It was attempted once before a month ago. The boat was intercepted in the channel and sunk; but our enemies have learned from their mistake. This time they will not attempt a landing at the great London docks. This time they have chosen one of our more remote counties. Their destination is Cardiff. From there the plague will spread with infinite slowness at first through Wales. The storm clouds will gather slowly but fear will precede the actual plague like a great wind before the blasting storm and lashing hail. Fear is the actual agent that best serves the purposes of our foes." Holmes was silent gazing in grim determination at the fire.

"But these matters will not reach a head tonight, my dear Watson. It is time that we slept for I assure you the summons may come at any time in these next few days. I am happy that I have two guest rooms so that each of my guests may enjoy my humble hospitality. We will resume this discussion on the morrow. Until then I commend my manuscript version of my travels to your earnest perusal should you be awakened by the storm during the night."

Book Two:

The Journey to India

From the Journal of Sherlock Holmes

May 14, 1891 - The Mediterranean Sea

The ship was held over for a few days for provisioning which was as well for me. It gave me time to obtain the mountaineering equipment from Bergamo which it is as well to purchase now. While awaiting these deliveries I have had time to enjoy the truly astonishing local cuisine. Each night I am to be found in a local Trattoria with a crisp bottle of white Genoese wine, some of the oven-scarred round breads, and delicious shrimp pasta. My thinness is being much supplemented by such delights and begins to take on some of the contours of my erstwhile aide de camp, Watson. When at last we departed from the roadstead and I felt the sea take the vessel there came over me a sense of the most marvelous freedom. The smell of tar and canvas mingled with the pungent smells of shore life. The many tuberous life-forms made an undersea garden that slid from under us as the boat left the granite shores to seek the deeper waters. I stood and watched as the marvelous stone city slipped away in our lee. A strong easterly had caught us and would soon take us by the Corsican isles. A journey of many weeks lies ahead. The forced inaction might tend to grow oppressive but I shall use this journal to elaborate those theories that will be tested in the coming months and years.

Perhaps the reader is already curious about these "transcendental researches" that I have mentioned. We live in this latter part of the 19th century in an age of materialism and determinism. Herbert Spencer and August Comte are the patrons of the age. Each has, in his own way, elaborated a view of the society of the future as also have the great dialecticians Hegel and Marx. The common element of all of these theories is that their view that man has no inherent dignity based upon God but is rather a cunning beast. If he survives the drive of his appetites and creates culture, it is only because his pride exceeds his lust and greed. The result is that there is little room for talk of dignity or virtue in modern philosophy. The mass of mankind may be domesticated under a stern rule but never converted to a higher order of thought and conduct for if man is to be the measure of all things then all standards must return to man for validation. For this reason atheistic thought always begins in pride and ends in disgust and despair for history always succeeds in rendering the ambition to make of man an absolute both null and void. There is always too much of the unregenerate ape still within us. Not that Christians have always been optimistic. One need only look at the absolutism of St. Augustine, the Jansenists, and the Calvinists. Augustine despaired early of the potentialities of men if left to their own resources. The result was that emphasis upon Original Sin that was later to be so ardently embraced by John Calvin who consigned all but the elect to the flames of hell.

Against these grim advocates of the view that man is innately flawed and sinful, we have those who exalt the rationality and dignity of man, from Pelagius to Nietzsche to the positivists of the current day who place the burdens of personal and social elevation upon unaided human nature and effort. Such men glorify the individual and ignore the question of instilling general virtue in the great supine mass of mankind. But note that all of these are western thinkers working out of a tradition of Judeo-Christian law and assuming a relation to a Supra-rational being, God, if only to rebel against it. Once take away that belief in a single, central, organizing force, writing as Winwood Reade wrote in his The Martyrdom of Man, that man stands alone, then the entire spectrum of western thought changes. We move then from the concentration upon metaphysics to the triumph of epistemology under men like Immanuel Kant. No doubt the great German thought that he had buried metaphysics once and for all in his discussion of the various powers of pure and practical reason, but not so, for he left us with two ghosts of metaphysics: his noumenon (the unknowable true essence of things) and his categorical imperative, the remnant of what had been called the divine or the Holy Spirit in man. The result was that man was not yet closed in upon himself and his own mind. The transcendent still beckoned. Man cannot be satisfied by worldly knowledge alone in any form, because it is we who are doing the knowing. Man must probe the nature of his own knowing apparatus if he is to rest assured that he does not distort reality in the very act of knowing. What is that knowing finally but a pondering over his particular state and nature? What we desire is to escape, to get beyond all monkey-knowing, all that can be grasped by our opposable thumbs and to know without the limitations of a body in space and time. We tend to respect knowledge in proportion to its abstract nature and its immunity from all desire even if such knowledge finally becomes so attenuated that it becomes irrelevant to human concerns.

Man is a constant reproach to himself. The entire problem of atavism, of man returning to the ape, as shown by the brutality of his own history, haunts mankind. But there is an opposite folly, to turn into a thinking machine where man becomes a cipher unto himself, diminished by his own creations, and loathes to meditate upon his own condition and the limitations that it imposes. All of which is to say that man must remain a human knower and to honor the compassionate and emotional in his nature if he not to so alienate himself from his world by a premature objectivity that the intentional nature of all knowledge disappears. Man must therefore seek the transcendent if only to validate his own being. He must! Even I who have been described by Watson as the most perfect thinking machine that the world has ever known must pursue those vague phantasms that come to us, not clothed in thought but in desire, a desire for what, I have often asked myself and answered at last, that I hunger for a responsive voice from the empty abyss of time. Some outer being must tunnel down to us where we cry from our tombs with our mouths full of clay, or else we shall despair of our own existence? As Sir Thomas Browne said, "It cannot be long before we lie down in darkness and have our light in ashes." Show me the man that accepts gladly his own extinction? The peace he may desire leads not even the suicide to such despair that he would not desire one last momentary sigh of comfort before oblivion claims him. How much less can such men as Moriarity and I, who desire to write their names across the sands of the ages, accept either a fleeting fame or a vaguely constituted promise of a celestial home, when we desire certainty and immortality? We are the restless ones, plagued by thought. We test eternity daily by our actions; he by embracing darkness and I by unmasking evil and dragging it into the light. Both alike are engaged in a struggle and we have reached a position of parity at last. I cancel the man out and he me so that the net gain to the world is zero. There is thus a certain poetic truth in our supposed joint death, as Watson will no doubt report it, locked in each others arms and dead at the falls of Reichenbach. But can it really be admitted that goodness cancels evil or evil cancels goodness? We are, after all, not dealing with mere mathematical concepts. Metaphysically speaking the two concepts of good and evil are incommensurable; they do not appear upon the same level. They are scaled differently. Good doesn't oppose evil, for if that was so then God would surely have extinguished evil by now. No, goodness works in another way entirely, it rips apart from the dilemma that evil poses for good by taking evil upon itself in the person of Christ, at least so Christian metaphysics has always maintained. The dilemma of God confronting evil is to use evil to defeat itself for what is evil finally but the very definition of power, if that power is not used to promote the good. Goodness operates by leaving evil free to do its worst and then making that worst irrelevant, by setting up a dynamic of pure love. It is in powerlessness that good steps, as it were, beyond evil into a zone where evil cannot follow. The change is not of an order of magnitude but of entirely separate dimensions. This is what Jesus meant when he said that His Kingdom is not of this world. A similar thought appears in the Old Testament when the prophet was assured that God's thoughts are not man's thoughts and that as high as the heavens are beyond the earth, so high are God's thoughts beyond those of man.

Such thoughts are a summation of my position at this time as I set forth upon my journey. Such is my faith, but to prove this position to the Professor, ah that I cannot do at this hour, all of the exposition I have just given is mere supposition with me and as I have so often said to Watson, it is a capital mistake to theorize without data. So it is that I go in search of the data, not of my own experience and reflections alone but to the general witness of the composite faiths of all mankind. The task of the individual and his fate is caught up in the salvation of all. One does not enter into relation to God who does not relate first to God's creation and to his fellow pilgrims of this exile. In contrast to this view of mine is that of Moriarity, the supreme individualist. He presumes to judge all things while he alone remains to set the terms of his own universe, created in his own image, all of which is to say that he is a proud man. But am I any less proud in thinking that it is I who shall lay before him a proof that will turn him from his course, to deflect that vast river of his own speculations? What of my own motives? Is it God I seek or is it my own vindication and apotheosis? Who after all is the man of reason? Is it by reason that we come to God? If so then what becomes of the statement of Christ that unless we become like little children we shall not enter the Kingdom of Heaven?

It is not good for me to entertain such doubts though of the purity of my own motives for I must face many dangers on the path that lies before me. It will hardly do to begin in a half-hearted spirit. I must use my own vanity perhaps to carry me along, for if a man waits until he is worthy of the task before beginning, then the beginning shall never be made. May I be purified along the way that I must travel! I must go to those cultures beyond the comfortable British complacency, represented by such men as Brother Mycroft. I must proceed as though I doubted all that I believe. I go as a modern Descartes to discover, if I may, the limits of my own experience and just how far faith must precede reason if the troubled thinker is to find certitude and peace at last.

May 18, 1891 – Mediterranean Sea

The first problem facing the philosopher is whether reason has any hope of grasping the cosmos? What are our meager formulas to the vast activity of so great an entity? Newton assumed that the same laws govern the motion of particles and galaxies. He attempted a shorthand version of the great discourse of the planets. What does the universe care of our efforts to comprehend it? Shall I stand on the molten surface of the sun and measure it with my thermometer? Do the vast gaseous storms of Jupiter await my estimate of their force and direction? How then shall I speak of God? Would I not do better to set my pen down at once and fall to my knees or re-read the Book of Job, rather than to undertake this journey? Even prayer, according to St. Paul, is inadequate; so that the Holy Spirit prays within us as we should with unutterable groaning. Has God been mourning the loss of His creation since Eden? Who will

126

comfort God? It is questions such as these which haunt me and have driven me perhaps half-mad. Woe to the man who seeks to grasp God before God grasps him for he may grasp an idol instead! The measure of our grace should govern our aspirations as well as our accomplishments in all things. Yet I continue even if my very continuance is a vanity at last.

May 21, 1891 - Mediterranean Sea en route to Gibraltar

Already I have grown accustomed to the motion of the vessel that contains Colonel Moran and me. How strange it is to know that Colonel Moran is aboard, yet perforce to keep our distance until we may be sure that we have not been followed. The Professor explained the entire arrangement and I agreed on our last night together at the Inn. I need a guide for my proposed journey to the east. I am, after all, a creature of London and not of the mountains, the deserts, and the jungles. As for the Colonel and I, our acquaintance must grow gradually if we are to respect each other. So far we have been merely thrown together in the Grand Salon and at meals. I have no illusions regarding the danger that this man may pose to me. During his time in the east, his Eton and Oxford roots yielded to what I can only call a loyalty to the eastern mind. Though he fought valiantly against the Muslim tribes in Afghanistan he became impressed, for so the Professor explained to me, with the subtlety of Hinduism and can quote freely from The Upanishads. I was aware that the Professor had made him chief-of-staff, as it were, of his criminal organization and it was Moran who I suspected in the case of the death of John Douglas of Birlstone Manor. I also saw his hand in the death of the widow and heir to the great tea plantations in Assam of her husband, the late Mr. Stewart of Lauder and Edinburgh. Her husband was a Scottish trader whose tea importing business relied upon the slave labor of thousands. Their efforts had made the man one of the richest men in England. His widow had enlarged his already vast acreage. She was apparently of the same mold as King Leopold of Belgium and would suffer gladly any atrocity meted out to those who tended her plantations as long as such atrocities might add to her already vast fortune. She was found strangled in her mansion in Lauder. A statue of Kali, the death Goddess was found beside the body and a circle of tea surrounded it as well as a cryptic sign. The message was clear of course; it was a warning that her death was some sort of retribution for her mode of establishing and preserving her tea empire. I recall that I was consulted in the matter but could prove nothing. Colonel Moran was in England at the time, but departed soon after for the Indonesian islands. The estate of Mrs. Stewart escheated to the Crown since she had made no will, at least none that could be found. As Crown Land an administrator was appointed who looked into matters and I heard from Mycroft that conditions for the laborers have markedly improved since Mrs. Stewart's death. It is a strange coincidence perhaps, but the Vermissa Lodge was also one dedicated to vengeance for economic wrongs. It is an unfortunate corollary to industrialism that the labor that is most necessary to a society, whether that should be farm labor or coal mining, those very activities that are most essential to the common good, always fetches the lowest wages. The highest wages go to support life's superfluities and luxuries such as entertainment or banking and finance, and to support those persons who trade in intangibles who get the highest rewards. It is therefore a peculiarity of higher societies that they finally require either slavery or its equivalent in order to maintain these tributes to national vanity manifested by social excess and nominal nobility.

In order to attain these ends of excess by means of slavery two forces are useful: first, wages must be kept low enough to ensure want as well as to ensure fear and second a system of social force through prisons at home and warfare abroad must exist to compel the masses to obey and widen the sphere of empire. The flow of resources and benefits must always continue in an upward direction. Every great civilization feeds the center and makes war on the peripheral lands that surround it. When the disparity of resources and their utilization for war and those allocated to peaceful expenditures becomes too great, the center itself begins to starve in order to maintain the garrisons in the field. Finally insurrection or secession at home breaks up the empire and a period of common warfare begins until a new power arises elsewhere. This is the cycle of empires and civilizations that determines history. At the present time, the central role is held by England. The world bears tribute, and has throughout the reign of Victoria, to British supremacy. I myself once carved the wall of Mrs. Hudson's rooms with VR for Victoria Regina. Watson's readers have undoubtedly assumed that I did this as an act of homage to the queen. If so it is strange is it not that I did so with bullets? This is not to say that I am not a loyal Englishman, for I follow John Locke in the belief that the social contract is a surrender of individual sovereignty to ensure the common good. I myself have kept a certain codicil though, reserving separate choice, in order not to violate my own conscience. I have been able to do so because, as a consulting detective, I am not part of the official police force. I live by my wits. I am certified by no organization. My stock in trade is a solution to human dilemmas in whatever guise they may present themselves. Where I differ from Mycroft is that he has a single client whose interests he must always serve or resign his unique commission. He determines policy by charting that course of least resistance between conflicting alternatives. He is allowed no personal views. It is not his province to have them. His mind is a purely technical device for resolving conflicts. He shows what consequences will flow from any given course of action and what departments of the government will be impacted. He is a conservator of the conservative and an expeditor of whatever is adventurous in Imperial Policy. Above all he understands how to broker sufficient force to intimidate other imperial powers such as the Empire of Germany and the Empire of Russia. He has assured me that war between the great powers is inevitable but that no small part of his efforts is to avoid it, or at least to delay its outbreak, at least during the course of his tenure in office. That he has been successful in this was shown when England avoided being involved in the Franco-Prussian War. Not since the defeat of Napoleon has England been involved in a general conflict of the European powers. To maintain personal peace with Mycroft, I keep my own attitudes to power in check. I would as soon aid my own nation as another and have done so and will do so again. This is the extent of my patriotism.

But what have such mass problems to do with those little closet-dramas that hold all of the interest of life for me? If we are reduced to mere engines of consumption and production as the politicians and economists would propose, then where are we as human beings? In all of Watson's narratives the attentive reader can glimpse my character by the problems that claim my attention. How many involve a love interest, a crime passionelle, and the jealous seething of the human heart? How frail we are in our envelopes of tissue confronting the perilous workings of fate. As such I expect little of human virtue. Would I behave differently in the same circumstances is always the test of my conscience. It is this which makes me suspicious of the easy virtue of the prelate who can espouse a moral code that would condemn the majority of human beings to eternal fire. Certainly if I could find the transcendence that I seek in the easy bosom of the Church of England I would remain at home and confine my researches to the Book of Common Prayer. Even that very Mrs. Stewart, who, if my suspicions are reliable, was done to death by Colonel Sebastian Moran, was after all, a regular member of the Church of England. She might not have cheated a tea-monger out of a rupee consciously, but she saw no problem when the Irish tenant farmers were evicted in the 1840's from her husband's estates. Few realize that Ireland exported food throughout the famine years because the Irish, who grew the food, could not outbid foreign buyers. Mrs. Stewart was only a bride then, but when her hardness of heart continued towards the estates of her husband in India the die was cast. No doubt she appeared as a member of the predatory class in the eyes of the Colonel rather than as a mere frumpy British heiress. In any case, it was as a tiger in the bush that he brought her down, viewing her as a dangerous beast of prey. But perhaps I overreach myself in interpreting the Colonel's state of mind. I cannot see him though in the guise of a mere murderer for hire. Could the gallant soldier and graduate of Oxford fall so low? No. Character for good or ill is not the fruit of a day or of a season but the result of years. I must ask the Colonel though if I am to hear from his own lips his political philosophy. So far I have kept my distance and awaited his overtures. Certainly there is time to cement a further acquaintance since we shall be at sea for over a month before we reach Bombay.

May 30, 1891 - The Atlantic Ocean

We sailed though the straits of Gibraltar just after dawn. The sea acted as a great sluiceway and the vessel sailed out with the withdrawing tide. The mighty rock hung over the ship in the melting mists as we favored the Spanish side to avoid the Barbary Pirates. I was on deck and staring over the rail when suddenly, the Colonel was at my side. He had approached with the stealthiness of a great cat and only the sudden advent of his shadow alerted me to his presence.

"Magnificent, is it not?" The Colonel remarked. "I can still recall viewing it as a lad when I made my Grand Tour of the continent. I was just out of Oxford and seeking my way. I had taken a first at Oxford in Oriental languages and I thought to go into the state department and be seconded to some embassy or other but the idea of transcribing dull diplomatic correspondence did not appeal to me. I had read Lermontov as did so many of my generation. It was he who stirred my romantic blood. I wanted to be a soldier. I dreamed of routing Cossacks and wedding a Princess of the Caucasus with dark eyes and Circassian skin." He sighed. "But you see me today, sunburned by tropic suns, a bachelor, and put to the indignity of acting as guide to a laconic Baker Street dreamer and police adjutant."

This was our introduction. Though his words were insulting, he smiled and I sensed at once something of the charm of the man. He was of medium height but immensely strong, clean-shaven but with a massive cleft chin. His teeth looked as though he could gnaw bones. Yet for all his fierceness there was a certain reflective quality in him that surprised me.

"You left England shortly after the Professor?" I inquired.

"Yes, we took opposite routes. I crossed to the Continent from Hull and proceeded via The Hague to Paris then Strasbourg and finally though Switzerland to Italy. I met with the Professor after you parted and we arranged that I am to keep you in sight and since an absurd game of hide and seek would be unseemly, since you must have known if I would be following you, we decided that I am to act in the open and affirmative capacity of being your guide."

"You do not resent such a role?" I smiled.

"I am always happy when I am traveling and the Professor assures me that you will prove an interesting companion Mister, I believe the name is Sigerson," he smiled.

"Thank you Colonel. Well then, our first destination is Northern India after we land in Bombay."

"Then perhaps it is as well that we discuss the Hindu mind before we land since this is your first trip to India. The Hindu mind is quite comfortable with two ideas: a multiplicity of Gods and a cosmic inscrutability. It is not law based. It has no abhorrence of images nor is it burdened with comprehending the mind of God or the purpose of things. The Hindu learns to accept life upon its own terms as a given. There is no linear relation to time. Hinduism expects eternal duration and embraces easily the lack of control of man over the cosmos. No eternal seat of judgment awaits us but rather a daily adjustment and placation of the forces of life. There is an essential lyricism to the Hindu relation to Brahma. I trust that you have read the Rig Veda, the ancient hymns? If not, then I advise you to do so and the Upanishads as well. You will find a far more sophisticated concept of the ultimate than the prosaic war-god of the Hebrews."

"I am surprised to see you so knowledgeable of the tenets of any faith, Colonel Moran."

"No doubt you think of me as an unprincipled scoundrel. I have my own principles."

"I would be interested to hear your philosophy," I replied.

"I desire a just world by any means humanly attainable, to make it so."

"Like the murder of Mrs. Stewart of Lauder, for instance?" I asked pointedly.

The Colonel was silent for some time before saying, "Shall I put a case before you?"

"Pray Proceed."

"Imagine not a single obnoxious old woman but picture instead a great disembodied force that results in the death of thousands. It is mindless but intrusive into the very home lives of the poor. See the bodies of children dead in the first dawn of life so that this mechanism can send riches to some great central node. Now imagine that the process may not be disassembled. It can though be stopped at the center, not by a war involving any number of inane strategic decisions with the price of young lads dead who will never personally benefit from the war. By the death of one person, that node of distribution and acquisition (and she not innocent mind you but collaborative in every way with these evils) may cease to work its evils. Is that murder or war, the only war that may be claimed to be truly a just war?"

"All of this is very clean and pat in the way that you state it, but you killed her though in cold blood." I stated severely.

"And by doing so, I saved thousands." he answered calmly. "Surely the net gain justifies the crime. But, in any case, I played by the same rules as she had always done and her husband before her. She had long since committed herself to live by force alone and not by mercy, not dreaming that she would meet one equal to the forces that surrounded her and guaranteed that her own pillage would be seen as respectable and justified. He who lives by the sword shall perish by the sword. Is that not somewhere in the gospels?"

We were silent, gazing at the sea. I saw in the Colonel the vast logic of the Godless universe, of force meeting counterforce. I thought of the sharks in the ocean around our ship, gliding soundlessly through the vast deeps. I thought how accustomed is the earth and the sea to the deaths of its denizens. I pictured the depths of the past with the great saurian's eating each other through geologic ages. Certainly God was patient then to await the advent of men. Great glaciers had to recede to make room for our animal clad ancestors. Who stood by us in the night when great beasts roared outside our domiciles? Was God present to the dim night consciousness of man? Long before the parsing of cubits in Noah's arc or the Mosaic Law touched the common fate of the great Gentile hoards, was God speaking within the human cranium when mere survival was the only rule? Perhaps the Colonel learned the price of survival on the Pashtun peaks of Afghanistan and in the fetid, green bamboo jungles of Indonesia. Did this knowledge make him a savage or merely a man of honesty before the world when seen as it

133

truly is: a battleground, a jungle of contending forces? His sad eyes had more of the nature of the beast which knows how far fear may yield to mercy without putting its own existence in peril. The Colonel took my silence for dismissal, nodded, and we parted that first day of our acquaintance.

Later-

I cannot close this day's entries without some comment upon the arguments raised by Colonel Moran to justify what might be called a targeted elimination of evil at its source. The metaphysical problem lies in the contrary approach followed by God who does not eliminate evil even when its source can be foreseen. Since God is capable of foreseeing all evil and must also be presumed to be able to take effective action to prevent or limit its activity why does He not do so? The world that we observe is one wherein Evil seems to be positively drawn towards goodness and holiness by a strange inverse affinity. It is the very disproportion and violence of evil that shocks us for evil is incomprehensible to the very degree that we do not ourselves participate in it. Is goodness fated always to play the role of the victim? The fate of the Holy Innocents comes to mind, those male children put to death by King Herod in the attempt to prevent the future ascendancy of Christ as King if the Jews. If Herod had only known that his own power was secure for, Christ did not desire to share in the apparent victory of evil but to take it upon Himself; by doing so to render it null and void. This is not to say that this simple arithmetic of cancellation works out on this side of the grave. The death that awaits us all demands of us a final affinity to good or evil. Who then is to be pitied, the innocent led to slaughter or the man who must face his God with his brother's blood fresh upon his hands? We hunger in our righteous ire for retribution and wish to be its agents. The result, alas, is the long parade of vengeance and reprisal that makes up so much of the record of human history.

June 6, 1891 - Across the Equator

As my previous entry shows, it would appear to be the fate of the man of virtue to need to endure evil both around him and within his own inner heart. Evil cannot be objectified as though its root system did not extend underground to include us all. The burden of original sin is universal.

As Watson has recorded, it is my own inner sense of right and wrong, that has time and again dictated my policy in the information that I share with the police and when I have allowed even the criminal to escape the clumsy clutches of the law. The law is of course prescriptive in nature for without norms we would be a sea. But even the sea, which seems so uniform, has its currents and eddies, its tides and yes, its storms. The man at sea who shall navigate truly must consider more than the celestial position he occupies, he must feel those forces that will constantly shift his position before another sextant reading is possible. Moral choice is far more often a choice between evils than it is one between good and evil. What is clear from the pulpit becomes instantaneously refracted in the foggy London streets. Would that every day was a clear day 'at a Bedfordshire country house and not a dank midnight by the Limehouse docks! It is not that the poor should forsake morality (since often they are the only ones who find it); it is that choice itself is often a luxury in the blind seething struggle for existence. Perhaps this is the source of Colonel Moran's unique brand of morality. How often have I seen in the opium dens some poor soul throw a ratty blanket over the quaking shoulders of a fellow inebriate whereas, when I was a lad in my father's house among the landed gentry of Yorkshire, I listened to gentlemen discuss Irish evictions over their drawing room port while the vicar shared a pleasantry within earshot of a discussion that would doom an Irish family to starvation by degrees after eviction.

As younger sons, Mycroft and I knew early on that we would not share the fate of Sherringford our elder brother and that we would have to live by our wits. This gave us both a certain empathy with the tenants of the estate. We are today always welcome at the Manor of course and as to our education, nothing was spared. I never took my degree though, preferring those courses and techniques that would be of immediate application in my chosen line of work. Watson commented extensively upon my deficiencies in some departments of knowledge at the time that he wrote, A Study in Scarlet, his first book about my life as a consulting detective. I must confess that I exaggerated my areas of ignorance to prove a point. In reality I am something of a scholar in my way and my monographs on various Chaldean scrolls and medieval land tenures have drawn scholarly notice in the highest academic circles. It is Sherringford though who has been confined to the East Riding of Yorkshire with his days spent discussing oats, parsnips, and sheep-shearing. He seems happy as a rural lord and an occasional letter serves to inform me of the condition of the Holmes Estate. I am always caught up though in some case or other and my visits home are few. My promises of months have been extended to years. Mycroft of course lives in a world that consists only of his rooms, of the Diogenes Club, and the Home Office. While for me London life has been my university far more than Oxford or Cambridge ever were.

Yet how different was my life in England to the youthful colonial existence of Sebastian Moran must have been. Whereas many colonials come to despise the people among whom they govern while they adhere to class distinctions more severe than the Home Counties; the Colonel appears to have embraced the democracy of the battlefield to an extreme degree. Having served with native orderlies and infantry he perhaps developed that breadth of vision that ensures command across languages and cultures. Each of us has, in our own way, developed democratic sympathies. Each has seen how the masses of our fellow men and women are caught up by systems they can neither understand nor control. These systems extract raw mineral wealth or wealth from the weaving of textile fibers while returning high priced manufactured goods under the eyes of an occupying army and navy who ensure that no imperial possessions may produce homegrown products to compete with the imports from England. We both deplore the injustice. Still, I have tried in my way to serve the crown, putting my doubts as to policy aside. I bow my head though before no Lord of the land since I am also of the gentry. I know at first hand that a fool in a cravat is still a fool. But would I extend my abhorrence of injustice to a shot from an air-gun at Mrs. Stewart as she sipped her tea on her terrace? I am a democrat but not yet an anarchist.

Still, I spent many days turning these matters over in my head after my first discussion with the Colonel. By day the green shores of Africa appeared at intervals off of our port bow. The ship was

136

gripped in a deadly heat by day and it was only at night when the stars appeared in the heavens, more stars than I would ever dream of seeing with such clarity in England. Then I would seek respite from the heat in my cabin with a walk on the deck. Already I dreamed of the snows of the high mountains. Is there clarity in thinner air or do the mountain people grow shrunken within themselves in the eternal chill? Where is the ideal man dreamed of by Herbert Spencer or Winwood Reade to be found? And if such a man evolves, shall his posterity bear his virtues translated from the heart to the loins? Do great men appear only intermittently? Does the species evolve by certain shared virtues in the face of which the contribution of any given individual mutation is negligible? In the case of the human, only generations out of time will see the final result, just as a brighter plumage appears on the bird over time or a thicker armor on the rhinosaurus. When shall we see greater virtue or a clearer reason in man?

June 12, 1891 - The South Atlantic

The smells of Africa blow out to us at sea. I have been spending my days on deck lately. To one accustomed to the confinement of city buildings, fog, and the smoke haze of London the freedom of these days is like a new birth. If it was not for the need to be present where the problems are most likely to present themselves in the great metropolis, I would long since have retired to those regions where nature manifests itself in all its grandeur. Though I have a horror of the isolation of the country where the social constraints of humanity may yield to the secret darkness of the human heart and petty despots may dominate the helpless inmates of the family home and its servants, I love the great desolate regions of the earth. However charged with terror may be the hurricane or the avalanche, that terror is not an evil in the true sense. There is no malice in nature, but rather, a vast indifference to the human order. Whether this insensibility shows the indifference of God or whether it shows that we must seek our solace in the company of men and women is perhaps the primal religious question. Is the human a mere afterthought of a blind creation or is it the core and purpose of all that we see before us? When the great saurian beasts of the Jurassic Age gorged their mighty gullets through millennia, was God patiently waiting for our primate forebears to rise to the level

137

of Original Sin? Or were man and his counterpart mate existent in some distant world of the spirit? Were they then plunged at the moment of that sin into this primal swamp of passion and disappointment of the world that we know so well? In that original state of grace when we walked with God in the cool of the Garden of Eden in a place beyond place in a time beyond time, was all lying before God's mind in contemplation? Had He already seen the furthest concatenations of all events? If so, what must be the endurance of God, watching what has already been foreseen! Think of the horror of the dripping eons. Surely no thinking being could endure to live twice, first in prospect and then in actuality. Even joy would be anguish in such a state. For this reason the theologians place God outside of time. Religion cannot probe the mind of God but only the mind of man. Whether those glimmerings that we call religion can find their source in God cannot be verified from God's side but only from our own. If God himself does not pierce the veil it must remain for us an impenetrable curtain. We hammer with fists of flesh and sinew against a rock wall. If granite became soft as eiderdown and we clawed through it for generations, even then, it would pose an insuperable barrier to us as an image of the journey to God. Unless God were to assume our very form the human would be forever alien to anything but itself. The Incarnation is then the opposite of transcendence. It is God wishing to know the experience of man as man. It is for this reason that we hunger for transcendence in turn, so as to know ourselves through the eyes of God. A human existence on its own terms is an oxymoron. Man cannot be defined in terms of man alone. The criterion of religious truth must then be beyond the human. But what is that criterion? Place man in the original position prior to choice and affirmation of any one religious faith and what will move him or compel his assent? Does he then create the truth in the act of assenting? Do we get the God that we deserve? But if there is actually a God beyond our own creative act then he creates us in so choosing just as we create the gods in our own image if there is no actual one, single true God of all. This is the reason for the Christian belief that salvation is an act of Grace - God chooses us before we choose Him. Grace gives us the ability to assent prior to the act by which we claim what has already claimed us.

138

How strange, if these speculations of mine are true, that so many men and women create the human at the Jurassic level? How often have I wandered through the dank streets of Whitechapel or Limehouse past the entrances to cheap music halls, bumped into the gin-soaked bodies of women who offered themselves for more of that self-same gin or seen through the opiate haze of a Lascar operated opium den the haunted eyes of the lost men. Yet is God not closer to those who are at such an end of human resource then He is amidst the pomp of a summer garden party in Surrey or a diplomatic gathering in Pall Mall? If God is not to be found but must find us then perhaps all that we can do is to seek the image of God in men and women. We must set the transcendent aside even as God has done if Christ is indeed God. A true religion must help us doctrinally to do so. But doctrine has that not itself always been the problem? We are at sea amidst absolutes clothed in such various and manifest appearances and formulae! We seek to formulate what lies beyond all formula and then demand acquiescence from unbelievers to what cannot be verified! So for now I turn from these reflections and seek again the blue distances of these waves whose eternal motion is perhaps the heartbeat of all we can ever know of God.

Dr. Watson's Narrative Continues

I read the above entry just before falling asleep. The sound of the crashing storm made Holmes' little abode like a ship at sea. I wondered how he knew of the pending arrival of the Dutch ship Friesland. I could not doubt that no ship would attempt a landfall until the storm and the sea swells that it had generated should subside. It seemed strange that the crew on a boat engaged in such a mission of destruction would consider themselves bound by its own charter to arrive at Cardiff if they knew the true nature of their cargo. I also wondered what would keep the disease in check aboard the vessel itself. Would the rat only be infected with the pestilence after its importation? That must surely be the case or else the crew must surely die before bringing the ship to port. These and many other questions beset me. What events would the following days bring?

I had hoped that this period of respite from the trying exertions of recent years would merge into a quiet if premature retirement. Through the years Holmes had vetted various ideas for his retirement years when they should come at last. Among these was that he might purchase the old Baker Street rooms from Mrs. Hudson and there he planned to maintain a small museum containing various artifacts from his long career and maintain a school in the art of detection. He would lecture there for a small audience drawn from the police agencies of both Europe and America. The fees collected would support him in his retirement years. He already possessed a substantial investment income and there was always his share in the patrimony of the family estate at Sigerside in Yorkshire, so financial cares did not trouble his mind at this time. The simplicity of his life combined with several munificent cases in 1896 had finally given him the financial security to pursue other problems of interest and to make up for his generous waiver of many of his professional fees through the years. Young Cartwright of the Baker Street Irregulars was now himself with Scotland Yard. The expenses his education had been quietly paid for by Sherlock Holmes. He had also established a home for some of London's many orphan boys and purchased a country retreat and school for them near Whitby where they could breathe the clean bracing air of Yorkshire; this latter endeavor was made possible with Mycroft's help.

I could see though why Holmes preferred Devon as a retreat over Norfolk or Sussex. Ever since the affair of the Hound of the Baskervilles and the matter of the adventure of the racehorse, Silver Blaze, Holmes had loved the bleak beauty of the western Moors of Devonshire. I was also not immune to their charm. Even on the frosty morning of my arrival I could sense in the dying year a poignant reminder of earlier days when my companion and I had pursued the chase on this same ground. Never though had the stakes been higher than those which met us now. If the boat slipped past us with its deadly cargo it would mean the peril of countless lives and the collapse of the economy of the Empire. I had always admired my friend's strange capacity for detachment. Even in the midst of an adventure he could lose himself for hours at a concert by Sarasate before resuming the chase. It was that faculty that allowed him to find repose now while outside the storm lashed the stone house and

140

the dead ivy ripped like skeletal hands at the lattice. As for me, action was the great anodyne. I found myself prey to fancy and terror in proportion to any delays I might encounter. Perhaps only an old soldier who has known the agony of waiting for the attack, that he knows will come, can imagine how different was the dreamy, abstract, problem-solving approach of Holmes compared to my own swift and decisive nature. It was for this reason that Holmes often hid from me those elements of the case that might have led me too soon to an apprehension of what might lie before us. This policy no doubt explained why he chose on this occasion of most immanent peril to entrust to me the reading of his memoirs of his years of absence and spiritual questing in the Far East and the Islamic lands to distract my mind while we awaited news of the ship.

It was only with the greatest effort that I was able to follow his theological conclusions though I recognized their insight and brilliance. My experience with a Jezail bullet was not such as would leave an open mind to devotees of Mohammed but neither was my Christianity as settled and formalized as that of Holmes whose theological speculations and conclusions might have made of him a great prelate had his vocation led him in that direction. While not sharing Holmes' initial skepticism at the time of the case of The Sign of Four, I had not sought my life's comfort in religion as he was later to do. Instead I found solace in routine, discipline and the order of medical practice combined with the comforts of marriage. My esteemed wife, the wife of my early years, the former Miss Mary Katherine Morestan, was my moral ideal. My own nature demands more than mere words and dogmas however inspiring and convincing to provide a basis for life. Still, I could sympathize with that questing nature which Holmes possessed and his passion to decipher the greatest puzzle of all: why all things are as they are. It was with such musings as these upon the infinite that I fell at last asleep.

I awoke the next day to a strange silence. The wind had dropped over night only to be succeeded by a dense fog rising out of the moorlands that surrounded us. My first thoughts were of the conditions at sea. If the fog was not merely a local phenomenon but extended to the seacoast as well, then it would be madness for the vessel Friesland to try and make a landfall. The rugged Devon and Welsh Coasts left small margin for navigational error. The vessel would have to stand off and wait for the fog to lift. I dressed quickly and descended only to discover that Holmes was awake and already active. He had built up the fire in the sitting room and the homely smell of baking bread filled the downstairs area. Holmes was laying out thick slabs of bacon in a large frying pan. Three place settings were visible in the breakfast nook that looked out upon the waves of moorland, now shrouded in drifting mists.

"Ah Watson, you are up at last. I am afraid that I do not keep London hours. The Professor still sleeps, as befits a man of his age, and we may have a few moments to ourselves. Help yourself to the tea, an excellent Yunnan and you will find the Devonshire cream to be excellent."

I did as he directed and he poured a hearty helping also into a large pottery mug before sitting on the leather couch by my side.

"Well then, how is your reading coming along?"

"When I left off you were approaching India by sea."

"You are making excellent progress then. I trust that my theological reflections are not overwhelming to you."

"They are complex," I stated, "But I have been able to follow your thought. I must admit that I never knew that your reflective mind would take the particular course that it has."

"If you look back upon your own narratives you will find many cases where I have wondered about the deeper origins of the darkness in the human heart and speculated upon the purpose of existence. Besides, my dear fellow, there is a time of life, which we are both entering, where these matters may no longer be put off. The days grow shorter before us as age progresses and we cannot be unaware that the terminus draws near. At that time the question of the personal meaning of one's life supplants the place of early passions and of the pursuit of honor and renown. One turns instead to one's place in a higher order of events and the possibility that one's many failings might be transmuted towards a higher end before it is too late."

"But why turn to religion for this? Surely, the life of a noble English gentleman is sufficient," I replied.

"Ah the noble dead, Westminster is stuffed with them. But where is the point of reference Watson? If there is no final absolute, no Greenwich Mean Time of the spirit then virtue and vice, guilt and innocence become matters of self-definition or of one's social group. We become savages grimacing across a stream dividing our respective lands. The metaphysical drive will not be so easily silenced. But you will have quite enough of this in my manuscript so let us leave the subject for now so that we may move on to the events that lie immediately at hand."

"The vessel Friesland..."

"Precisely, I do not anticipate a landfall in this fog."

"Nor do I; but what then shall we do?"

"I believe that we should go up to Ilfracomb and see that all is well upon the motor launch. I regret leaving the comfort of home but we must be prepared for instant action. You will find the local port to be quite charming and I have arranged for lodgings for us in an excellent inn."

"When shall we leave?"

"I think after noon. We shall go to the village halt at Coombe Tracey and catch the express train for Ilfracomb. But you must allow me to resume my duties as cook for I hear stirrings above and the Professor will no doubt join us presently."

A short time later we were joined by the Professor who nodded to me when he entered, no doubt still sensing my reservations in his regard. We sat down and over the hearty Devon fare listened as Holmes outlined what lay before us.

"The launch has been ready for days since the Friesland was spotted by one of her Majesty's vessels off the coast of Gibraltar. It anchored off for a day off Lisbon and telegraphic communication was made to London. Our own vessel then set sail from Plymouth and rounding the coast took up its station in Ilfracomb where it has remained. The vessel is well-armed with heavy guns. The incoming Friesland will be arrested in our territorial waters for carrying contraband cargo and placed in quarantine while medical officers board her. The ship will be gradually evacuated and then the vessel burned to the water-line."

"But you said before that ship and all aboard were to be destroyed," I reminded Holmes.

"Yes, because I expect these men to resist boarding. They who are desperate enough to attempt a landing with so deadly a cargo, will they be likely to surrender without a fight?"

"The crew, if any remain alive may welcome medical aid."

"Then why did they not put ashore in Lisbon? Much depends upon whether the disease is running through the ship's company or whether the contagious animals have been kept in some way confined, only to be liberated upon landing. I believe that the latter course is the most probable. If that should be the case we may indeed anticipate some resistance on their part but we are well armed."

"I cannot but imagine that their may be repercussions from the Dutch or German consulates. If we fire upon the vessel, there will surely be an international incident." I objected.

"My brother Mycroft is already working on that eventuality. The result we hope will be that the objection will be pro-forma. The Captain of the Friesland will no doubt refuse a customs boarding and that resistance if coupled by arms will justify any action on our part."

"But what if he permits boarding, surely we will not climb aboard such a deadly vessel."

"It is my belief that the Friesland does not anticipate that its approach will have been foreseen. It no doubt intends to land its cargo in one of

144

the smaller ports and then to withdraw again to sea. This coast has always been a noted area for smugglers and the technique is not unknown. The Captain will be surprised therefore when we place it in immediate interdict and may respond by firing upon us. If on the other hand he is an honest seaman, why then he shall be placed in quarantine and his crew evacuated over time. Have you anything to add Professor since your opinions may be of service?"

The Professor raised his great head and in his usual quiet tone stated, "You intend to proceed I see in proper British fashion. You must presume that so desperate a venture requires a desperate crew. I would anticipate that the Baron's agents have seen to manning the ship by seamen willing to risk death for a large promised reward. They no doubt know that they may be called upon to offer resistance and since they are smugglers. If their sole cargo is crates with these creatures aboard they have had to be fed and watered by some remote means no doubt to prevent contagion until these shores have been reached. In my plans with the Baron I left details to him. In unloading the cargo it will be a small matter to Baron Maupertius if these men catch the disease as far as their mission is concerned. If, on the other hand the disease has already spread among them they may be operating with a reduced crew who may in desperation seek to land the cargo and then either to withdraw quietly again to sea or to disperse upon the land while a small contingent destroys the vessel. It will then go reported missing at sea. The disease will then spread gradually inland until it reaches Cardiff and from there it will spread to Wales, to London and finally in all directions. The rodents are prolific so that a few mathematical calculations would indicate a small initial spread of the illness in remote districts followed by an exponential spread to larger population centers and a growing terror in the public at large. It may take as long as six months before significant numbers of deaths occur but the very horrendousness of the symptoms will breed a terror disproportionate to the numbers of actual dead. This terror will be the actual weapon used to disable the country's economy."

Holmes and I had listened with interest to this remarkably concise forecast of events. Holmes nodded, "An admirable exposition Professor! No doubt you may imagine how you would proceed were you Baron Maupertius. This event has been long in planning and his prior premature attempt about which the Professor was not informed in advance which attempted to land a similar cargo but was lost in a fog just such as this, has no doubt taught him better how to proceed now. I do indeed anticipate resistance but now I must ask of you both the immediate question which is, will the Captain ignore this fog and attempt a landfall? As I see it we must anticipate just such a daring move and be ready. For this reason Watson and I must proceed to Ilfracomb while allowing you, Professor, to return to Kings Pyland. When the affair is concluded we will of course come over to inform you of the course that events may have taken and in the process be able to review your most excellent stable of racehorses. My groom will see that you are taken home by my two-seater dog-cart. Meanwhile, Watson and I will set out within the hour. Watson, are you game for a foggy drive across the moors and a jouncing steam locomotive?"

"Of course," I answered.

"Then holloa, gentlemen, the game is afoot!"

The Professor was taken to King's Pyland and when the dog-cart returned it departed for the larger village of Coombe Tracey with Holmes and me aboard. Dartmoor and Exmoor are in a way similar to the ocean. The great barrens exist in waves of land; deep valleys are followed by high ridges. Over all great storms of fog were blowing and the even in late morning there was no sign of the sun. The heavy mist soon covered my raincoat with the damp. I hunched my shoulders attempting to withdraw into its dark recesses the better to escape the bitter chill. Our dogcart made slow progress. The fog surrounding us seemed to stifle all sound but the slow plodding of the horse's hoofs upon the well-worn track. Holmes had just broken the silence to assure me that the village was not far distant and that we would surely make our connection with the London and Southwestern Railroad connection when a most strange and unsettling event occurred. Suddenly from over the great expanse of the moors came a most mournful sound, a sound that took me back some years, a sound that chilled my very blood. It was the sound of the distant baying of a great hound!"

146

I turned to Holmes at once, "Holmes! Can it be?"

My companion wore a look of concentration in which was mixed an element of consternation and wonder. He shook his head after a moment.

"We must not give way to portents my dear fellow."

"Have you heard it before?"

"Yes on occasion but only in recent days."

"To what do you attribute its advent?"

Holmes smiled. "Well we must not eliminate the possibility of coincidence and find pattern where there is only serendipity. No doubt one of my neighbors is a hunter. Sight-hounds are not uncommon in this country."

"Have you made inquiries?"

"There has been no time. The pressing matter at hand has taken precedence over the search to reassure any superstitious fears that I may possess. No, Watson, I believe that we have only one hound from hell in our archives, we need not seek another." Holmes lapsed then into silence but I must confess, I who knew him so well, could tell that his senses had quickened and that a train of reflection had been set into motion by the event.

We soon arrived at the station at Coombe Tracey. Our baggage was unloaded and a short time later the small local train groaned into motion and we were on our way to the port where our vessel awaited us.

Holmes sat back against the stiff green leather seat and placing his finger tips together began a desultory conversation as we proceeded on our way. "Well, Watson, having read some of my manuscript I am sure that a great many things may have become clear to you. I have at last reached the summit of my career, a career that has not been a uniform one. You yourself witnessed the lean times when it was only my small share of the estate income from Yorkshire remitted to me by

147

my brother Sherringford that sustained me. As the eldest of the Holmes brothers he succeeded to the family estate in the North Riding of Yorkshire upon the death of my father. My mother, alas, had succumbed to an early death from tuberculosis during my boyhood. I was away at school at the time and I am yet to be able to speak of the matter without pain. She was a most extraordinary woman, Watson, of French Huguenot extraction. Her people lived very near the area where I conducted my later experiments in coal tar derivatives for the French government that you will eventually read of in the manuscript that you are perusing now. She had a most artistic turn of mind and it is to her that I owe that pattern of minute observation that became first a habit and then a profession. My father was a man of his class and time, devoted to his tenants, fond of the pleasures of the hunt, and with a most excellent stable of horses. Even now horses from our stables are coveted by the steeplechase riders of England. But not to digress too much and to return to my career, the point that I am making is that after my early career there came the Moriarity incident which in a sense formed a great divide in my affairs. My involvement with the case, followed by my untimely end as recounted by you, made me not merely a household name but gave me an international reputation so that when I returned all Europe was at my feet and the number of remunerative cases flooded in as you recall. You will also recall the matter of the Vatican Cameos stolen from the Vatican Museum. I was happy to render the service of facilitating their return to that enlightened gentleman, Pope Leo XIII, a man I deeply respect. It is not easy you know to be the Holy Father and to guide the Church. These are troubled times and many look to texts for proof of God or to deny Him. Faith though is not a deductive matter or a mere matter of philology. Faith deals with wonders, Watson. Ah once again I digress, it is the habit of age. The main point being that the Moriarity affair was for me personally invaluable. I was finally able to exercise my talents on a world sphere and to see results that would affect the lives of thousands. This is not to say that helping any one person in any way is not a great benefit, but how satisfying to think that one's life might also have swayed history from its usual blind and brutal course. So, descending as it were from the mountains of Moriarity, the great flood plain of my latter years spread before me. I had completed by great journey to the east and to the Moslem lands, I had seen my early interest in medieval palimpsests bear fruit in some most interesting discoveries at the Abbey of Cluny, I had done work on coal tar derivatives in my laboratory in France, and then to receive commissions from Royalty and from the highest levels of government, both from civil governments and from the Church; well, my career was complete. I had even, for form's sake, completed my long promised work in entomology on the segregation of the queen in the honeybee hive (for we must not forget the small in the large my dear fellow). Without pollination there are no crops and without crops, why then we all starve and our great guns and bridges and other elements of the hubris of man become irrelevant. A foreseeing providence in this matter reminds us to conserve all things, for all of creation is interrelated and interdependent. This fact is brought home upon me more each day. We cannot neglect anything as insignificant nor treat any life as less important than our own. We are now engaged in a matter that may save the lives of perhaps millions. That so small a vehicle as a microbe and its rodent host may kill so many, well, one need only think of the Black Death of the 14th century, that killed a third of the population of Europe, to be impressed with how fragile is our species' purchase upon this earth."

"But what if the vessel should slip through our solitary blockade," I inquired. "Why is not the entire navy mustered to prevent a landing?"

"Ah, that would never do. We must recall that this is a foreign flag vessel, Watson, and though the Baron is Dutch, the actual ship registry is German. One does not sink in these unstable times a German flag vessel with British ships and in British waters even if it is under a Dutch charter. The incident might lead so far as to provoke a general conflagration such as the current striving empires might in their folly welcome, but that would be a world tragedy of truly extraordinary dimensions and might shake the very order of western civilization. My travels in the east told me you see how short and shallow is the west's claim to predominance of the globe. The ruins of empires litter Asia."

"So then our task is to interdict or arrest the vessel, Friesland?"

149

"We have at least, as I have stated, a launch at our disposal, armed to the very teeth and quite fast. It shall be our business to immediately disable the craft to prevent any possibility of escape. We shall drop off from a separate vessel small boats to accommodate survivors who will be placed in arrest and quarantine upon landing. The vessel will then be sunk and hopefully presumed to be lost at sea. Our own vessel bears no flag or name, which is to say, that we, my good and noble doctor, and I the distinguished consulting detective, will be for the next few days from the standpoint of international law, pirates."

"But we act on the government's orders," I objected.

"Yes but nations still exist in that world of savages described so well by Thomas Hobbes. Since we are not at war we are technically pirates if we sink the vessel Friesland. For this reason, I can but hope that the other vessel fires first upon us."

A several hours later we stepped out upon the fog-shrouded platform of the station at Ilfracomb on the edge of Exmoor. We soon found a public conveyance that took us down to the waterfront where we checked into the best hostelry in town. The reception area adjoined a charming Tudor era dining room and it was there that we met the Captain of our vessel. It was a smart cutter named the Albert John. Holmes had summoned him by a short message carried by a page. He saluted us briskly before sitting down.

"All is in readiness, Mr. Holmes."

"Have there been any reports regarding the Friesland's location?"

"Not since the report, which I am sure that you possess, that it was sighted in stormy seas by a fishing vessel in the Bay of Biscay. The observing vessel was in the guise of a fishing smack so as not to arouse suspicion."

"I assume that no landing reports have come in from further down the Devon coast or Cornwall?"

"There have been no reports. We still believe that an attempt will be made on Cardiff or the vicinity. The storm conditions have been

150

quite severe and now this fog...well, I would not care to attempt a landfall. Still, the fog is a two-edged sword. It makes excellent cover. I have dispatched several fishing dories into the channel now that the storm swell is abating. The wind has dropped and the vessel may be becalmed and awaiting the precise moment for a freshening wind to carry her home."

"It would of course be ideal if we could approach her under the cover of fog ourselves. Should we have to fire upon her there is the question of observation. We do not want any of this reaching the German authorities. You are aware that the ship is a German flag vessel?"

"Yes, and of our unique status but we are not at war though and this being a commercial craft I must say that I am perplexed as to the reason for such extreme degree of concern exercised toward its apprehension."

"Let me assure you, Captain; this craft bears aboard its timbers an armament of the most extraordinary potency which is capable of causing great loss of life to the citizens of this nation. We will of course attempt to aid survivors, should we need to sink the vessel, but I assure you, no vessel of war ever deserved less mercy from the arms of your own vessel. Do not hesitate to sink her if need be."

"Very well, sir. My ship and I are at your command. Will you and your companion be aboard?"

Holmes smiled grimly, "It is necessary. There may be a need to communicate matters through you to your crew in case of certain developments. I trust that they all are volunteers and that they know that they may encounter great risk in this enterprise?"

"They are volunteers to the man and all very discrete, sir. You may be assured, Mr. Holmes, that they will do their duty."

"Excellent! So may we all, for Queen and country! Well, I believe that will be all for now, Captain. For the present my friend, Dr. Watson, and I will await your summons by day or night here." The young officer stood and saluted us again before withdrawing.

Holmes was silent for a time before continuing. "This is a most delicate affair. I trust that our enemy will not slip through the net. Well, Watson, we have no choice but to wait, an activity that will bear heavily upon us both. Let us eat something now for our efforts may be demanded at any hour. After that you may sleep or continue to peruse my manuscript account my eastern travels as you will."

From the Journal of Sherlock Holmes

June 18, 1891 - the Cape of Good Hope

The days of our southern journey have been quiet ones. After our initial contact, Colonel Moran kept his own counsel. He often prowls the decks by day like a restless tiger. I am amazed at the sheer vitality of the man. He obviously is one who seeks no counsel but his own fierce convictions. What a pair we will make on this quest. I shall have no admiring Watson to confirm with alacrity my every deduction but rather, a morose and haunted man, one who is unlikely, if it be not too early to judge, to sympathize with my web-weaving, the luxury of a London philosopher. His world is so confined to the mere antinomies of death or survival that it must appear the height of self-indulgence to seek a personal meaning to life. What use is the personal, he will argue, when the fates of thousands are decided daily simply by lack of food? To such a man as the Colonel, mere human laws and our impressed awe and reliance upon our governors must appear the height of folly. To him dialogue with an opponent is simply unnecessary; once your opponent is viewed as irremediably evil he or she need only be killed. The great pattern then continues to weave, unaware of the insect-like absence of your enemy. Convenient, yes, but right? Doesn't the enemy also deserve some consideration? Is not final judgment for God alone? But then Moran would say that the quiescence and mercy of the average man is misplaced. For him the essence of the thing is to stop evil not await its transformation, but then how does one fight evil directly without becoming evil oneself?

These are proper speculations for the harsh and sunlit lands that constitute Africa with the Cape of Good Hope on our port beam. The deep rich red and green of South Africa beckon, but alas my

152

journey is to the east. Already India beckons. I have read with great interest the English translation of the Upanishads and the Bhagavad Gita, for at my age to learn a new language to study the originals takes more time than I have at my disposal. I mentioned to Watson at the time of A Study in Scarlet that the mind has little space for diverse but useless knowledge, but there is a caveat to that dictum: one can never be certain what knowledge may prove essential. To the student of the human condition everything is essential. This of course raises the problem that perhaps the human condition cannot be explained within itself even if one were privy to all cultures, that all knowledge is in fact self-referential. All that man knows is but a series of self-portraits. We cannot abstract from our own knowing apparatus.

If, as Christian doctrine maintains, our origins are clouded by a different intent of the creator, viz. that we were meant always to share the very life of God, why then all of human history and our drives and aspirations, our unruly passions and our partial loyalties are shadows on the face of that divine intent. Christianity is then a religion of reparation and restoration. It posits as real an order of things and a destiny that reaches beyond the present and what sense of justice or of limitation we might aspire to from within our own senses. Since it does so, we are often confronted by the absurd in the demands made of human nature by God. When we see around us every indication of gross failure we are tempted to set up an order of things such as the one proposed by Karl Marx in his work, Das Kapital, so as to realize heaven upon earth. We are tempted to rely upon structure to reform human nature, to find some great god of procedure that will make virtue unnecessary and make of generosity and love mere appendages to an imposed justice. In such a world, sin or virtue would be mere personal affectations of no consequence and the only crimes would be those against the state or whatever absolute might substitute for a transcendent God. How pale must Christianity appear before such an enforcement apparatus as that of a secret police? Christianity instead turns the mind back upon itself to evaluate its own shortcomings. It has always seemed a great paradox to me that the Saints are always reproaching themselves with their own sinfulness. Do they never compare themselves with their fellows and observe that on the scale of virtue they far exceed the norm? They do not.

153

Why then do they not? The reason is simple, because their point of comparison is from that ideal reality of trust and the loss of self-regard that sees all things from the point of view of an order existing only in the mind of God. It is the prerogative of Grace that it convicts us only to increase our hunger for God. Finally all remedies fall short of the very life of God, for the saintly desire God alone. The great nakedness of desire for what lies utterly beyond us forces upon the soul an attitude of appeal. The Saint knows that the very means of its own acquiescence lies beyond its own resources. This creates an agony of spirit that only those willing to venture upon the path to sainthood will ever know. This is the great Dark Night of the Soul spoken of by San Juan de la Cruz.

Is there no Hindu version of this blind searching? Though less fleshed out, this sense of the limited is there too. Though Dharma is imposed upon mankind and though our destiny is union with the all, the Hindu belief is that through Yoga and other disciplines we may already share in that eternal order. It is essentially Pelagian. The great Hindu literature peoples with a multiplicity of gods the great temples of the Eternal order. In this there is a mythological component and a desire at once to keep, as in the Upanishads, a sense of the inexpressible absolute but also to create a pantheon of deities to which one may intimately relate. Hindu beliefs even have a version of the Christian Incarnation in the coming to earth of Krishna. In addition the very culture of India draws the individual forth into the masses. The borders of individuality that create such isolation in the west are tempered by larger categories to which the individual belongs irretrievably.

How contrary to, say the Mormon belief, which so exemplifies the American spirit, a spirit which deifies the individual through a pragmatic program of deliberate elevation. The Mormon Doctrine of Spiritual Progression implies that each man may himself become a primary deity and that the God we worship was once a man like ourselves, not by stepping down, as in the incarnation, but rather through a continual stepping up to Godhead. There is a pragmatic and mechanistic nature to this approach to spiritual perfection that must appeal to a people who have spanned a continent with railroads and look to human inventions to create the good life. Indeed, if I were to characterize the American spirit I should say

154

that the primary virtue and vice is its worship of the individual and its corresponding degradation of larger human entities such as the clan and village. Americans as a people learn to distrust one another and the world at large, for in the pursuit of individual happiness a great race is set up and every man's pursuit may interfere with another's similar pursuit. To such a people charity must appear foreign, since the weakness of the other, economically speaking at least, may make him a more proper avenue of economic exploitation. This may explain the rise of the commercial upper-class in what the American writer Mark Twain has called the Gilded Age. No doubt the American experiment will someday founder upon the people's mistrust of one another and lack of a cohesive body politic. When they do so, the people of America may find their very democracy will succumb to paralysis as one group resists the vision of the nation held by an opposing party. Perhaps a new civil war may erupt, or what is more likely, the vessel of the state will sink into inaction. America's salvation must come from without, since its own contradictions have been made an absolute. Even the legal order will not save it. America will no doubt drown in laws until the parties who can afford the true invocation of the blind Goddess of justice are only the wealthy. Pragmatism will finally discover that it is not practical and that a door must remain ajar to a non-self-determined world. It will no doubt take a great humiliation for them to collectively realize this.

It takes an older civilization, such as India's, to know the full tide and cycle of events; so perhaps I blame too harshly a new nation such as America. As a product of the 18th century enlightenment, America had the youth and vigor to explore, not a geographic continent alone, but to posit man as his own deity, in practice if not in theory. In this quest they have met with singular success, but at a great price to the immigrant classes. The great question for every American must always be, "When will I arrive at my idea of America?" There is little reliance upon God in this question. Each man looks only to his own definition of happiness. Ah, but I digress only to digress still more in each day's entries in this my journal; but then, this book of reflections is my own notes to aid me in my quest for what has eluded me for so long. Surely every option to the abiding faith of man in himself alone must have its voice and be considered in turn if I am to refute those two latter-day Pelagians, Moriarity and Moran.

June 30, 1891 – Off the Coast of Persia

The past two weeks have been uneventful. The waters of the Indian Ocean grow warmer as our vessel proceeds northward and I have spent recent days on deck gazing at the sea. The brooding presence of Colonel Moran has been the other omnipresent reality of my life on board. He paces the deck like a tiger day and night. On one occasion though he did more than briefly nodding at me in passing and even so far varied his usual practice as to sit down at my side in a deck chair and to inquire what my intentions might be upon landing.

"As for me, my instructions are clear, Mr. Holmes. I am to act as your guide and translator on your journey. A sum has been placed at my disposal to cover all of my expenses. You, I believe, are also well provided for, so that we shall not be forced to proceed with our eyes on economies. The Professor mentioned in a cable to me before we left that a private wager exists between the two of you; but it did not enter upon details. I am therefore prepared to do your bidding."

"You have summarized the situation admirably, Colonel Moran. You will, no doubt, be happy to see India once again," I replied.

"Yes, but my true desire is to return to the islands off of the Malay Peninsula. I am a solitary man, Mr. Holmes, and the great tides of humanity in India I find to be oppressive. To place one's own will against fate and to triumph has no place in the acquiescence bred of the Hindu mind. I do not care to be absorbed in the great mass of humanity even if it is done under the exalted name of Brahma. Give me my own land and allow me to lead a select few to a better life out of squalor and penury and I am happy. Besides, I detest the caste system and the sense that one's life is determined by a prior life. I am a deep believer in free-will and the ability of the man of substance to determine his own fate in the one and only life that he has."

"Ah but Colonel, even the great man must bow at last to old age and death must he not," I queried.

The Colonel ground his teeth at this. "Yes, but with resentment, Mr. Holmes, with resentment."

"Would it not be better to make peace with pain and suffering and to imagine its vindication from an outside source than to begrudge a hostile universe?"

"No, Mr. Holmes. There is too much suffering and much of it blind and visited upon those least able to bear it. The universe was not designed after all only for philosophers; there are the innocents to be considered as well."

"Perhaps you are making that decision for them. Even the most simple of souls have found great peace in a graceful surrender to the will of God, knowing that they are the objects of his love and concern."

"A poor concern seeing that it is so inefficacious. But why does God so will? That is the question. Why must human nature be thwarted at every turn? We suffer desire and are bid to be chaste. We hunger but are bid to fast. We are injured but forbidden revenge. We desire certainty and are told to have faith. We are discouraged and told to hope. And finally, we die and are asked to look at the frozen and silent visage of death and imagine that there will be a resurrection or a rebirth. Why all of this frustration of normal human intentions? Why bid us to be humble rather than proud in our own self -reliance?"

"Why the degradation of the Cross of Christ, in other words; I believe this matter was discussed at length by St. Paul," I answered. "God does not leave us to suffer alone. May there not be some purpose to innocent suffering after all? Who may ever say the force that may be generated by a forgiven wrong?"

"I am not unfamiliar with his writings," answered the Colonel. "I was raised in a pious Protestant home, Mr. Holmes, and though my people were of limited means, I received an excellent education. I

157

was forced to work at an early age though. I enlisted after coming down from Oxford in the army to fight for my country overseas. I saw at first hand the price in death to obtain and keep an empire and to maintain it, to keep the flow of goods coming to England at cheap prices and to force our colonies to accept British manufactured goods at high prices. This practice creates over time a great inequality of trade. The mass of persons serves the few. Inequality is the great original sin. When I realized fully how my own efforts were serving the ends of this inequality I retired early and living on a small pension, I returned to England and placed myself in service to a man of will whose crimes paid by exploiting the wealthy citizens of the empire. I felt that there was a certain justice of return in this. I considered myself to be an agent of nemesis for their complicity in the ruin of nations."

"But you prospered, did you not, Colonel Moran, as did the Professor for it is no doubt he of whom you speak. Your organization paid well and as its heads you both reaped great rewards. Have you in turn redistributed to the people your gains?" I inquired.

"You may be surprised to learn that I have," said he. "I knew that no private organization, no matter how large, can hope to repair the depredations of nations. I took the money that our way of life created though and invested in a plantation on an island in the South China Sea. We grow tea, rubber, cacao, jute, and vanilla as well as cocoanuts and spices. It is a feudal plantation but I live simply as do the tenant farmers on my lands. By paying a fair wage and by selective marketing with America through San Francisco I have enabled many to escape poverty. There are no exteriorly imposed laws on my island and beyond a small tribute to a local Malay chieftain I bear no allegiance to any state. When I meet with pirates or robbers I dispatch them on the spot and such is the certainty of reprisal that my own peaceful tenants are seldom molested. I have not found justice in this world, Mr. Holmes, but I have found an island of contentment based upon tribal unity and personal loyalty."

"So you contend that the small state is necessarily virtuous. But much is based upon fear and loyalty to your own dynamic self.

What will happen when you die? Will not internecine strife break out in choosing your successor?" I objected.

The Colonel was silent for a time. I had clearly raised a difficult point. At last he spoke.

"The matter has troubled me a great deal, but I believe that I have found a solution. I will in due time name a successor and pass on my own duties while I still live. I will so strengthen a new set of loyalties that my own death will be silent and, insofar as possible, a most quiet affair. I desire not to be buried but placed in a native canoe with flowers and then solemnly burned as the sun sets and as my frail craft seeks the great open sea which is perhaps all we will ever know of God. From the sea all life came and to the sea we return at last. It is a belief adequate enough for me."

With those parting words, Colonel Sebastian Moran, nodding to me briefly, stood up and resumed his walk, leaving me to ponder his words in silence.

July 10, 1891 Bombay, India

We have arrived at last! The heat from the land blows outward to the sea with the heavy smell of the mass of humanity, animals of transport, and the humid earth of India. I have brought with me little in the way of luggage because the next weeks will entail all modes of travel and I hope to obtain appropriate clothing and supplies along the way. I met Colonel Moran on deck and we passed through customs together. I carry a letter from Mycroft which expedited proceedings immensely and my own assurances sufficed to dispel any difficulties which the Colonel may have encountered alone due to his past dealings in the country. We repaired at once to the British Consulate to obtain all necessary papers for our proposed journey and the Consul took charge of my Bank draft for deposit. He will be able to arrange that all along my proposed journey it will be possible to obtain funds through drafts drawn on the Sovereign British Bank which maintains branches into Persia, Tibet, and even as far as Samarkand. The Consul was in addition quite cordial.

"We have of course heard of your reputation, Mr. Holmes, and will do all that we can to aid you in your travels. You realize of course that these are troubled times. There is always a danger of an uprising and the Tuggee worshipers of the Goddess Kali emerge from the hills on occasion and wreak havoc and terror."

I spoke up, "I realize of course that I am far from my usual ground of London, but I am not unacquainted with danger. Besides, I have a most able guide and linguist in the person of Colonel Moran."

The Consul looked awkward, "I will not of course question your judgment, Mr. Holmes, nor that of your esteemed Brother Mycroft who has conveyed to me by your hand a royal pardon to cover any and all past offences, but you are aware that Colonel Moran, though convicted of no actual crime, was at least suspected of, well if nothing else, irregularities at the card table unbecoming an English gentleman."

I answered him, "Sir, your kind warnings I deeply appreciate but I assure you that I have no intention of playing cards with the Colonel and his unique gifts will be of inestimable value to me. His knowledge of dialects and fluency in Hindi, Farsi, Arabic, and Tibetan will be of immense help. And as to courage well, his record as a hunter of tigers should allay all doubts that he will prove an invaluable guide."

"We are aware of the Colonel's reputation as the best heavy game hunter that the eastern Empire has produced as well as his former distinguished service with Her Majesty's troops in the Punjab in the Afghan Campaign as well as his distinguished lineage. We will assume also that he may desire to make amends for certain pursuits of some most distinguished ladies, ahem." He stopped speaking.

The Colonel looked up fiercely, "I am a man of appetites Sir, and having spent my life among people who do not adhere to the artificial constraints and conventions of monogamy, I seek my alliances where I will."

The Consul continued loftily, "Well be that as it may, it is of no immediate concern to us, but we exercise a unique function in

India. We must at least appear virtuous in order to dominate so diverse a land. If we appear in a weak or scandalous light we become less credible and our rule less secure. You can understand that of course, Mr. Holmes. What I am saying is that we will be more pleased if Colonel Moran passes swiftly northward to the less critical regions of Her Majesty's reign. I see that you plan on entering Tibet."

"I do and of spending time at the Lamasery in Lhassa. I will be traveling in the guise of a Norwegian explorer, Knut Sigerson."

"That will be a difficult guise to maintain under a British passport, but I believe that I can work something out with the local Scandinavian Consul and obtain papers that would indicate that you have been given the status of an Honorary British Citizen to expedite your travels and we here can issue a separate British passport under your assumed name."

"Thank you. You answer all of my concerns. As to your recommendation that we move swiftly northward, your suggestion is entirely in conjunction with my intentions. As a Londoner I find this heat somewhat burdensome and I desire to place a great distance between myself and any chance pursuers. I have been involved in a complex case prior to my departure."

"Please feel free then, Mr. Holmes, and, er yes, also you, Colonel Moran, to lunch at the Consulate. We have also arranged for your rooms while you remain in Bombay, unless you prefer one of the Hotels, but you will find our cuisine to be of the best and the balcony of your rooms overlooking the harbor to be most attractive. You will proceed, no doubt, by rail as far as the frontier."

"We will require a great deal of mountain equipment prior to leaving," I interjected.

The Consul debated with himself, "Well, as to that, I would advise that you to obtain supplies closer to the actual start of your Himalayan excursion. No doubt Colonel Moran will know in advance what you will require."

With that we were dismissed. We shook hands all round. It was a relief to me to dispose of any difficulties of an official nature that we might encounter. Colonel Moran had done a most excellent job of reining in his passions under the brief scrutiny that we received in obedience to the Professor's injunction to him not to cause me difficulties. It is extraordinary the power that the Professor retains over so formidable a man as the Colonel even at this immense distance and deprived of the power to retaliate directly and immediately.

We repaired at once to our rooms and after an excellent lunch of huge prawns cooked in cocoanut milk with lime leaves and an excellent red lamb curry we repaired to our rooms. I have written this overlooking the harbor. I look forward to a few days here of rest so as to lose my sea-legs prior to pressing on.

Dr. Watson's Narrative Continues

Another day dawned and still the fog continued unabated. I had spent the previous evening reading before turning in early while my companion sat smoking in his chair by the small coal fire. I could tell by his manner and by the intent look in his eyes that his nerves were trimmed to a fever pitch as were my own. We spent the daylight hours expecting news momently. When the afternoon hours brought no word from the Captain, Holmes' impatience reached a peak.

"This is intolerable! I cannot help fearing that they have slipped by us, or worse, that I have missed some hint and that they have redirected to another destination. I have had every reason to believe that they intended a west-coast landing, but circumstances aboard may have necessitated a change. They might have chosen the south coast. Disease may have broken out on board and they might have sought the nearest English port that they could reach. I have reasons for doubting this though. The entire point is to land their infected cargo without the advance notice that being laid up in quarantine would provide. How they will manage this, I cannot say, but precautions against contagion to the crew must be in place on so long a voyage. There would be the risk of panic aboard and premature abandonment of the vessel. No, I am certain that only a handful of

162

trained attendants actually come into contact with the animals for food and water while the remainder of the crew remains ignorant of the deadly nature of their cargo. But in any case, being this near their destination, and with success at their finger-tips, they will feel a great anxiety to make a landfall. Already they have been delayed by the storm and now fog. What do you think Watson?"

I was flattered that Holmes asked my opinion of the matter. I spoke cautiously but I think accurately when I said, "I can think only of their own natural desire to be rid of the danger posed to themselves by having such creatures aboard. Would they not wish besides to take advantage of these very conditions to make their landfall and to escape? Is there any port short of Cardiff that still has an adequate population where the plague could establish an initial contagion base and spread inland prior to detection? If so, perhaps they will make for it. Besides, in reaching a smaller port they might elude any possible customs inquiry upon landing that might reveal their cargo."

"By Jove, Watson," said Holmes rising from his chair, "Really, you excel yourself. Your medical training and perspective in this case seems to have led you to the precise conclusion that I had reached by a more discursive path. There is just such a landing place close at hand, the village of Lynmouth. The coastline is straight near-by and no really adequate harbor exists but it is just such an out-of-the-way place where such a landing might be attempted. In any case, our efforts are wasted here in simply waiting."

He walked over to the bell pull and a short time later his summons was answered by a page of the inn. Holmes had meanwhile scribbled a short note.

"Deliver this note please to Captain Walker of the Albert John down at the harbor," he informed the page who had answered his summons. The young fellow touched the brim of his cap and departed. "And now, Watson, let us fortify ourselves briefly. There are some cold kippers and some bread on the sideboard and do you dress warmly and in the sou'wester that the Captain has provided for each of us as we may spend considerable time on deck. The Captain will require an hour to build up a head of steam and then we shall depart."

163

The walk to the quai was bitter.   The fog seemed to penetrate our
very bones. My companion was silent but I could feel the nervous
energy that our errand aroused in both of us.   How were we to find a
vessel in the open waters of the Bristol Channel?   It is normal
procedure to sound a horn at intervals but would our target vessel
comply with normal maritime practice? On the other hand would it
take the risk of being run-down in the fog?   When we reached the
pier, the Captain was waiting for us.

"I have the vessel below, Mr. Holmes, if you and your friend would
climb down this ladder.   The tide is at low water just now and we
shall have to fight to get around the breakwater against the incoming
current."

I looked down into the murk and could just see the outline of our
vessel below us.   It was a smart rig with both sail and steam power.
It did not appear to be a military vessel but I knew that several
cannon were aboard and that it carried a Gatling Gun under tarps
mounted on the bow. To maintain our civil disguise, none of the men
would be in uniform.   Holmes swung over the empty space and
clinging to the ladder descended to the deck. I followed him grasping
the rusty iron rail that was slippery in the mist. A short but perilous
descent brought me to the gunwale of the boat where two-seamen
helped me aboard.   The Captain followed and immediately led
Holmes and I to an enclosed wheelhouse in the aft part of the vessel.
Our mooring lines were cast off and we began to move slowly into the
channel.   Our horn sounded at 30 second intervals but fortunately
harbor traffic was light.   Only a few brave fishing vessels might
venture out under such conditions since they knew the coast almost by
feel. I could just see the black stone breakwater in the fading dusk as
we cleared the harbor waters passing on our port beam. We were
going quite slowly at 3 knots.   Our plan was to get out about a
quarter mile and then parallel the coast in an easterly direction. We
would ply the waters between Ilfracomb and Lynmouth relying on
our compass and the general angle of the coast to maintain a parallel
to the land.   With each turn we would in theory be in deeper water
thus avoiding the necessity for constant soundings for depth.   The
current ran parallel to the coast with few eddies and only a few reefs
and sea stacks, most of which were closer to the land, to avoid.   Still,

it was a risky business and only the sheer necessity to find our target justified us undertaking so great a peril. I possessed an excellent pair of field-glasses which I had brought and I stationed myself on the bow. The mist allowed only occasional observations though and the constant wiping of the lenses finally forced me to give up my efforts. I rejoined Holmes and the Captain just outside the wheelhouse. Our engine was remarkably quiet and there was only a small residual swell from the recent storms but little chop since the breeze was still.

The time passed slowly. The mist would lighten on occasion and I would be able to glimpse the black and inky waters surrounding our vessel and see the small bow-wave drifting into obscurity. Then we would re-enter the thicker mists and a great isolation would descend again upon us. We had ourselves ceased to signal our position by a horn so as not to announce our approach to our enemy and I prayed that we would not encounter any fishing dory by accident. We had proceeded in silence for some time with all ears listening for the slightest sound. We had made several turns and must now be out about a mile into the channel. I had just turned to Holmes to announce that I would be going below to the galley for a mug of tea and to ask if I might bring him anything upon my return when Holmes' thin hand grasped the collar of my coat. I heard nothing at first but within a minute I caught the slight whisper of waves hitting a boat. The Captain gave the order for the vessel's engines to stop and our screw ceased to turn. Our motion gave us still a slight headway but all was silent now around us. The sound was clearer now. Evidently a vessel was laying a-hull broadside to the slight waves and swell. It appeared to be slightly inland of us off our starboard bow. Was it waiting for the fog to lift before proceeding inland? We too came to a stop and the bow swung slowly off of our course until we too lay broadside to the waves. Had we been heard by the strange vessel? Was it the Friesland or simply another vessel taking the prudent course and waiting for the mists to disperse before proceeding? I had not long to wait for an answer. The Captain had given the order and a small skiff with three men aboard was lowered to the water in order to reconnoiter.

I whispered to Holmes, "Do you think...?"

165

"Hush, Watson. I don't like this. These men will have to maneuver around the ship to read its stern without being observed and..."

A barrage of shots rang out that seemed to be louder in the conductive, moist air. The skiff returned immediately and I could see that one man had been wounded. The two others helped him aboard. I saw to the man immediately. I had him brought below and for the next quarter hour was busy staunching the flow of blood and dressing the wound. When I returned on deck we were under power again and in full pursuit.

"Is it the Friesland, Holmes?"

"The men were not close enough to say but since we have been fired upon, it is a fair inference that...halloa!" The mists which had been showing occasional gaps lifted suddenly and we were able to catch a glimpse of the vessel ahead. It had put on all steam and, due to its longer length and greater hull-speed, was pulling away from us quickly. I pulled out my field glasses and was able to read on the stern the legend, Friesland, and to see where the German flag waved from the masthead. I was about to exclaim to Holmes my finding when our own vessel opened fire. Two men had thrown off the cover of the Gatling gun, threaded in a belt of bullets, and with a staggering noise the stern of the Friesland and its helm were raked with fire. I could see bits of wood flying as the bullets hit home and a man slumped at the wheelhouse. His place was soon taken by another though and the vessel swung to port. It was then that our own vessel was brought under fire and a shell hit the water just off our beam. Holmes and I sought cover and for the next few moments could only act as witnesses of the fusillade between the two vessels. Another belt was loaded and this time the side of the vessel was raked at the water-line. A short time later a third belt was loaded and other vessel's cannon-port was hit and the firing upon our vessel ceased. It was then that we also turned broadside and our own cannon opened fire. Whether we scored a hit I could not say since the mists closed in again around us and the vessel was again lost to sight. We had no choice but to proceed and to close upon the vessel before it resumed headway and was lost in the mist. Even as I tried to scan through the mists as we approached the vessel, it began a slow turn until its bow was facing towards us. This reduced our target area considerably, but this was of little matter since return fire had ceased. In any case it was extremely difficult to see the ship. Even as the mists had opened for a time they were closing again, swiftly.

"Mr. Holmes?" the young Captain inquired, "I await your instructions."

Holmes was silent for a moment. "Let us proceed to close with the vessel, Captain, but slowly. We cannot be sure that the vessel may not again open fire again upon us."

The Friesland was now entirely lost to view. Even sound was muffled. When last sighted it was turning towards us.

"I don't like this Watson," muttered Holmes. "Why are they not making a run for it under cover of this fog? Perhaps, they are tending to the wounded. Their rudder may be disabled or....yes. Captain! Steer to starboard quickly!"

There followed a minute of confusion as the Captain gave the order to turn the helm to starboard and to move ahead with all steam, but it was too late. The high bow of the ship rose up out of the mists and began to close with us swiftly. Our own vessel had begun to move forward and our bow swung broadside to the oncoming ship. The gallant lads aboard who were not involved in the actual operation of our vessel immediately opened fire with the port-side cannon. Their aim was good and I saw a great opening appear just at the water-line in the bow of the other ship. A second shot imbedded itself in the bow stem. I did not see the third, for Holmes had grasped my shoulder. "Jump Watson, jump for your life" he cried.

We each leaped overboard into the freezing channel waters. Had we not been wearing heavy life-buoys we should have been lost immediately but as it was we bobbed to the surface just in time to witness the ship as it plowed over the Albert John virtually severing her in two. Even now I can see the great bulk of the Friesland looming down upon me so that I thought for a moment that I should be immersed by the great hull. The ship had gathered speed as it advanced upon us. At the moment of collision there was a terrible sound of breaking timbers and I could see that fire had broken out on the Friesland. As the debris of our own vessel was pushed aside I could see that the Friesland was riding low in the bow. The speed of the vessel combined with the gaping cannon wound in its bow had caused it to take on water precipitately. It is odd how swiftly the mind works in such circumstances, but I found myself speculating on the effect that plowing over a substantial cutter like the Albert John would have on a weakened bow stem and whether our third shot had increased the damage. These thoughts soon became of a second order of importance though, for I also realized the great peril of our position. I called out at once to Holmes. He answered and was swiftly alongside of me. "We must keep in close proximity with the others, Watson." He had pulled out a police whistle and was using it to signal our whereabouts in the mist. As the one point of verifiable direction our little group became the point of assembly for those sailors who had escaped destruction, among whom was the Captain. Already, I could feel the effects of nervous exhaustion and shock. I could only speculate as to the time that we would be able to remain afloat before hypothermia set in and with it our last, cold sleep. We could still see the Friesland as the fire aboard had spread. It seemed at once to melt the mists surrounding it and to create a strange aura of light in the further reaches of the mist. Were the circumstances less terrible, I should have called the effect beautiful. We could hear sounds of screams from the vessel and not a few men entered the water from that vessel. Some were clearly set ablaze by the flames. They fell like cinders from the great central pyre. Several explosions could be heard and there could be no doubt that the ammunition aboard the vessel had detonated under the influence of the intense heat. If the gallant Albert John was to sink, the vessel had had its immediate revenge upon the Friesland. There could be no doubt that the ship was doomed and it was a great comfort to me that if Holmes and I were to perish we might at least rest assured that our mission had met with success. The deadly cargo of the Friesland would not survive the fire and sinking. England would be safe.

This left at issue the question of her crew. We could not see the ship clearly so were unable to tell if its crew had been able to abandon ship. Perhaps they were fighting the fire, attempting even in this last hour to save their deadly cargo. Would any of the rats be able to escape and swim for land? I had heard tales of rats swimming for immense distances but by dead reckoning though we were at least five miles out into the channel when we encountered the Friesland. Besides there was the fire to contend with and I hardly thought that these immense rodents were allowed to roam the ship at will. They were undoubtedly confined to pens or cages where they would meet their end with no recourse to swimming. These considerations passed through my head at the time and helped to distract me from our own perilous situation. We were immersed in deadly cold waters out of sight of land and shrouded in a deadly mist. Holmes had continued to blow his ship's whistle and using it as a central gathering point a number of the ship's crew that had avoiding sinking with the Albert John had gathered about us with those unscathed supporting the wounded. There had not been time to launch the ship's skiff but a number of deck planks had survived the sinking and now formed a loose debris-field surrounding us. Several of the crew had managed to get a hold on some of these and paddle them to our central gathering point. The buoyancy that they offered allowed us to gain some height above the water-line and reduced the need to exert excess effort to keep our heads above water in the slight chop that had come up.

A light breeze was blowing the mist over our heads in ghostly wreaths and with it came the smell of burning and charred materials aboard the Friesland. The ship now appeared as a huge blaze and the waters around us glowed with a red and yellow glare. The mist grew gradually lighter as the wind pushed the thickest clouds away. At last we could see the ship clearly. Its bow rode low in the water and its stern was high in the air. It was burning like a candle that had been tilted askew from the inky waters that surrounded it. The heat scorched our faces when the wind shifted towards us and the contrast with the chill of our immersed bodies was startling. The smoke ascended with a mighty roar. Surely, any men who had succeeded in swimming free must have been roasted by the heat. Suddenly the ship, the steel of which must have been molten, split in two in the center. The fire was quenched as the bow sank from view and a short time later the stern sank also. There followed a strange and uncanny darkness. Not even an ember remained and the sea flowed over the spot where the fiery remains of the Friesland had gone down. We had not been able to take our eyes from the flaming spectacle during the time involved in the sinking. The light provided and the sound of Holmes' whistle had made us able to gather the Albert John's survivors. We floated now in a loose convoy of timbers and debris and prepared to meet our own quieter but inevitable fate in the chill seas. Already I could feel that deadly numbness that is the prelude to deadly shivering followed by unconsciousness and death from hypothermia. Could we hope to last another hour? The Captain was attempting to cheer the crew. Holmes swam alongside of me and though I could not see the lean face I recognized the old confident tone just touched with a sharp and stoic humor as he said, "Ah well, my dear fellow, surely this is a small price to pay as regards ourselves, two aging British gentlemen lost to save a nation, and the lads aboard the Albert John have lived up to the highest aspects of their profession. No single ship has better deserved the thanks of a grateful nation. Unfortunately they will never know the danger thus narrowly averted but Mycroft at least may erect some small monument when the time is proper to acknowledge the business we have done today."

To this I could only mutter my own assent. It had indeed been a gallant exchange, worthy of the Elizabethan days when galleys and men-of-war had lain broadside blasting with cannons their joint route to eternity. After Holmes' comment, we were all quiet for a time. Each man was alone with those thoughts that precede death, reviewing the course of life with its joys and its bitter regrets. I recalled my marriage and the excellent woman who had chosen to share her all too brief life with me. I had learned from her how to accept death. She had shown remarkable courage in her last decline from an illness from which even a Harley Street specialist could not have cured her. My own small savings had been depleted in her last month in the effort to save her life. I can only rejoice in the trip that we were able to take together the previous year. I can still recall the fresh spring mornings sitting out on the piazza of our villa by the sea. How bright was the sea then, reaching south to the great sand deserts of North Africa! We would have our coffee together before taking a slow morning walk. In the evenings we might catch a brief concert or dinner party with the small colony of British ex-patriots that inhabited our local village. The afternoons were long and slow. I would read on the piazza on a settee erected underneath a small tent or awning that shaded us from the midday sun. I would glance up from time to time to find the dear eyes of my spouse gazing at me. Did she wonder even then if I would bear up should I ever lose her? Can life's call be constantly frustrated by the specter of the death of those who die too young and leave one unscathed? Does medical training make facing death easier, or does it not bring a greater bitterness that even one's ministrations and all of science cannot retain the dull organic processes that sustain our bodies and with our bodies, our souls? How strange that in an hour or even a minute all of the vast sea of memory, the labors of a lifetime, the friendships, the loves, the tiny preferences that are personality are suddenly eclipsed and their remains only the silent breath and the glazed eyes to bear witness to the vast succeeding silence...Death.

I must confess that these were my thoughts when suddenly there was a sound and a flare lit the sky a half mile distant from us. Holmes immediately reached down and placed the whistle in his mouth. Though his long, thin form was weakened by the cold, he was able to respond. We waited. Soon another flare went up, closer this time. Again Holmes whistled in response. The vessel from which the flares came soon closed upon us by gradual steps nearer and nearer. At last we could see it clearly. No doubt it had seen the flames from the Friesland and had come out to seek survivors. At last it was alongside us. Rope ladders were thrown over the side and seamen descended to aid us. Those of us who could manage let go of their places on the planks and swam to the side of the ship to be hoisted aboard. The Captain, Holmes, and I were the last to board since the charter of the voyage had been ours. It was proper that the crew board first. A short time later we found ourselves blinking in the light of the wheelhouse and drinking a warm beef broth while blankets were wrapped round our shivering forms by kindly crewmen. Upon inquiry we were able to ascertain that no members of the Friesland crew had been rescued. We were soon underway on the return journey to Ilfracombe. Holmes drew me aside.

"It is normal maritime procedure Watson for an immediate investigation to be made in the case of a marine collision. There are

171

insurance matters to tend to and in this case we have a foreign flag vessel striking a British vessel. The situation is most delicate. The proceedings in an Admiralty court will be public knowledge and an international scandal could ensue. We do however have a point in our favor, the Friesland has sunk and in deep water. It is non-recoverable and as far as anyone knows we were struck by an unknown vessel. Our own vessel has likewise sunk and our crew is sworn to secrecy. It is a chartered vessel and the owner would no-doubt accept a check for an amount above the vessel's value. Now here is what I propose: the captain and the crew of the vessel that rescued us have no knowledge of the existence of the Friesland. All they observed was a fire which drew them to the scene. I have already told our own captain and through him to his crew to say nothing of our mission. The loss of our vessel will be put down to a fire that broke out aboard our own vessel. The British government will reimburse the insurance company for the cost of any losses and arrange a finding with the Maritime Board of Inquiry. The only record will be that the cutter Albert John sailed into a patch of mist and that nothing more was heard of her."

"But the Captain and crew of the rescue vessel, surely they will speak."

"They will only report that they rescued a small band from the Albert John after it was struck by an inbound whaling ship. The whale oil ignited and both ships were lost."

"But there will be an immediate investigation when we land, we will have to produce ship's papers or at least identify the vessel and its proposed destination."

"A brief wire to Mycroft will bring all such inquiry to a stop. We have the British government with all of its resources at our disposal my dear fellow."

In this manner the incident was resolved at last, an incident that might have had the most appalling international consequences. All took place even as Holmes had outlined. The bustling little official from the Port of Ilfracombe who met us in our rooms at the inn after we disembarked was at first suspicious.

"Do you mean to say sir that you and your friend, landsmen both, were out in a dory on such a foggy day as the day when and were rescued by a boat that had gone to the aid of a government cutter on maneuvers?"

Holmes smiled ruefully before replying, "Well perhaps we were imprudent, but my friend, Watson, is a most avid fisherman, are you not Watson? We had drifted rather far out with the tide and were able to observe the fire aboard the whaling vessel soon after it broke out. We hastened to row towards it to render aid and I am afraid that in our zeal to pull one of the men aboard after the sinking of the whaling boat, we managed to upset our own vessel. Had the shore patrol rescue boat not come along shortly after, we would surely have been lost."

The little man scratched his head, "Well now, so you say. But as to this whaling boat, I have not been able to get the name of the vessel. That would be three boats lost today for the cutter Albert John is also missing. It ain't good for the port's reputation; that it ain't."

"Would you care to join us in a glass of Brandy?" Holmes inquired.

The man hesitated, "Well in my official capacity..."

"I assure you that my friend and I are men of the most absolute discretion."

"Well then I will," he assented, "Thank you kindly, sir."

The brandy seemed to warm our visitor. He was regaling us with the awesome responsibilities of managing a small British Port when a telegram was brought up. Holmes read it laconically and then passed it to the Harbor official. He read it and gasped, "Well I never."

Holmes spoke sternly, "This matter as you can see, stops right here. There will be no further inquiry nor will you speak of the matter informally to anyone. There will be no report as to the fate of the cutter Albert John."

"No sir, absolutely not sir, but this telegram...."

Holmes smiled, "You can see that the matter is in most excellent hands. All will be arranged and any seeming neglect on your part will be repaired at the highest levels. There will be a small news item stating that a fire broke out on an unnamed whaling vessel and that is all. The rest will be resolved in London. Go now and rest assured that you have rendered a signal service today that will be remembered by your superiors."

The harbormaster bowed and withdrew. Holmes tossed me the telegram. "It is from the First Lord of the Admiralty, my dear Watson. Our local official was suitably impressed."

"So it would appear. But what should be done now, Holmes?" I asked. "If this ship Friesland is no more is that an end of the matter?"

"Hardly that, Watson," replied Holmes grimly. "We have stopped the threat posed but it may be repeated unless we bring the matter home to its perpetrators. These are deep waters Watson, as deep as any that we have encountered in the course of our labors together. We know the principals but proof, ah there is another matter. Courts of law require proof so that the arm of the government can render justice. There are cases where even the long arm of the law can never reach and when they occur, action of another sort is necessary. I have therefore desired to consult an expert on the extralegal, Professor James Moriarity. We will return for a few days to my home near Grimpen on Dartmoor to lay our plans. Then, Watson, we may need to go to London and from thence abroad."

"Why abroad?," I asked in amazement knowing that Holmes did not enjoy travel since his return from his long absence of 1891-1894, the only exception being an occasional brief trip to France or Italy.

"We must go to the Netherlands unless I misjudge the advice that we will receive from the Professor to confront Baron Maupertius with his crimes."

We spent the next day in resting at the inn after our ordeal and in receiving a visit from the Captain who assured us that no further inquiries had been made, that his men had recovered well but that he would remain in Ilfracomb to see the burial of those gallant lads who had lost their lives in apprehending the Friesland. It was then, two days after the adventure at sea that Holmes and I found ourselves in a small steam locomotive on our way back to Coombe Tracey by the circuitous eastern rural line. At my age one does not recover quickly from so rigorous an experience as immersion in a frigid sea and I could see that even Holmes' constitution had also been strained by the ordeal.

I resumed my reading of Holmes' manuscript of his Asian travels on the seemingly interminable train ride home. Each country halt allowed the train to be loaded with additional freight of farm goods. Meanwhile, reading the journal took my mind from the boring train journey across Devonshire and from the tragic loss of life on board the Albert John. Holmes smoked his pipe in a corner of the compartment and gazed through the window as the bleak expanse of Exmoor and eastern Dartmoor rose like another grim sea before us. What was to prove our most extensive and convoluted case had just begun.

From the Journal of Sherlock Holmes

July 18, 1891 - Enroute to Kashmir

We left Bombay behind us after several days spent in purchasing necessary items for our expedition. The embassy has granted us the maximum of comfort during our stay, a comfort that we spoiled Englishmen will not know again for some time. I might have stayed longer but I could feel the strain on the chain by Colonel Moran who seems to literally thrive in conditions of hardship. His leather-like skin speaks of tropical suns and of bitter mountain chills. I am a man of endurance but I can already tell that I could not hold a candle to the Colonel in combat. It may seem folly to trust him, but strangely his own lion-like nature raises him above petty perfidy and fraud. Professor Moriarity only used him in cases of the most extreme nature and where, no doubt, the Colonel's own peculiar moral sense would suffer no violation. The man has a conscience although not a Christian one. He appears to see the world as a set of opposing forces and he would no doubt be as ruthless towards an enemy as he would be heroic in defense of a friend. These qualities will make him an admirable guide and ally, for I have planned to enter regions that will be most inhospitable to an Englishman. I will require just such a man as Colonel Moran at my side.

I have been impressed by the sheer crowds of humanity in Bombay. The people of India are truly beautiful, with luxurious skin and white teeth and flashing eyes. It only makes their fate as a region more tragic. I could not look upon the often skeletal children or witness the ever-present signs of famine without the most bitter remorse. Surely England could do better for its main colony. But then, even in the case of the Irish potato famine of the 1840's just before my own birth, England had thought more of maintaining crop values than of feeding the helpless population. When the public works were shut down in 1847, those desperate Irish who had not yet emigrated were left without money to purchase food. It does not matter how cheap produce may be if a system does not generate the funds in the people so that they may purchase that produce. England concluded that it had done what it could for the Irish by sending over Indian meal and was tired of the whole affair as the famine persisted year by dreadful year. How much evil in the world is the product of just that weariness in dealing with the constant demands of charity! I believe it is St. Paul who says that charity is patient and kind and endures all things. It perseveres to the end. One wonders if Christian people ever ponder those words. If so how quickly do they conclude that they have done enough.

The land surrounding Bombay was alternately lush and green and brown and dry. Our train pushed at times through barren hill regions and our train swayed perilously as it seemed to me on the uneven tracks and settled rails. The sanitary facilities left much to be desired and I learned swiftly that India is at peace with human alimentary functions that would draw a blush from the denizens of a British drawing room who speak awkwardly of drains. Still, I adapted as one must to the ravages of necessity. I marvel at the patience of the people under adversity. No doubt their Hindu faith that this life possesses the quality of illusion makes them better able to bear the gross aspects of daily life. There is also a remarkable social stability born of the caste system that, however appalling in itself, at least prevents much violence and social upheaval. It also makes the Indian people patient under British rule. Otherwise a rebellion would succeed by sheer mass in throwing off our arrogant discipline of a noble people whose history and antiquity dwarfs our own. The people of India were building temples when Britons were living in grass thatched huts and stone homes. How strange really are the vicissitudes of history!

Gradually the great plains of India receded as we approached the Hindu Kush. We could glimpse them long before we crossed the border regions, towering beyond the dusty tracks where cattle-drawn plows stirred the red clay soil of the Punjab. The heights that are our destination are one of the great nexus points of civilizations. If Europeans found their ideological destiny mediated by way of the philosophy of Greece and Rome, so Asian thought has been penetrated by associations from the Hinduism and Buddhism of India as well as the Confucianism and Taoism of China. All of these doctrines meet in the great mountain chains of central Asia. The doctrines sweep over these lands like oceanic tides. They wash up against the mountains, are partially contained, yet drift over and combine in strange eddies. Once reaching Japan they were taken over by that unusual and insular race which combines the paganism of its Sun King, its reverence for ancestors in Shinto, and the unique brand of Buddhism known as Zen. I am sorry that I cannot travel so far and sail from Japan to America. Even America of course has devised its own unique religion, one in keeping with its independence and pioneer spirit. Unwilling to take on the God of the Jews and of Christianity, yet unwilling to break all ties with Christian tradition, the Mormon faith, in that fashion so typical of American ingenuity, simply reworked and adapted Christianity into a new industrialized religion under the aegis of Joseph Smith.

His first action was to give a body to God the Father thus eliminating any distance between the physical and the spiritual realities. Having thus disposed of the mysterious existence of a transcendent God by making Him physical, and thus unified with His creation, Mormonism moved on to its next great doctrine. Rather than a mystical participation in the life of the Trinity a different eternal destiny is posited whereby male members in eternal marriages can themselves become co-equal deities and populate their own universes with immortal spirit children. The One God of revelation and western philosophy becomes the start of a long succession of similar deities in one long celestial progression and multiplication. Human nature meanwhile, no longer exalted by participation, becomes instead in each male believer a new departure towards a new deity with its own frontier universe to settle with descendents. What could be more typically American? The Mormons hope by a sort of reverse colonization to spread their message back to the worlds of Christianity and of Judaism from whence they derived the roots of their own new and synthesized religion. They will no doubt find resistance when their claims wash up against the ramparts of Islam with its own book also supposedly derived from a divine original copy residing in heaven.

What faith so many religions put in words as though any mere vocabulary could contain God! Surely, if there is a God, then we have the origin of everything in Him including intelligibility itself, of which the written word is but one form of language. Mathematics and music, are these not also languages with their own particular content. For myself, I have often come closest to God listening to music. It is formed formlessness, surely that is the essence of God and to lose oneself in the contemplation of a great symphony, to witness how each part is coordinated with the whole, to feel the unity in its diversity, to proceed beyond judgment to direct experience, and finally to lose oneself in the oceanic bliss of the moment....surely there is more of eternity in the language of music then in the discursive definitions of these discordant faiths. The same may be said of mathematics. Why even Professor Moriarity sees the charm of the quantitative sciences. Is the universe finally some vast equation? Were the Pythagoreans the best mystics after all? Could not one final formula perhaps describe each event down to its most minute permutations? Do we live within a vast crystal, each face of which is a force? Are our own existences mere molecules drifting within a supersaturated solution and assembling themselves gradually along the faces of that great crystal? Will the chemists and physicists be the new prophets of a religion, that finally emerging from its anthropocentric forms assembles all consciousness into a greater whole? Does God exist or is he rather coming into being, as Hegel states, at least insofar as

He may be spoken of by men? Must essence yield to existence when we speak of the divine?

But stop. The temptation to a new Gnosticism must always be present in a consulting detective such as I am. Perhaps it will be this very need to solve the problem of the nature of God that will lead me into heresy and finally reduce God to my own measure. To receive heaven, not as a possession but as a gift, surely that is the nature of Grace and to reach out to pluck the fruit of knowledge and be like God, knowing good and evil, surely that is familiar ground....the original sin.

To reach backwards and to discern the original intent of God towards our primal parents, would that not make all clear if we could achieve this? But alas, that intention of God and the route to what that destiny might have been is lost to us! We have instead to witness the great mopping-up efforts of God, the effort of restoration that is history. We cannot recover humanity's natal roots or hope to hear again the infant cry and see with the clear eyes of our dawning. We only know that we were once, comfortably face to face with God and that God created a first community, a duality to mirror God's trinity in human beings. Beyond this we reach in vain in Christian thought. We are asked rather to look ahead with crosses laid across our backs and to await a restoration not of our making, but of our willing participation if we are Christian. Can a consulting detective hope to penetrate the designs of God or penetrate nature so as to reconcile our aspirations with our fate? That is the question that I pose for myself. Perhaps it was inevitable that I would pose it. How could I as a detective trace the strange twists of human nature and of criminal motivations and not seek to solve the greater mysteries of human virtue and vice, of good and evil. Crime detection finally becomes merely a matter of seeking motive through the twists and turns of circumstance and then finding the means chosen to commit the crime and to avoid detection. But the motive is usually one of the great constants of human nature: greed, fear, jealousy, envy, spite, desire, revenge, anger, mistrust, pride, or despair. But virtue, ah here the greatness of humans emerges. Not only are the vices turned on-end and opposed by their opposite virtues but a new dynamic seems to come into play. Grace seems to awaken a human potentiality not lost by

179

original sin, or rather more accurately to show what our unsullied destiny might have been and to glimpse through the veil of time into those natal regions when we walked at peace with God and with ourselves.   The mists part and we glimpse around the pavilions of our happiness a destiny that might be eternal.   Surely this is easier than to imagine than that both vice and virtue, unnoticed by any higher force and life greater than our own, finds a common destiny in the compost of time.

Though heaven or hell may alike seem unworthy of us, surely some judgment beyond our own seems required, some unbiased pronouncement of the entire universe upon our thoughts, actions, omissions, and errors there must be.   Otherwise events are mere motions and duration the mere ticking of a clock and all of human meaning descends into nothingness.   Professor Moriarity may feel able to live with such a view of life and death but not I.

These thoughts coursed through my mind as our train approached the great heights of the Hindu Kush and the Himalayas.   Surely these are more than mountains.   They were produced by the collision of two continents.   One can only imagine the energy produced and dissipated by such a mighty collision.   The great height attained by these mountains is a measure, not of the total but of the residual force.

This one tiny planet in a vast universe shows in miniature the much greater forces that extinguish stars.   Surely if human life were to seek some image of its own significance, then we may not turn to nature which shakes us off like a fly from a quivering flank.   We must seek God within and not residing beyond the stars and the vast empty cosmos.

It is a pleasure though for one such as I, a thinking man of our age, who has lived amidst the seeming independence of trade and industry, of mining, commerce, weaponry, and diplomacy to see that to the earth itself, all such human endeavors are trivial.   The great problems of life remain not without but within us.   I have always agreed with the great poet, Alexander Pope, who said:

"Know then thyself. Presume not God to scan. The proper study of mankind is man."

Yet am I not doing precisely the opposite of Pope's injunction on this journey of mine as I seek to scan out the parameters of God? But no I answer, for my effort is but to scan the paths of religion. I wonder, are we ever really closer to God through our doctrines or are they rather a distorting lens to blur the true image of God with our conceptions of Him? Is religion the residue of our immature reflections in the face of events rather than a portraiture God himself which would surely entail the sin of idolatry? Do we mistake the way for the destination and in exalting the way lose what dim intuitions we may have of our goal? Even here in a purely geographical sense I can see that as I come closer to the mountains and begin to ascend that I lose perspective upon them. I can no longer grasp the great range of peaks, let alone individual mountains as the train climbs among them. Instead the view is of titanic faces of sheer granite threaded by innumerable streams and waterfalls. Suddenly all falls away and lush valleys spring to view. The terraced farming of tea planters yields to occasional figures grazing sheep or goats. Even Switzerland's mighty Alps seem like a child's glass winter-scene of falling artificial snow, a mere diorama compared with the immense scene that lies before me. Already the air is chill. The train will not be able to take us much further, which is reassuring, since gazing from the windows into these appalling chasms is trying upon the nerves. I only wish that Watson was along to lend his picturesque language to describe what we are seeing. His romantic nature would rejoice in the prospect and even more in what I am sure will be the austere beauty we will soon encounter. We will disembark at last on the Himalayan frontier and travel by animal transport. Tibet lies ahead!

July 21, 1891 – Kashmir Valley

Truly this is a land isolated from the world. After disembarking on the frontier from our train, we spent a day obtaining further supplies and equipment and arranging for transport. The first part of our journey was in a unique wagon drawn by Yaks. The road is rough and rutted and our progress is slow. We are met continually by local peasants who have various items for sale, but as we are well supplied and would be stopping constantly and as space as so limited, we are forced to decline many of these offers. We are already at an immense height. If this were the winter season, the road would already be encased in snow. The winter landslides have brought down huge boulders that occasionally block our way. As swiftly as they are removed it seems that a new slide brings down more debris, so that each traveler on this road must clear his own way. It might be a metaphor for life itself in which each of us meets again the great standing perennial problems of human existence. Do we ever make progress in resolving the great questions? Have our many records brought us closer to the inscrutable mystery of our short days or as Thomas Brown speaks of them so eloquently, our "winter arches" in his magnificent work, Urn Burial? Often have I read with pleasure the books of the 17th Century authors. It was a bitter era. The writers of that period in their magnificent baroque prose examined human life with a scientific detachment and honesty as well as an unparalleled eloquence. They had no hope for a long duration in this world and so had no time for the dishonesty and euphemisms of our days.

What a ghastly time I live in! How cheapened is the human spirit with crass commercial activity, as though we were ourselves corporations and business agglomerates and not mere flesh and blood after all. Our buildings promise a spurious immortality and our elaborate trade-relations spread the earth with refuse. I am going to austere Tibet in part to rise above such things and to confront for once the essential. It is my hope that in Lhassa, if I make it so far, I may find the secret. I hope to see the Head-lama and to discuss these many matters. One hearing me speak as I have already done in this narrative of Christian belief may wonder why I am going to those who we refer to as the heathen for answers. Surely our revelation is not only adequate but sufficient. To this I might reply that nearly two thousand years of history in Christian dominated Europe has yet to witness a sustained period of peace and charity. Perhaps the relative stability of China has something to teach us. Our own history is one vast carnage scene of Christians killing Christians. How abstruse are the speculations of our theologies yet the mere categorical command to lay down our arms or perish by them remains yet untried! What wars may not the

182

new century bring! How have I longed for a land not yet fertilized by the blood of our fellow humans! How lovely finally is the earth itself. As the great Jesuit poet, Gerard Manley Hopkins, states, "It flames out shining like shook foil." But the same poet says also that, "All is bleared and smeared with toil." It bears man's very smell. What slug leaving its mucous trail could compete with us in our trail of refuse upon the earth? Everywhere we are the agents of imbalance so that creation, which wears the guise of eternal harmony, is spoiled by our ministrations. Who can look at a city and not see the great pollution of mankind enmasse? Yet stand one solitary being still and gaze into the eye and there is eternity there and a dignity, that though often marred by time, still speaks of our divine origins. Perhaps the Christian dawn is yet ahead of us when we might somewhat deserve what we hold to be a unique revelation to us by the God of truth and justice. We should not wish to hasten the millennium lest it catch us unawares. Let us give ourselves a chance for some meager token return to God before the foretold great apostasy and end of the world occurs. Each age has expected that the return of Christ would be in its own era because everywhere there was apostasy and atrocities. Yet the great apostasy is delayed, perhaps because apostasy means a falling away which is hardly possible when one has not been fully Christian in the first place. Had the world of history not been fertilized by the seasoning of saints, perhaps Jesus might have already long since returned. But for them, the rule of apostasy or lack of lived-faith would appear to have been almost universal among Christians. The saints prolong the earth's drama, perhaps by awakening in God the hope of a more universal penetration of virtue among men. But perhaps I am being fanciful. It is God's Grace that strengthens the saints more than their own efforts as men and women. Still, if we pleaded in prayer, not for an easier life but rather for greater virtue, would not all of our prayers be granted, even as Jesus promised?

So I go to Tibet, not seeking a substitute revelation to the Christian revelation, but to obtain a refracted angle upon my own tradition and from a distant culture to catch a deeper view, to find startling new dimensions, and to rid myself of the dull mold that so encrusts in habit and in rust the two-edged sword of Scripture by mere familiarity with it. I would like to speak with members of a tradition with a different conception of the problem of human nature, if indeed it is a problem to them in the way that we conceive it. The western mind conceives of the problem of good and evil since the time of the Persian Zoroaster as a struggle between two equal principals for the fate of the world. Evil is thus personal in nature as is good and each has its champion. In Zoroastrianism the creator is spared the indignity of such petty moral squabbles. He exists in splendid isolation like the god of the deists of the 18th Century. The dualism of Zoroaster has even filtered into Christianity through the heresy of Manichaeism. The Revelation of St. John acted as a bulwark against the spread of the heresy in that it posits a final victory of good in the person of the Lamb of God, but even to the present day there is a tendency to dignify the evil principal and to ignore the defeat and ignominy visited upon Satan by the cross of Christ. That Divine Sacrifice is held to be efficacious precisely by its action in remitting sin and, as it were, welding together all of the faithful in the very person of Christ in his deity and humanity, thus restoring human nature to the status of God the Father's original intentions for humanity.

By the Sacraments of Baptism and Communion, individual humans are incorporated into the very body of Jesus Christ. At the same time the language is used of spousal relations. As the Bride of Christ, the Church as a single body of heart and mind enters into union with Christ. The members of the One Church of believers are to share this eternal union of God with all. The resultant salvation is meant to be a resolution of the primal fall that severed human beings from their own true nature, an original sin bred of mistrust of God and the attempt to grasp as a possession what can only be obtained as gift and under the conditions appropriate to our nature. In a sense the original sin is one of impatience. There is no sign that God the Father ever intended to forever deny to humans the fruit of the tree of life or of the knowledge of good and evil. Indeed it might be credibly maintained that moral knowledge is a prerequisite for understanding the magnitude of the gift that God wished to bestow by creating humans in God's own image.

Does that mean that the original sin was inevitable? No, I do not so believe. The sin was two-fold: first it implied a lack of trust that God would know the time and season for His own elevation of humans to deeper knowledge; second the sin's malice was to attempt to be like God, not in merely knowing good and evil, but as the determiner of good and evil for man to provide, independent of God, the very criteria of good and evil for himself. The mere image of God is by its nature derivative of the original, it cannot hope to, as it were, set up shop for itself without being a reflection of its source. As such, the original sin was stupid and futile metaphysically in its very incipiency. There was never hope of success. What there was, indeed, was the prospect of eternal frustration to realize a nature beyond its own inherent limitations. In that sense it was a blessing for God to banish our primal parents from the garden of his original intent before in addition they mutinously ate from the tree of life. Death was a blessing in that the frustration bred of our arrogance which would continue at least until salvation restored our true nature, would have a term limit. Death would always keep us humble and by this means restore our ability to petition God for a restoration, not to our former status, for alas innocence once lost is lost forever, but to a conscious and willing cooperation in our own restoration, our salvation. Original sin changed forever God's initial plan and required a new initiative on the order of our original creation. No, more than that, it required a deeper penetration of the Triune Godhead into humanity. God in effect in the person of the Second Member of the Trinity, the primordial, the Logos, the Beloved Son, begotten of the father, but not, as in the case of humans "made." Jesus Christ took on human nature Himself through the Incarnation.

It was as though He had stepped into a mirror, into the image of God to rectify a distortion, a lack of true identity in that reflection, bred in the mirror itself by the freedom of the image to attempt for itself a self-determination but without God and hence of necessity beyond God. Once having done so humanity was metaphysically incapable of its own sovereign restoration, trapped in a pit of its own making it was only from within God as the one and original to restore what could not be unilaterally re-claimed by man.

Finally, it is death itself, death in all its indignity and squalor, death that temporary refuge for recalcitrant human nature from eternal frustration, death that is conquered by the very act of accepting it, first by Christ in His crucifixion, and later by all who would follow Him, that results in salvation. This is the Divine Choice of the very

185

person of the Immortal Logos. The immediate disproportion of Divine Life and eternal death is immediately evident. Death could not triumph over Life; it must break asunder like a vessel that cannot contain so infinite a content! In this we see the resurrection not as a mere magic trick of God, but as a metaphysical necessity for the less cannot contain the greater; death cannot contain life. Christ must rise from the dead.

Yes, but what of us? Can mere belief and our tiny virtues hope to entitle us to a similar fate of eternal life? Surely the input from our side is inadequate to the result; we simply do not deserve salvation. It is this realization, based as it is on the mere metaphysics of the situation of man and of woman, that makes some sign necessary to signify the divine, unilateral gift of salvation, thus we have the sacrament of Baptism. Its function is to show what God alone may by gift effect: a new status of humans, a deeper reflection of the image of God than might have been, had we never sinned at all, oh felix culpa! Evil then is not merely defeated; it is incorporated as the very means of our greater elevation! If our fall is due to an instrumentality of a more Primal Evil, of Satan and His Angels, then that agency is frustrated in its effects not by man's merits but by God's mercy. Whether that very frustration of nature might breed a similar repentance and a similar initiative in their regard by God towards the fallen angels exceeds the borders of revelation, though Origen at least speculated upon the matter. Certain it is that a final severance from God is, by definition, eternal death. It is a metaphysical possibility for any creature that would attempt to snatch at God's own essence to create as it were an auto-exaltation into hell. To persist in this attempt (despite its futility) would be the metaphysical equivalent of attempting to lift a mountain with a teaspoon, and that forever and with the certainty born of insanity that at any moment the mountain will begin to rise. To a mere consulting detective, this is as close as I may come to solving the intimate puzzle of primordial angelic evil. But how are good and evil conceived of by the people of these mountains? Does the rarified air of these heights give them a unique perspective on the human condition unlike that vision of our origins and destiny bred in the desert peoples of the Mesopotamian basin? This is the question I hope to resolve as I enter the Tibetan snows and valleys.

Book Three: Tibet

From the Journal of Sherlock Holmes

July 31, 1891 – At the gates of Nepal

We left the Kashmir valley of India behind us with its rich rice fields and terraced farms and have now entered a region which if I might say so is cruel to the aspirations of human nature. Who can live in these granite defiles? Who can withstand the icy winds that drop down upon us from these peaks inaccessible? Even the passes are of such great altitude that they frustrate our endeavors. Great snow storms descend upon us without warning. My head buzzes through sheer lack of oxygen. I hope that I shall soon shake off the languor bred of a plains existence and of a life spent in the fogs of London. Even Colonel Moran is showing signs of fatigue. We shall have to take a break in the city of Katmandu before pressing onward into the wilds of Tibet. It has always been a source of wonder to me how certain lands are settled by certain peoples. Is there something in the soul that resonates with a particular landscape? Or is it rather that in the wars and migrations of the primal tribes of man that people become stuck in a region and gradually acclimatize themselves to its particular demands? The tides of humanity flow over the earth sometimes in great rivers, more often by a slow diffusion of language, arts, and influence. They come to feel that the land is their own possession but ever and again there are the great invasions, the empires that rise to a point of magnificence only to decline, to fragment, at first at the edges but then often in the very center through practices of indulgence and luxury. The military on the frontiers gradually surmounts the civil power at the center. Force comes to determine policy and the Senate must yield to the standard bearers at the fringes of battle. When empires break apart, it is often with a great suddenness. The ligaments which have been long-strained through diverse acquisition and greed snap. Afterwards the remnants are either absorbed by other great powers or sometimes the seed of a new empire is born in what was once a mere colony.

China is a good example of my theory. At present it lies in the domination of the great European powers but one need only look at the delicacy of Ming pottery or read the exquisite poems of Li Po to see another time when China was its own empire and not the needy opium cistern that our policy has made it. If the British Empire should dissolve, as remote as the possibility may seem to us now, might China rise again; might its rich river valleys seethe with agriculture and finally with commerce? Even if this should occur though I trust that the people of Tibet will be immune from outer influence and domination. If ever a people had a dominant passion for the land it must be the people of Tibet. Who would choose the bitter chill of these mountains or the arid hill regions that surround them if it were not to see life without illusion or regret? Have the Tibetans discovered a secret way to peace that takes no heed of mortal ambitions but rather adapts utterly to circumstance? To see good and evil without reference to ourselves, would that not be the highest attainment of truth? But then, how can that be? Human inquiry makes little sense if the universe is indifferent to our fate. The human mind cannot weave its web, however elaborate, without a few fixed points beyond itself to serve as anchor points. Among these anchor points are the concepts of good and evil.

To say with Nietsche that we alone are the creator of values may lead us as these views led him to the very height of absurd stoicism by positing his Eternal Return. Nietsche claims that if we may only embrace our fate to the extent that we would relive our lives willing, even if we had to repeat it in every joy and sorrow an infinite number of times, then we will have deserved the title of being the Overmen and presumably also overwomen who may determine good and evil. The madness, if I may say so, in this lies in its vast solipsism. If every man and woman may determine the very nature of good and of evil then there is no point of verification to resolve differences. Each person would then inhabit their own universe. Finally, even communication would be impossible, for if one may determine even good and evil, then surely one might assign the meanings to all concepts. Words would lose their fixed centers and language drift set in at the microcosmic level. The result would be first anarchy, then cacophony, and finally a great silence. Human society would become catatonic. No and again no, Mr. Nietsche. Human meaning emerges from within cultures; all is mediated by

188

the possibility of discourse. Tear that down and the human mind turns within itself and rots away. The problem of the transcendent is the guarantee for any human meaning at all. This is why humans will always need a path beyond themselves, what Lao Tsu calls The Way in his writing, the Tao Te Ching. That which western tradition calls God the Chinese refer to as, the way. But is it the way to a destination or is it merely a path? Is there a god in oriental thought that might be addressed as Father? But oh, if a path exists without destination, then surely we have returned to the problem posed by Nietsche. The path must end in something in order that the end strands of the web may be mounted to some ultimate fixed points. But who has seen God? There is a quote from scripture that bears on this, "To whom has the mind of the Lord been revealed?" Prophecy and revelation thus become necessities to the human mind, but a peculiar type of prophecy, one that knows when, like the wings of the Seraphim, we must veil our faces before God. I should say that one of the primary tasks of all religions is to remind us of our essential limits.

August 4, 1891 --- Katmandu

We have arrived in Katmandu. We are at one of those border regions that have played so large a role in history. It is at these great intercourse points of commerce and of culture that historical fault lines appear. Just as the earth's crust is not stable but made of ever-shifting tectonic plates, so do cultures, races, religions, and art forms collide, merge, and blend. Sudden great shifts may occur, often under the force of armed conflict. Desire and greed in turn may cause vast migrations. The urge to dominate may reduce native populations, supplanting them with others that will in turn be displaced.

All is change; nothing stands still but in pause and suspense, not in final rest. The great Greek philosopher Plato desired that all might come to rest in the contemplation of static forms. His concept of the eternal led him though to neglect the particular, the special, the unique, and the individual. All of these were but shadows of the only real thing, the eternal forms. They were imperfect beings but not Being itself. His thought filtered deeply into the early Christian Church and some would say that the Church has never emerged

189

from his influence, though he had no standing as an Apostle or as a Church Father. Heaven itself, in the Church is still seen in static terms, as the Beatific Vision, an endless contemplation and worship of Divine Truth in the Persons of the Trinity. Indeed, the only dynamic in heaven appears to be the response of worship, led by the choirs of the Seraphim, the highest of the Angelic Choirs, to which are added all of the voices of creation at the last day. All is to be ordered to God and that order is one of worship and of love. This vision flows through all of Apocalyptic Literature and though beautiful, has always seemed to me top be more of a function of a literary device than of the necessary and absolute order of God in relation to creation.

Indeed if we look at nature we observe precisely the opposite of this mode of proceeding. It is God who acts as servant, who stands back, so distant in his own essence that many doubt God's very existence. Others, desiring to bridge that gap of apparent absence, adopt a pantheistic attitude; by looking at all beings, they subsume God into the vast totality of creation. Both extremes are essentially Platonic and both lead to a distortion of what I believe to be the truth. The distinction of Being and of beings is accurate and in this Plato was correct. He was likewise correct is saying that Being is one and uncreated while beings are multiple and derivative from the source of creation. The insight of Scripture though is that by being made in the image and likeness of God a great abdication took place on the part of God. He surrendered control over what humans might choose; humans might choose to define their own essence in opposition to God, which was the original sin.

The Church defines the Nature of the Trinity as Three distinct Persons in one God. This is a non-Platonic idea for in Platonism the attraction of the One destroys all diversity. All is subsumed into unity. But observe nature and we see an order of multiplicity engaged in cooperation and adaptation. Vast interlocked communities are the rule and unity in the sense of final similarity is only known in death. Yet even decay is a servant and a prelude to greater diversity. From death life re-emerges, often in changed forms. The universe that we know is one of diffusion and of multiplicity. From whence then comes this desire to return to unity when Unity itself is Triune?

190

Then there is the question of why does God create images of Himself in human beings? Does God require mirrors then to view His own perfection? Shall we visit upon the nature of God the vanity of an aging dowager who must be constantly assured of her own unchanging beauty? Surely both Scripture and experience would argue the contrary. God appears to rejoice in the divine artistry, to stand back and to admire the goodness in creation rather than wishing to suck it back into his own divine essence. Creation must then always stand in some sort of metaphysical opposition to God. Nature is a constant birthing. Is it too much then to say that God behaves as one who engenders and disperses gifts not that they may be recalled but rather that the individual might in all freedom render back, not a debt, but rather an original gift in return, gratuitous love for the Creator? By making worship a matter of duty rather a spontaneous return, has not the Church made what might have been a joy instead to be a great burden? Is God lost in the many restrictions and sub-covenants? Are not daily codicils being written to add to the endless contract between God and humanity? Do not even the Sacraments themselves finally become a pro forma celebration which is the essence of magical rites rather than the living reality of persons in relationship? When will we escape Platonism and return to change, leave the static for the living, the dynamic, and cease to contemplate and begin as Christians to participate in the cosmic dance?

The God of the Hindus, Shiva has many arms and even dark Kali slaughters only that life may re-emerge while Christian thought has been paralyzed into statuesque immobility since Plato. Christian thought anxiously awaits a historical coming that will silence the choir of creation that is all that we know of life! Change will become changeless in the vast cold halls of eternity and the glory of a sunshine meadow be reduced to an affirmation of a text. If the Spirit of God gives life and that abundantly, then it is to change and abundance that God seems ordered. To take a single metaphor of a Kingdom and to forget that much in Scripture is ordered to the more Dionysian image of a Wedding Feast is to distort the Christian message. It is to be like Buddha, who growing tired of the suffering of creation and wishing to slay Kali as the Goddess of change and destruction, thought up nirvana, the great Platonic ending of

191

Eastern thought whereas the Chinese kept the doors of diversity and change open in the great "I Ching."

One must turn to Heraclitus to see this preoccupation with change in western philosophy. To Heraclitus even natures were not static. One could not even swim in the same river twice for already the stream had moved on! Even Nietsche, the great god-spoiler is a Platonist at last in his idea of an Eternal Return for anything repeated an infinite number of times without change or variation must be viewed as static. Change demands variation and from variation comes diversity. This creates a problem in explaining what an ideal state would be like. If the idea of perfection is univocal, then of course any variation implies a stepping down from the perfect state. For this reason Greek philosophy as it penetrated Christian revelation tended to freeze virtue and its reward of heaven into twin static conditions and contemplation of either tended to slow time into the standing still of the eternal moment. Eternity then as a concept became either the timeless instant if our present sense of time as succession was to cease in the realm of the eternal or if the category of time was to be retained, then eternal time must be the same as time without end. Both ideas destroy the true mystery of eternity by implying that we can ever understand it. I suggest that just as the phase changes from a solid, to a liquid, to a gas are unique and categorical in the realm of matter, so eternity is a phase change of time such that it cannot be comprehended from our present frame of reference within time. For this reason heaven and hell are alike incommunicable except through metaphor and images.

For this reason only a closed system can posit an eternal return, while in an open system, nothing returns as it is, but rather it goes on developing, but not in isolation. No, for Christianity believes that God is with us and indeed more than simply with us; He dwells within us. Jesus says that the Kingdom of God is within you! Let us take an image here from the Gospel: What, Jesus asks, did we go out into the desert to see, a weed blowing in the wind? What voice did we hope to catch, the voice of the weed? No, we would hear the wind itself only by the opposition of creation to its passage. Salvation history is the story of resistance to the voice of God here likened to the wind. Scripture is the gradual growth of clarity in man's relation to God. Though God is in Himself absolute and unequivocal our perception of Him is modulated by time and circumstance. For this reason salvation history (and the Scripture writings that record it) are not severable as though any event or passage can be understood without relation to its place in the whole.

We may seek more certainty at the hands of God, but alas, until creation is touched by the wind it has no voice, at least not one that we can hear. God is known by indirection and revelation is filtered to us by His implicit action rather than by strict causality. Nature is indicative rather than categorical in its relations to morality. One may never be sure whether the aspect of nature to be used as an authoritative precedent is a product of fallen nature or is in fact some fragment that was immune to our primal fall. For this reason I am skeptical of proofs of God's existence from ontology or teleology. I find more persuasive the bare fact of our yearning and desire. If God is love then surely it is our desire for love that is the best proof for the existence of God.

By desiring prematurely to silence creation into a static certainty of the content of faith, we cut ourselves off from the Divine Voice that has chosen to speak through creation. Is it not time to listen to that voice before our depredations and our static definitions silence it perhaps forever? How strange it is that we dream of other worlds, but have yet to do justice to this one. Even our ideals, clothed as they are in generalities, miss the fact that it is only in the particular that virtue or vice can be seen. To wake each day to the unique set of opportunities in which character must manifest itself is to know what life truly is. Nothing is accomplished once and for all until death. To fall or to rise are daily options. Herein is the terror of human freedom.

Each day I ask, shall I remain closeted by my hearth or set off for the antipodes? Shall the wanderer continue wandering or shall he seek again those souls known to one's youth to see how they have prospered or declined and seek his home again? For what is the Odyssey without the return to Ithaca? What suitors may have insinuated themselves there in one's absence? Besides, is all not finally a great circle? What new land is reached but to discover that it is the old land to its native inhabitants? To the wanderer it is adventure, promise, and youth, but to those who have always lived there the land in question is only what they have always known. Do they imagine a journey to that land from which the traveler has just come? Does it bear that same aura of promise and of dream to them? Do we but exchange hearthstones and ash-pits and all in vain, for where is the final revelation that we seek, "Wo ist das Land wo die Zitronen Bluhn?" Surely Goethe speaks in this line of that magic land of flowers and of dreams that we all seek to find.

Watson has claimed that romance has no claim upon me. Hah! It is that I have always resisted it the better to see human nature clearly, from that marvelous distance maintained by Shakespeare. The true artist must hide behind his works. There is a constant temptation to autobiography and to take one's own views as dispositive of all of human nature. Even in religion this is so. What, for instance, is Lutheranism if not the autobiography of that tortured soul who could not trust his own contribution to his own salvation and therefore must attribute even his will to the action of God? How, he wondered, could God love him in his innate depravity? Similarly what is Calvinism but an autobiography of Calvin himself? John Calvin, the master bureaucrat, who would single-handedly build an ideal, seed community in opposition to the universal Church with all its failings.

Perhaps the Catholic Church, realizing this tendency towards power in us all, wisely posits but one Pope, so that every member of the Church who would wish to be a Pope unto himself, might concentrate instead upon God. Time cancels all partial certitudes, even of Popes. The universal Catholic Church, guided by the Holy Spirit, levels all roads before the second coming of Christ.

So it is that to be a Catholic is to finally submit to something, not out of despair, but in the full vigor of one's power. This should be the definition of belief and of a mature faith. Is that not what I have intended by this mad rush to the heights of the world in my search to find a basis for faith that might make the commitment something, not plastered on only to fall away at the first doubt, but rather springing from my own inmost being? How else shall I set before the Professor upon my return that data that will forestall

194

whatever plans of ruin he is forming in my absence so as to obtain from him a commitment to cease and to come over to the position that I have chosen?

Perhaps the entire matter is a sign of vast hubris on my part. Perhaps evil must finally find its own resolution on the very terms that it has set for itself and that no outside force except Grace may be operative upon it. Still, there is surely the force of example. What are our lives but books in which may be read the startling intersection of moral forces under the regime of grace? Others must learn by the paths that we tread together to emulate or to shun our example. But the ways are so various and so convoluted! This is why we turn to religion, to reduce the particular paths to a single great highway, to shed our dreadful isolation and to find finally a home.

Ah well, enough of these speculations for today. Colonel Moran, that great certain beast of a man, would call all of this a mere spinning of spider webs. For him, actions are simply themselves and they yield results and he takes those results as they are without a backward glance or a pang of regret. But, I wonder if even he is immune from the wounds of conscience. I wonder if, before he acts, if he must not first weigh his motives if only to direct his own mighty will. From many such willful men have great saints arisen. Think only of St. Ignatius Loyola, St. Teresa of Avila, or St. Catherine of Siena, or even of the great St. Paul himself! Sainthood is not simply a matter of automatic virtues or of insipid, teacup versions of sanctity. Sainthood means facing life calmly and squarely, of seeing it bordered between birth and death, that short interval between the twin eternities on which our tiny island of sensibility rests, and then, in the darkness of faith, reaching into the infinite. Such is not the action of a feeble soul.

But the opposite position takes a certain courage also: to see oneself as a bewildered beast, saddled with rationality, squeezed into this brief tangle of life, only to die and to watch all that one may have gained by living becoming in an instant humus, no different from plant and animal matter, to be sponged off the face of this lovely earth and not even once in all of futurity to awaken, if but for an instant, and to recall oneself and those who were dear to us and to

195

mutter before sinking again into endless sleep, "Ah fair face of earth, how I miss thy every pulse beat!" Who, even in the face of suffering, would embrace nirvana if a possibility of happiness remained in our unique and individual selves? Are not even our sufferings precious to us as showing the way we have come and the occasional moments upon life's mountain-tops when we stood, as I stand now, actually near to the very rooftop of the world where I might shake my fist at fate and claim my status as a man, proud, and finally immortal? I scorn to be a stoic like Epictetus and to despair of life in an easy acceptance of death, if I am to be robbed of these moments of glory by death forever!

I will mourn the loss of a grey dawn breaking over the sea. I will mourn the sound of an aria sung by a great soprano. I will mourn the yeasty taste of bread or the sting of brandy upon the tongue. I will not willingly acquiesce to my own extinction. This is why I must have faith: one that is real, not a matter of the stale sweat of wooden pews or the much-thumbed hymnals of a desolate chapel. But even this bare, non-conformist faith of the workingmen's chapels run by the Methodists, show forth the patient martyrdom of labor known by the British lower-classes. In each branch of Christianity, there is a quiet heroism. Not all must have faith of the grand sort nor must every church structure be a basilica. Some may drift to faith like leaves on a stream; others must fall like the great oak crashing to its rest after great resistance in the self-same stream. Surely, all alike, in their separate ways come to God. "In my house are many mansions," says the Gospel of St. John. May some lodging be granted then to me, to Sherlock Holmes!

August 5, 1891 --- Katmandu

Today we leave for Tibet. We are getting a late start for the season of the year. I have entertained hopes that I can make it as far as Lhassa where I hope to visit the very center of Tibetan Buddhism at the main lamasery there. If these sanguine hopes are frustrated though by the early snows, I may have to content myself by visiting one of the other monasteries that dot this rugged region. I hope to reach Persia by late fall and to spend the winter there.

Buddhist thought takes many forms according to the genius of the people who embrace it. The Tibetan form fascinates me because of the layering of an Indian faith over a pre-existing culture with roots in the Tibetan Book of the Dead and also Confucian influences from China. The resulting syncretism of beliefs will give me some sense of the cross-currents of belief systems out of which new religions appear to arise when seen from a strictly anthropological viewpoint. Of course it is my position that Christianity and Judaism before them are alone products of the direct intervention of God, but if I am to prove this I must be able to show Moriarity how true religion differs from anything that man might arrive at through unaided reason or natural mythology.

Colonel Moran spent yesterday putting together our expedition of Sherpa guides and bearers and conveyances. I was happy to have a day of rest for I am not yet acclimated to such altitudes and my constitution, though sturdy, is no match for Colonel Moran. I received a note from Mycroft before leaving Bombay. Professor Moriarity has taken up residence, under an assumed name, in Devonshire. He has purchased the estate and horse-stables at King's Pyland, a suggestion that I made to Mycroft as a probable future refuge for the Professor, by telegram from Florence. I have long been aware that the Professor's family has Irish gypsy blood. With that blood there descends an inherited love of horses. I once mentioned to Watson my theory that the individual is a function of all of the tendencies and aspirations of his forebears. The destiny of the family often takes precedence over whatever individual dreams a man may have, thus the legend of the familial curse or destiny. If such a phenomenon exists, then it is the curse of the Moriarity family to enjoy the thrill of gambling and games of chance as well, for they are adjuncts of the racing instinct. I had long known of the Professor's affection for playing the long odds. His original meeting with his arch-collaborator, Colonel Sebastian Moran, was due to a chance meeting at the casino at Monte Carlo. The Colonel has always preferred cards where the demeanor of the player can have some effect and victory can be willed by character. The Professor, on the other hand, has always favored roulette. He even has devised a most unique system for winning at that game. He has found a way of placing bets in a complex pattern so that the odds shift remarkably in his direction. His practice has been to hire confederates to place the bets while he sits in a corner of the great casino with a pencil and paper creating combinations of bets. This desire of his to win against heavy opposition was my first clue to the Professor's inner character. It meant that he could be counted on to play the game against me long after he might have retired and dared me to bring his crimes home upon him. Sooner or later he would make a slip and in the detection of crime even one slip is often enough. I was able to read the pattern and trace over a dozen crimes at once to the Professor's organization and to identify the men in his orbit.

But why and wherefore this need to tempt fate on his part? Why should the quiet scholar need danger and risk to give substance to life? Here I must reveal a secret to my journal. There are humiliations that exceed the moment and leave an intergenerational need to revenge a deep inner wound. The Moriarity family had been grooms and trainers of racehorses, first in Ireland and later in Yorkshire. How strange that the Professor and I should both come from that bleak northern county which has molded our respective need for solitude and isolation. The Professor was the first of his family to acquire an education. To be the first to break out of a family mold, even if the direction is upward, leaves a peculiar guilt. Abrupt change is anathema to the family's image of itself incarnate in the individual. The result is that there ever exists a desire to return to the family pattern and to share the family fate.

I have provided a place and a pattern for the Professor even as he has done for me by assigning Colonel Moran as my companion. Mycroft is to see that the Professor is not harassed by the police. The Professor accepted his new isolated domicile as I supposed that he would. He will find at King's Pyland that loyalty to the soil and to the horses and that love of place and of rootedness that has been heretofore lacking in his abstract character as a mathematician. It will be the first step to his restoration. Mycroft also informed me in the same telegram that Watson has returned to London and has written a remarkable valediction to my career entitled, The Final Problem, recounting my supposed death at the hands of Moriarity. Watson read the clues I left with his usual unique consistency and reached the foregone erroneous conclusion. Alas, poor fellow, was

198

all my tutelage in vain? But so matters must remain. I enter now into regions most remote and I must leave to England what pertains to England. I seek in another culture the universal threads of the human dilemma of existence.

August 14, 1891 - On the Perilous Trail to Tibet

I intend to write these next journal entries in the evenings in camp, for every hour of the daylight is spent climbing. Our first day of travel brought us closer to the pass through these great mountains. We have ascended another 2000 feet during the last two days. We have left behind the Buddhist Temples of Katmandu with their flickering candles and orange robed Monks. We leave behind also that fatalism and determinism of the Buddhist mind and seek the optimism of the Chinese. In the great I-Ching there is always the emphasis upon good fortune and how the superior man may find it. If the Buddhists are the oriental Augustinians, then surely the Chinese are the oriental version of the Pelagians. To create by one's own will a better world and an ideal society by proper subordination and order, surely this is the essence of the teaching of Kung fu Tsu, known to the west as Confucius.

Europe has never escaped the religious dominion of Israel, Persia, and the Arab lands. Just as the Greek and Roman gods were defeated as were the ancient Germanic and Celtic gods also as the Roman Empire expanded to embrace them. Only the Christian cult finally remained after Mithraism and the oracles of Diana and Dionysius fell silent. In China, Confucius and his school provide the same unity century after century that the Bible provides in western culture. Cultures find it impossible to escape their unifying mythologies. We cannot think ourselves beyond these primal cosmological conceptions. Is it possible then that the Chinese may possess a truly alternative view of the place of man in the cosmos? Is there a way beyond suffering?

We spend our lives seeking happiness yet knowing that perhaps the cruelest thing of all would be to attain it only to know that it will be snatched away by death. Against this the Jews believed that one might find comfort in the joy in one's children and their successors and in the final assured triumph of Israel against its foes, but that does not rescue the individual from oblivion. To this great truth of universal suffering the Buddha advises that we embrace our fate with full knowledge of this first noble truth. What we westerners term oblivion is, to the Buddha, but another name for the escape from re-birth called instead, not oblivion, but nirvana, a state to be aspired to and not feared? If the western mind clings to life and would welcome a succession of lives the eastern mind rejects rebirth as the very essence of the problem. To step out of the wheel of rebirth is the purpose of life to this way of thinking.

To the European mind this idea calls into question the point of all human effort. Why build monuments, why compose art, music, and dance if life is but a crawling hive? But even bees make honey and however utilitarian this activity may appear, they know how to dance as well! Against this Buddhist view we have the dynamism of the Chinese, the hunger for success, victory, and good fortune. Not all is suffering it appears. Instead for the Chinese, there is a great balance in life. All things follow a way and so may each man through the willing embrace of virtue. There is a better path to lead through the endless maze of circumstance. To know when to cease inquiry and to await revelation and to prepare one's eyes to meet it – that is the great human task. Meanwhile let us be busy; let us enhance the human fate by human effort! How similar this is to the admonition of Thomas Carlyle in his great book, "Sartor Resartus," where he says we must do first what lays close at hand; the succeeding duty will then have become clearer.

To turn back and to survey what we have done blinds us to futurity, rather should we press on even as the Colonel and I have done this day climbing these forbidding peaks. What is perfection finally but tranquility of form? To build slowly out of written characters, each pregnant with meaning, each word a unique entity with its own form, perfected in individuality, that is the genius of the Chinese language. With perfect denotation one does not need connotation to achieve meaning. Let the simple declarative suffice, let a single tree be a symbol for all trees. The Chinese have achieved Plato's dream of the universals. To perceive the vast order of things and to live within it, not as flawed and fallen, but as beneficent and sufficient, would that not destroy our preoccupation with evil and take from us finally and for all our Manichean roots and ensure the victory of God? For who possesses this grand order and is its origin if not God?

The Tao Te Ching of Lao Tsu speaks of the source of creation as nameless, but creation has a mother, and her we may approach. The Tao studies nature, our beloved earth, and does not seek beyond it the way to God, to God in himself. What is this admission of our limited ability to know the full mind of God but a refusal to imitate God, seeking the knowledge of good and evil, the province God alone, which is surely the Original Sin? For good and evil are finally to be defined only in reference to God as they bring us closer to God or farther away. The path is of God's choosing for only He is the destination. Not knowing the nature of God fully, how can we chart a path to Him by ourselves? This fact is recognized by the Tao Te Ching when it says that the way is uncharted. God finds us more than we find him.

The epistemology of the Chinese is to grasp the pairs of opposites and to see the tension between them, to grasp the relatedness together with the distinctions at once. Therein is the gate to the ultimate root of being. But self-interest must always blind us to this wider perspective to existence. How then do we transcend the self? Or need we do so? After all, the self is affirmed when it joins a greater whole, when it finds connection. Thus the great Confucian idea of order exists wherein all things have their place. Willing subordination is not slavery but the way itself. Happiness follows the man who knows how to belong, to leave the cacophony of desire and assertion that makes him an end in himself, for only God may say, "I am that I am." We on the other hand must say, "I am that I will be." For us the future is the ground of hope. We draw closer to an unnamed goal or failing seek the road again. We grasp that we might be grasped.

What is every religion then but the dance of bees pointing to their hive members as the source of the honey of existence itself? How does one break the primordial parochialism of our own pride in finding the truth when God alone can claim that he alone can be worthily self-referential?

Who will segregate the queen in the great hive so that she may be seen in herself? If we reach beyond the attribution of opposite sexes to God by reversing the normal gender appellation applied to God, only to then step beyond duality altogether, this will purge us of much of the false attributions applied to the deity. We find the Great Source, the unknowable, the word beyond all words, God, in the union of the creative and the receptive, in Chi'en and Kun, the two primary hexagrams of the I-Ching. Does God as beekeeper sleep listening to the primal Om, the buzzing of the hive of creation? It must be music to the ear of divinity to hear His hive in which each bee must have her place.

I write this by a guttering candle flame in my tent. Sleep must come soon now for we resume the ascent tomorrow to the pass into Tibet. The winds howl up the mountainside and the canvas walls of my tent make a strange music as though I were in a lonely barque at sea.

August 20, 1891 - The Lamasery of the Golden Moon

It has been some days since I have written in this journal. My only excuse is that I have been overwhelmed with the beauty of our present location and so caught up in talks with the head-Lama that there has been no time to write. I desired to gather my impressions before setting anything down. What a relief it was to descend from the mountain pass into this lovely valley. There is something terrible about snow, ice, and granite. Even the vast deserts of the earth are less inimical to human life than high mountains. The sudden windstorms that threaten to blow one like so much chaff off of the mountain's face combined with the sheer scale and magnitude of the vertical prospects, the gaping chasms, the groaning ice fields, and the sudden plunge of tons of snow into unsuspected crevasses. All are a source of terror. There are heights both physical and mental that should be merely observed with wonder. The attempt to scale them may bring a man into peril. It is a peculiarity of the human condition that we are constantly meant to exceed our limitations yet we are always reminded of them by the sheer resistance of material nature to the dictates of our will. To know when to act and when to withdraw is essential. Every civilization has had some system of augury, for who would not wish

202

to know what the future may hold? Beset as we are with peril though, and in light of the many accidents that may bring our most sanguine plans to ruin, is it not a blessing that obscurity surrounds us? It allows us our few moments of complete joy and triumph whenever all of our difficulties seem at an end and the prospect fair as far as our eyes can see. Such are my feelings today in this green and golden valley of the moon.

Colonel Moran and I have been assigned rooms in the lamasery itself. Our rooms are in a small edifice with its own courtyard surrounded by a low stone wall. Over the wall there is a steep fall to the terraced fields below. A small stream courses through the valley at tremendous velocity. The waters are clear and beneath them lies a virtual garden of stones set off by the lovely pale green of the current. Mossy banks surround the stream and grottos are formed by the dense trees. On the other side of the lamasery the valley widens into fields before another steep descent through a narrow gap to a deeper valley. Thereafter the prospect is of further continuous ranges of snow-covered peaks. The unique verdure of this valley seems to come from its location on a seam in the hills. Winds seem to bring airs laden with the scented spices of Siam to us in this distant place, but perhaps I am being fanciful. Certainly the charm of the place might justify such an air of romance. The Monks seem in constant good humor and we are met with great courtesy. Their simple robes recall the words of the Tao Te Ching that the wise man carries a jewel in his breast but goes about in poor garments. The head-lama is a man of about seventy though to see his eyes one might imagine in him the joy of a child. He radiates a quiet acceptance and humility and one might say that peace follows in his steps. I don't know what I expected from our discourse for I find that he speaks little. Instead, there is a sense of patient listening with full attention in his avid but not intrusive gaze upon one while one is speaking. He seemed at first to lack all curiosity as to who we were. We were simply admitted, assigned rooms, and brought to him after we had rested. I had at first thought to employ Colonel Moran as a linguist, but was surprised to learn that it was not necessary since the head- lama spoke English. He told me some of his surprising background before becoming a monk.

"I was once engaged in trade in Shanghai, dear sir," he said. "I am not native to these mountains. I came here as a traveler many years ago. I came first to the Lhassa to study under the Lama there, but after an active life I found that I could not find comfort in the Buddhist teachings practiced there. I am afraid that our past is sometimes an insurmountable burden to us even when we seek to abandon it. I could not accept the doctrine of many lives. My objection was that without conscious continuity what learning can take place between lives? I admit that it seems unjust that some live lives of sufficient length to invite contemplation while others die at the very threshold of perception, but so it is. Length of life is often not necessary to obtain what is essential."

I assented but inquired what doctrines were present then in the lamasery to guide the Monks.

He smiled, "Had you proceeded as far as Lhassa you might have found a more rigorous set of practices in place. Many travelers pass our little valley unawares as they press on to Lhassa. Others come here by accident and stay. I am sorry that you will not be staying the winter with us as it is a delight for me to speak English again. I understand though your desire to press on to the Pashtun regions before the winter snows set in. But we were speaking of our spiritual discipline here. We leave it to each Monk, those who can read look at the old books when they have time to do so, for we spend much time with the growing of crops and with our flocks. Much of life is simply surviving is it not? I myself am impatient of premature conclusions; they lead to great differences among men, to disagreements, and finally to violence. Surely, truth may take care of itself."

This diminished concern for absolute truth surprised me so I asked, "Surely a man of God must be concerned with truth? You made few inquiries of me when we arrived, but simply gave us the hospitality of the lamasery. My question is not an idle one. I am in England what is called, a consulting detective. I have made my career that of listening to a series of facts and tracing the larger pattern that those facts manifest. By this practice, I have been able to affect a measure of good, to help people. Over the course of my career I have observed again and again the role of the passions in

204

human motivation and how little any abstract value system can alter fundamental human motives. I have often wondered what is intended when men of religion speak of truth as though they were certain of every statement many of which are mere codicils to the most basic tenets of their faith. I have found that the circumstantial and the particular alter almost every human situation. Still, there must finally be a ground for our assertions or we are the mere playthings of fate. I assure you that this hunger for an absolute is no idle inquiry for me, for I have in hand at present a most difficult case. I must find an answer that will satisfy not only me but another man, a man of great intellect."

"Is the man that you speak of your companion?" the Lama inquired.

"No, but he is an associate of the man about whom I speak," I replied.

"And you believe that I may have an answer for you. Perhaps because I live on top of a mountain and wear robes and because I read Holy Books and have time to think about what they contain, you think that I am a wise man. Ah, dear sir, if it were only that simple. I was once a man of action, a merchant. I had a fleet of ships sailing in my name and many lives were dependent upon me. Here I am now in a land that is not even my own, for I am Chinese and we are in Tibet. No doubt you think that you have chosen the wrong lamasery and the Lama in Lhassa could give you the answer that you seek rather than an old merchant. We are good friends though, the Lama of Lhassa and me. I believe that he would smile at you, even as I am doing, and bid you to return into yourself for your answer. The decision is yours as it is the decision of each man how he shall relate to God and to his own life for that matter. Did not Jesus once ask his Apostles, 'But you? Who do you say that I am?'"

"Then truth has nothing to do with it all; there is to be no final arbiter for divided absolute positions? Surely it does not matter what we say of God – either God is or He is not independent of any position that we take," I objected.

"I do not say so. Truth in fact has everything to do with all but to accept this truth, to live in this truth, to risk all for this truth, to love this truth, to face one's own death in this truth; this is most difficult. The result you may well ask? Most men will spend their lives in partial assertion of what they say they believe. They will seek authority as a short way to inner conviction. These men do not know that the question of Jesus to His Apostles will finally be put to them by God himself. I am not unfamiliar with Christian writings you see. Did not Jesus again and again ask his followers, "But you, who do you say that I am?" or again to Saint Philip, "Do you not believe that I am in the Father and the Father is in me?" Why is faith necessary if it is merely a matter of truth? If truth has such meager credentials as to leave so much room for doubt, then what aid can it be to belief? No, Jesus put the emphasis where it belongs, in commitment prior to certainty."

"But if this is so, how will the contradictions of the various faiths be resolved?" I asked. "Surely we should have more tangible proofs for an absolute commitment of our very lives."

"No proof would satisfy all where God is concerned, for to have it one would have to comprehend God, to get around God and view him from all angles so that no tiny gap remained through which God could escape. God must then be stripped of all mystery. What would then be revealed? Who would dare such a violation? Does God alone deserve no privacy? Does he owe us to stand naked before us so that we may judge Him and decide whether he is worthy of belief? Shall we put him to the test? Shall He walk a line that we draw in the sand? Yet, I believe that he allowed even this when he asked St. Thomas to probe the wound in his side after the resurrection."

"Still," I said, "Jesus does speak of Himself as the way, the truth, and the life and assures his hearers that no one may come to the Father but through him."

"So he does and so it may be that no one comes to the father but through Jesus, but surely the way to Jesus and the means of invoking His agency may differ," replied the Lama quietly.

"The only means would appear to be by keeping his words and by belief in Him leading to an adherence to his teachings." I answered.

"So you assert that the process of faith acquisition may be achieved by a series of steps. For the sake of simplicity I shall list them. I do so in order to suggest that faith is organic rather than systemic in its origins. Here then are the steps: 1. Evaluate Jesus' credentials for truth; 2. Believe in Jesus; 3. Assert that belief; 4. Receive Grace; 5. Follow the teachings and should you fail repent and return to the course; 6. Attain access to the Father and the reward of heaven."

"It is a cold formulation, but I believe that you have stated it correctly." I responded.

"Then I suggest in turn that a man seeking truth will never get past step one."

"And why is that?" I inquired.

"Because Jesus has told us as much, do you recall these words of Jesus? 'No one can come to me unless the father draws him.' It is not then a matter of truth but of love. God the Father must already be speaking within the heart for one to find faith. The Holy Spirit precedes God the Son in His action on the soul. It is for love of that still and quiet voice that we believe. Belief then is a matter of prayer and not of intellectual investigation and the weighing of alternatives. What is prayer but desire? God is God because we so desire Him."

"But what is God in himself?" I demanded.

"Ah you are daring in inquiry are you not, Mr. Holmes?" he smiled. "What God is in Himself is a matter for only God to know and He must reveal it when and as He chooses or would you deny freedom to God? If God allows man the freedom of unbelief, does not man owe God the respect of allowing God to keep his own counsel in many matters? Or do you believe that God has nothing more to reveal? He will not contradict what he has said, but to believe that nothing remains to be known in due season is to reduce God to our own ideas about Him."

"But surely He owes us something, after all as creatures we are His responsibility or else we are mere playthings!" I objected again.

"It is precisely here that trust comes in. We must trust that we are not, as you say, mere playthings and that God's discretion is well-based. He has told us enough, he has done enough, and that must be sufficient for us."

"But how then can one compel belief? I have wagered the Professor that I can prove to him that his way of life is wrong. He is a great scientist and he will respect proof," I spoke as if to myself.

"I do not know your Professor, but I fear that you will lose your bet if it is based on the terms that you have stated. You may however reach the same end by a different route," replied the Lama with a smile.

During this entire interview I had felt like Watson when hearing one of my own demonstrations. It was not a pleasant feeling to be so at sea.

"How then can I prevail for I assure you that lives hang in the balance?" I cried.

"Go and think about it, Mr. Holmes, for I hear the bell ringing and we must descend to our repast. I trust that you like lentils. We eat a great many of them here." He smiled again and stood up. Together we descended to the refectory where the Monks gathered for their common meals.

Later-

After luncheon with the monks, the body restored on the simple produce of the earth, I returned to the terrace alone. I felt for the first time a fear that I might not prevail. I had been so certain that I could convince the Professor with a proof of mathematical certainty, but I was always thrown back upon the nature of the human condition and of our need to trace everything to a common source. Was this innate need due to the nature of things, or was it a peculiarity of human thought, a grain of sand in the human oyster that forces us to make up religions as the oyster makes a pearl? Why could not man be simply a happy animal? From where then comes this whole problem of sin, for instance, if there is nothing to sin against but our own vanity? Why speak of the mountains of eternity at all from the valleys of time? Could we not reach a modus vivendi at last with the human condition and accept gracefully our destiny of a mouth full of earth and a glazed eye?

No, no, and again no, for who, having once glimpsed divinity in a human eye, can imagine the perpetual extinction of that light, even if it is only glimpsed in the eye of the beloved? Is it not even more of a vanity to imagine human virtues enthroned on so feeble a substance as short-lived man? The stoic philosophy has always seemed to me the height of human denial. It escapes the problem by denying the problem: grit your teeth and accept oblivion, fine, hah! But will the fine stoic then bid the gasping child to do the same? Shall he gaze at the pangs of childbirth and council forbearance should the prospective mother sicken and die of fever and infection? Is human life a mere channel to pass to our heirs our own dismay? Will none ever stop and demand of the silent heavens: Why?

Why what? Why everything. Always we return to the cry from the cross, the thirst of Christ, not hunger but thirst, of the two the more tormenting need, the more basic. We do not hunger for life; we thirst for life that our blood, which is the life, may continue to flow. Awake oh sleeper, spring must come again, all must not be the sallow weeds of death, the sodden and discarded leaves of our days must not blow into the gutters of time so that our memorials fade, our brave dreams, our loves, all vanish to appear again nevermore. The whole edifice of our aspirations topples without God and without aspirations what mollusk is not luckier than we? What moss fulfilling its nature is not more to be envied then us in our travail?

But do we give religion birth or is not religion a voice from without, blurred perhaps by our capacities to receive it, but still a signal from the beyond and not merely from within us? But why do I speak thus? What if it does come from within? Are we not nature also? Who cares wherefrom the voice comes so long as it be a voice? Are we not the best medium for the message from futurity? Is not our very desire the best proof for its fulfillment? Can we not then rest and say that our very bones lie in repose for as the Psalm says, "You will not allow your Holy One to see corruption?" Thus does the individual finally ask the final question of his forbears and arrives at the same answers as they did though they are gone where none may find them in the quiet earth. The rock is pushed along to another age, but the weight of this rock, is it not heavier than we can bear? To articulate the question is to awaken to its agony? Should we not then spend our short days like flowers in the sun, vain creatures of beauty and of desire knowing in the pangs of joy our only heaven?

Ah, but even then, for us these fair creatures of an hour, as John Keats said, must be a poor substitute? What deified beauty but wears within the charnel rose? So the thinking man turns to science finding in its formulations, finding in the language of mathematics, the dry perfection and immortality of thought. The thinker becomes an object among objects.

To reduce the whole to a single equation, that once set down would encompass all things in a perfect unity; that is the dream of men such as Professor Moriarity. But having done so, having pillaged thought for the great assembly of feeling men and women, and standing back like a god but to review one's handiwork, would we say, as God has said, that our work as mere scientists is good? Have we not merely traced over the drawing of God with our own pale imitation? Is giving an account of the world in sheer physical succession adequate? Will the scientists not find themselves sooner or later back up against an unyielding absolute that will be probed no further?

For what is human knowledge but mere succession? We come late to the feast only to gather the crumbs and sip the stale leavings in the goblet. We are too far from our origins. A great gap precedes the Pre-Socratics and even Abraham and epic of Gilgamesh!

Who was present at the Triune council that preceded creation? No witnesses may be called! We, poor chimpanzees, strut across the table of time and foul the precious linen pages of history with our absolute certainties. For what is our history of wars, crime, pride, but not a great excrescence? We foul eternity with our very presence, yet God is said to love us. Silence then is our part before such great matters, mere contemplation and acceptance of the gift of having been at all. But if that is enough for me, will it be enough for Moriarity? Are we not back at stalemate if I can prove only what we cannot know of God?

August 14, 1891 - The Lamasery of the Golden Moon

It had been several days since I had been able to obtain an interview with the head-lama. During that time I had brooded over his words to me and the hope that he had extended to me: that I might still prevail in my wager with Professor Moriarity. This morning, when I again found myself in the simple but comfortable chambers of the Lama, I immediately broached the question and explained my concerns. The Lama listened carefully and then was silent for some time. At last he raised his head and spoke.

"If I may state your problem, Mr. Holmes, it is this: You desire to obtain an irrefutable and conclusive proof what we refer to as The Way. We believe that The Way is preferable to the path of evil and that a man does well to follow that path. You would seek some form of intellectual compulsion where we see freedom."

I agreed to his simple version of my side of the wager. The Lama then continued.

"You have told me something of the mind of this man you call the Professor, of his love for gambling and games of chance, of his mathematical mind, of his extreme independence and need for power and control, and of his greed for gain from his organization of crime. What you have not said, but what I infer from the above, is that he is a man with certain contempt for his fellow-beings. In other words, he believes that he is a superior man and as such that he has rights above and beyond others, that they may be prayed upon to satisfy his wants and for his own amusement. He is lacking in solidarity therefore with the universe. He does not see himself as a part of the nature of things, but rather as standing apart, by himself. He is a way unto himself and as such he does not know The Way because he does not feel a need for it."

211

Again I agreed to his excellent summation of the Professor's character and asked that he continue his remarkable discourse.

"Such a man is in great disorder, but as the great I-Ching says: a quality pushed to its extreme will switch with great suddenness to its opposite. May we not say that such a man is in despair and in great agitation? He cannot know peace, for he is divorced from all things, for all things follow The Way and he does not. You say that he is a mathematician, good! This may be the rivulet that leads him back to the river. Like every language, mathematics must aspire beyond itself for meaning. A language without referents would be mere grunting sounds. No language can be private. It assumes verification from without. No mind can exist within itself alone. Even the mad imagine and people their worlds with unseen interlocutors. This Professor is then reaching outward for a descriptive formulation. He may begin with a dull stone asteroid but end with the stars. He must climb the path of beings to the great Being itself. What is this but a description of the Way? To enter upon The Way is to be driven to continue upon it. From the idea of the other, the great outside-of-us comes a need for more and more relation. From glimmerings of affection one yearns for love and in love to find union with the all."

I spoke up, "But are there not many (I see it often in my criminal practice) who stop and will go no further. Whether through laziness or fear they stop. I have never been able to decide why so many stop short of God. How does one motivate internal growth in a man who seems satisfied to arbitrarily cease asking the final question?"

The Lama smiled, "Is that our task then? To, as you say motivate internal growth and compel men to God? Are we God? Are we The Way? This is where your definition of the wager was wrong-headed if I may so, in its first principles; because you wish to triumph so that the glory of victory shall be yours. Then you will say, 'ah well done Mr. Sherlock Holmes,' for you will have conquered the Professor, you will feel superior to evil! Do you not see that in saying so, you yourself become the evil that you fear, for now it is you who determine God's existence rather than God yours? God must now find a way to meet your formulation. God must adapt to your mold. There must be no leaking at the edges of your conceptions. Is this not what idolatry means? To form an image of God! But then, you may walk around God, you may comprehend him. But does not Scripture say, "The light shines in the darkness but the darkness did not comprehend it." What was the failing of the Jewish people in the time of Jesus Christ but that they did not know the hour of their visitation from God? Why? Because their religious certainty told them just how the Kingdom of God would come and what kind of messenger would appear. When Jesus spoke, His words were strange to them, outside of their formulation. What, we may ask, was that formulation and certitude but a manifestation of their desire for personal glory and the supremacy of a priestly caste, and not God's glory at all. So we here in this humble lamasery try, in our own way, to keep the path open, to allow The Way to speak to us and not to force our words into God's mouth."

"Then if you know the Christian Scriptures so well are you not Christian?" I inquired.

"Well my dear son, perhaps there are no Christians but finally only the one Christ in His Church and those who wish to take up their crosses after Him. There is but one vine and many branches. The temptation to define the outer region of the Kingdom of God seems though to make many who call themselves Christians bar the gates of the very Kingdom. These suppose themselves elect and oppose the mercy of God with the same bitterness as that of Jonah who was angry at God for sparing Nineveh. Christianity is not a status but an onward journey. Did you never read the words of Jesus that 'those who are not against us are for us?' The Kingdom of God is advanced by many who do so by simply not impeding its progress among men. The mission entrusted to the Church is not compromised by allowing God to speak within the hearts of those who can only be prepared for his final word by other means. God will find a way to reach their hearts. Are these people to be consigned to share the fate of the wicked when they have sought God by the only means at their disposal? Let me quote the Gospel again, "What did you go out into the desert to see, a reed blowing in the wind?" and again "Not everyone who says to me Lord, Lord, will enter the Kingdom but those who do the will of my Father in Heaven." God will not deny the searching heart and the humble

213

soul. We share with our brother monks of other faiths throughout the world this hunger for personal submission; we desire that we may be less, so that God may break through within us. We refer all things to God and claim nothing for ourselves and in ourselves. For what are we but containers of grace? All that is within us must come from outside. We do not wish to be like God "knowing good and evil" for that is not our task; it is rather to "discern good from evil" and to act upon what we hear to the best of our ability with the help of God."

"Are the concepts of knowing and discerning not identical?" I inquired.

"By no means are they the same! To know good and evil as God would require that we be God, that we be the measure of all things, but this, only God may determine by his own nature. God is the measure of all things and all things that live not in God are by definition nothing. There can be but one center to the circle. The center determines the distance to the circumference. To discern good and evil is to accept the determinations of God. That we may do; that we must do if we are to follow The Way. The Holy Spirit awakens us to discernment but not knowing. Thus is answered the much debated question of the sin of the blasphemy of the Holy Spirit, the only sin that may not be forgiven."

"I have often wondered about that sin since it seems contrary to the universal mercy of God," I expostulated.

"Not so, Mr. Holmes, it is rather a sign of God's mercy, though a sad one. The blasphemy spoken of that is against the Holy Spirit is to be hardened in original sin, in idolatry, in a great solipsism, in evil. Impenetrable evil is self-referential. It makes its own good the measure of all things. This blasphemy is to believe that the creature can be as God, sufficient in its own being. To do so is to deny love, for love always requires that one transcend oneself and reach outward to the other. To be frozen in inwardness, eternally, what is this but hell? To have lost all hope in the other, what is this but despair?"

"But does not God live in just this solitude," I asked.

"Christian faith believes in a Trinity; it would appear that God is not alone even in Himself! Love is forever out-reaching," was the answer.

"Can you explain the Trinity to me, then?" I asked since we had gone so far.

"I can only give you the answer of Jesus, "Do you not believe that I am in the Father and the Father is in me. How can you then say, show us the Father?" Jesus could speak in this way because there was no opposition in His nature. He and the Father were: One in the Holy Spirit."

"Does that not mean that the Father absorbed the Son after the resurrection?" I asked. "If so, then the separate identity of Jesus is lost and there is no Trinity, no communion in the natures of God."

The Lama laughed, "So, Mr. Holmes, you are not familiar with the early heresies. It took four centuries for the Church to work out the problem that you raise. The Divinity of Christ was always absorbing His humanity or so the Gnostics thought. God the Father always seemed to be absorbing the Humanity of Divinity of the Son so that the Holy Spirit was said, not to proceed from both Father and Son, or so the Orthodox Churches believe in contrast to the teaching of the Popes and the Council of Florence."

"I assure you: There is no carnivorous nature in God. God works through dispersing gifts. The Son is begotten but not made. God is expansive and prodigal, if we may say so. He does not retract his gifts. The result is that we have three distinct persons but one God. This is the faith of the Universal Church."

I began to see stirrings of the truth about the man who sat before me. "Surely, you are a Christian! You could not possibly know all this otherwise."

The Lama smiled. "What? Do even my words betray me as the woman said to St. Peter in the courtyard? It is true, my name is Chen Yugen and I am a Priest of the Jesuit Order of the Catholic Church. This place is my mission, assigned to me by the Father

215

General in Rome, to be the head-lama at The Lamasery of the Golden Moon."

I was frustrated and spoke up, rather heatedly, to the holy man before me. "But I have come all this way to find a differing account, another version of God. I wanted to be sure that I possessed the truth. I might have stayed in London and spoken to the priests there if I wished only to confirm my own Christianity."

"And here you are in the cold Himalayan Mountains, miles from home, and guarded by a man who was your enemy, as you have told me. But God did not ask this of you. You asked it of yourself. It was you who would make the path to God so difficult. The Way lay on the steps of 221B Baker Street, your home, just as the Way lies at the feet of all men and women. God is not found in excursion or in discursion either for that matter. Both are merely the ways that man exhausts his own seeming capacities to exist on his own terms. A journey begins with a single step. So does the journey to God, Mr. Holmes. That is what you may tell your Professor. Would it not be strange if all parallel lines finally meet if extended infinitely? The man who does not believe in God ends up by making himself a god as did King Herod. Similarly the man who seeks God with his whole heart will inevitably find him, even if only in death. You must ask your Professor if he is willing to be God, to people the universe with replicas of his own essence as a mere man. For a man to choose to be like God, he must create all men and women in his own image. He must choose to define human nature not simply for himself but for all men and women. He must will that all be as he is. Otherwise he is caught in a great inconsistency, a great lie of Being. If the Professor is, as you say, a man of reason and logic, then he will understand this and he will be forced to choose, as all finally must, to answer the question: "Am I to be God, or shall I defer to being merely God's image, to let the light of God shine through my individual nature, which is always referred back to God as the source of all things. To claim nothing for and in oneself; this is humility; this is repentance; this is The Way."

"Yes, but is this a proof for God's reality?" I asked.

"A proof as you say of God cannot be like a proof of anything else and still refer to God. The problem, you see is not with God; it is with us. We must decide our place in the order of things. Religion and particularly we of the Christian Faith believe that our scriptures reflect God's desire to communicate with us by revelation. This revelation is filtered through the consciousness of many people, first the sacred authors and later those who have based their lives on these teachings, under the inspiration of the Holy Spirit. To break from the collective wisdom of humankind and to set oneself up to find another way is to change human nature itself, for human nature as we have known it is inevitably religious. God is the one essential constant in the human soul. Every culture knows religion and there is a remarkable unity of insight as my time in the Lamasery of the Golden Moon has shown me. Perhaps this is because God speaks in our inmost being, both as individuals and in community. To do away with all of this and to set one's self up to be one's own end of all ends is to cascade downwards into the empty chasm of one's own being, there to face a great nothingness, to experience what it would be to live without Grace. Even the greatest sinners feel within them the urge from without to return to God. Their desperation in sin is a sort of madness. Perhaps some exist so changed from the usual condition of the human as to have no such awareness. We cannot imagine dwelling within such souls, so we may not judge them, but if it is true that all conscience is dead within them and they are prone to final impenitence, then are they most to be pitied, for they are then a separate species with the intelligence of man but the instinct of the beast. Real animals on the other hand are God's innocents. Even the crocodile carries its young in its jaws of death with tenderness. Perhaps there are beings born to seek hell or bent in that direction by horror in life and for them we pray, that even within death they may turn again to the dawn before the final eclipse of choice and be lost forever."

"Is your Professor one of these?" asked the Lama, "Who can say? You may though present him with what is at stake in his choices and perhaps his very clarity may force him to choose, for choose we finally must. In our nakedness we stand before the witness of creation in the love the Creator and beneath the Cross of the Son. Daily we claw through our passions and our pride all of our lives, sin and sin again, but only he who ceases to climb forever is finally lost as Goethe realized in his great play, 'Faust.'"

The Lama fell into silence then and I decided that it was time to withdraw. I had no more questions to pose that day and for many days thereafter. I left the presence of the Lama by bowing deeply. I returned to the terrace and looked over the valley to the mountain peaks and knew that whatever my expectations had been in coming to Tibet, I had not made a fruitless journey. It is not the place that determines the truth or our ability to receive it with inner assent; time and place may open us though to see with new perspective what we have always known. Truth is always signified by recognition, as though we always bore its message within us. It is the will that may be influenced by change of place and time or circumstance. The will is often chained by its own lethargy and habits, by its own long weariness and despair. It often takes a shock of some sort to dislodge the will from the habit of an easy and settled conviction that the partial may suffice for the whole, or that error may prevail over truth.

August 23, 1891 – The Lamasery of the Golden Moon

I can tell that Colonel Moran is restless. He is not one to enjoy the pleasures of contemplation. For myself, the insight and equanimity of the Lama is a tonic and I could spend many weeks here in peace and contentment, but Persia beckons and I fear that we must soon depart. Besides I must return to a city where I can receive word from Mycroft. I cannot imagine the Professor doing much harm in rural Devonshire but I can only hope that I have not provided him with an ideal retreat from whence he may weave his plots. What, I wonder, will be his next expedition into the world of crime? Will it affect nations rather than individuals, as the Professor has boasted? It is at the level of nations that the greatest of crimes occur? How calmly statesmen make decisions that will cause countless deaths, yet it is never called murder. How much theft and rapacity occur, yet we cannot call these statesmen thieves, for these expropriations are done in the name of whole peoples. With what pride and rectitude do these men in top- hats not keep their secret counsels! Can only history be their judge? When shall a greater tribunal be set-up to try these crimes that as yet have no name?

218

But, ah, how distant seem all of these matters to me here in far-off Tibet. The clarity of the mountains, the cleanness of these dry and desert airs bring peace. Peace, that strange word that in statecraft is meaningless. When states speak of peace it is only in reference to that time when their ambitions shall be satisfied and since that time never comes neither does peace. Peace for nations always means when the will of their leaders has been accomplished. Then peace is forced upon those whom they have conquered. What then is peace but slavery by another name? The victor, the regent, the ruler desires peace so that he may find surfeit at another's table, though he be no invited guest.

The poor do not speak of peace for they may not find it here. For them the Kingdom of Heaven is prepared by a God who comes as a servant. The peace of God is that He does not conquer even the soul but rather enthrones us even though from that posture of freedom we may deny Him. God never seems to reclaim a gift once given. Freedom is eternal. Thus all things have within themselves a property of divergence. All is a great dispersal. We live upon the scattered ice-flows of eternity. What shall bring us together at last in a great commonwealth of Spirit? To find that force and see it operative among nations, surely that is the task of humans upon this earth. If this is to be it must not be by coercion, but as a fruit of consent, a vast contract based upon a fundamental dignity between men. Alas, I have not the words to form jurisprudence on so grand a scale. What statecraft has not been able to achieve, neither has religion; for who can hear of the Crusades, the Islamic Wars, the Roman incursions into pagan lands, and not see mere oppression? But still, deep within each doctrine, a purer spirit waits, common to all, and rooted in the hearts of all, peace.

How strange that I should speak of peace here in Asia, where peace has never been known but only the vast migrations of peoples. What is the history of Europe but a great cycle of invasions? What is Europe but a great swirled-design of those who remained in the invaded lands to mingle their languages, their customs, their foods, and their superstitions? What ever started these great migrations? The differences in races and ethnicities argue for a pre-history of stability where these characteristics could gain a foothold in the great extended families and tribes. These differences that do not affect the basic nature of the soul still create sufficient difference that we find it difficult to recognize a common human dignity in one another. How attenuated are the sympathies of men and how long the memory of offences. Which people have not been guilty of atrocities? Who shall unweave the web of expropriation that is history and find that initial stasis that might be called primal justice? It is this loss of a starting point for justice that causes the Monks to return all prior to leaving the world. The Monks at the lamasery reject all in order to embrace all. They take upon themselves the losses, the penances, and ask only for space to reflect upon that common origin in God, lost in the mists of time.

Did man emerge upon the land from the sea as latter-day lizards, learn to climb trees and finally descending again to earth, learn to walk upright, so that our hands might be free, as Mr. Darwin is theory suggests? Is evolution directed always to a higher awareness, or might the phenomenon of atavism exist also? Perhaps the human race has found the burden of mind too much and turning from its divine destiny is already returning day-by-day back into the jungle. How long shall it be before we have scales again and return to the sea? But I am being fanciful; it would hardly do for the great consulting detective to be fanciful. Perhaps, I have set such a high store upon reason all of these years because I knew how thin the veneer of reason really is. Our humanity exists in that last surface layer of cells that float upon the great tumultuous legacy of the mammalian and reptilian brains that lie beneath. How frail is that delicate encrustation over the volcanic depths that lie just below! I laugh at those who would construct a science of man and of woman. Once we are beneath the microscope, what are we but microbes and virulent ones at that? To believe that we are more, we must look to art, to literature, to music, and from these deduce that we are more than time can ever contain. We create immortal monuments and how may that be if we ourselves are merely mortal? Shall my skull, sucked dry of all that is me as though I were a succulent snail, someday adorn the shelves of some arcane collector? Should I have been a canonized saint, might my relics, encased in gold, find repose within some alter in order to be nearer to the eternal sacrifice of the mass?

220

What do we finally do with all the bones in the world? Shall we not someday be drowning in cemeteries? Will humanity finally create vast trenches and bury bodies not individually but in hundreds, thousands? It will not matter then who one was, but in what great cause one finally perished. The great slaughter of the recent civil war in America is an example of this phenomenon of mass-death. What priest can minister the rites of the dying when death reaches such a scale? Yet we speak of peace and every day the number of arms increases. We live in the bondage of our fears and not in our dependencies upon each other! What horrors may yet await man from his own ingenuity? Is nature so failing in our destruction that we must devise other means to throng the halls of death? And all for what, for longevity, for dominion, for vengeance, for the passing glory of passion, or for possession of the many articles of trade? Alas for too many men, violence is their only bread and the means to draw out a life for another day.

Well, this day is mine. The lama has arranged for a private Mass and afterwards I shall gaze upon this pleasant valley and contemplate the mountains that are its home - peace.

August 28, 1891 – Last Days at the Lamasery

I have proposed to Colonel Moran that we remain here for the winter. We must make our decision soon for already there is a chill in late evening air that speaks of autumn and should we leave too late we may find ourselves snowbound as we cross the mountains of Afghanistan. How I should hate to try and survive a winter in some poor Pashtun village. Here at least there is to be found civilization, peace, and most stimulating conversations with the head-lama. With the spring I could extend my journey deeper into Tibet to Lhassa and perhaps reach Peking in the North of China. But alas it is probably not to be. The Colonel will have none of it. He is a creature of the tropics and deeply sensitive to cold. As he is my guide and since his presence is invaluable I must fall in with his wishes.

It is bitter to me that I must turn westward again. I should have enjoyed a deeper acquaintance with this hearty people and to be able to compare the Tibetan concepts of Buddhism with those of

India. I had even debated proceeding to Shanghai and going to Japan. I am learning firsthand of the great seductiveness of travel. It gives one the feeling of omnipotence. How bitter it is to turn about and to know that you may never return to the lands just glimpsed.

But is not each day like this? The dawn comes and the day lies before one with infinite possibilities and by night one turns about and knows through sad experience how little may be done in a day. So I must yield to necessity. Besides, I am curious about Persia whose great empire once encompassed the cradle of all cultures. What a place for a lover of the antiquities and of beauty! Besides, I am anxious to speak to some of the spiritual leaders there. To overlook the spiritual force of Islam is to misunderstand the world, for Islam is found everywhere. Even in London I have seen the women who proclaim their faith by their modest demeanor and veil. The west has not finished with the task of confronting, for good or for ill this supreme product of Asian culture. To assume the triumph of Christianity is, if nothing else premature. Will that confrontation, when it comes, be on the order of dialogue and mutual-forbearance, or will it involve the violent clashes of the past, ah that is for the future to reveal.

Dr. Watson's Narrative Continues

I put down the book of Holmes manuscript and returned to the mundane world of the train that jolted us along. I looked over at my companion who had nodded off to sleep. Had the mind of the great detective in those vast mountains of Tibet exceeded its own grasp or had it finally arrived at its goal to solve the greatest mystery of all, our own problematic existence?

In my first book wherein I have attempted to give some idea of the mind and habits of Mr. Sherlock Holmes I may have given the impression that Holmes' interests were narrow and confined only to the criminal and to the fantastic horrors of the age, that he had little knowledge of literature or of philosophy. This was certainly the impression made upon me at the time. At that time, however, I was yet to become acquainted with my friend's habit of humor and exaggeration which allowed him to underscore and emphasize his points and deductions. He would often assume a stance or a posture that differed from his real position or opinions in order to draw out his opponent. This technique, he no doubt adopted from his experience in fencing, a sport in which he excelled. I have seen him make up the most extraordinary stories on the spur of the moment in order to temporarily delay inquiry into a point that he desired to keep obscure. This is not to say that Holmes was mendacious. Rather, I would say that he himself was often unsure of a position until he had seen it clothed in the circumstantial. In those long hours in his many cases spent in a closed room at Baker Street smoking his vile shag tobacco, he would put himself into the minds of each participant in a drama in turn and imaginatively reconstruct the crime or series of events, looking always for any illogicality or discrepancy. The genius of his method came from his ability to detach from his own point of view. This is an ability that few possess. This commentary upon his methods I introduce now in order to show that Sherlock Holmes had rather than a limited set of views in philosophy, precisely the opposite. He combined the ability of the pedantic scholar with the very widest speculations. He could at once decipher an arcane meaning in a medieval palimpsest and engage in the highest realms of comparative religion. I will go so far as to say that Holmes desired to delve into the nature of nature, the being in Being, which is to say that he wished to know not merely the great how of life but the even deeper answer to the great why! He desired to delve into motivations and purposes not merely in the human mind but in that of God. I remember being at once shocked and concerned, as a man of solid if obscure Church of England piety, when Holmes inquired in his most laconic fashion one day in Baker Street why God had bothered to create anything at all.

"Do not be shocked Watson, I mean no offense, but surely any thinking man must finally ask as do I when faced with the countless problems that come before me as a consulting detective, the ghastly human dilemmas in which the criminal destroys not merely the happiness of others but his own into the bargain, why does such a man act so? Well then, turning to the mind of God, knowing, as he surely must know the ghastly ultimate fate that would befall so many souls, to say nothing of the offense to His own Majesty, He went to the trouble to create anything at all? Let us assume a state of primal bliss in the case of the Trinity and let us further assume, as the Church teaches, that creation was not owed to us, that we had no pre-existent right to be, for surely non-being has no rights, that creation was not a diffusion of being into the realm of non-being as the neo-Platonist Plotinus asserted, but rather a sudden and gratuitous act of God. Let us, as I say, assume all of this, you see the problem: why this great disturbance of the primal unity?"

"Really Holmes," I answered at the time with some asperity, "Now you exceed the mark.   Have you no sense of the proper scope of inquiry?   Perhaps a reading of the book of Job may be in order here for you."

"Would it surprise you to hear that I have read it, my dear fellow?   I found it singularly unconvincing.   To simply beg the question and brow-beat the poor fellow into submission, bah, surely that was unfair of the author.   Wait hear me out before you object!   It is possible that God was simply saying that the mind of Job was metaphysically so constructed as to be unable to grasp so sublime a truth as that which motivates God and that the poetic imagery is meant simply to convey that fact to the audience for surely it is the audience that is addressed rather than Job.   In point of fact we are Job for we share the human condition with him and each man feels justified in his own expectations from life. Job himself need not have existed as a separate human being.   He is rather, the type of suffering humanity.   His question is the great ringing cry of Jesus from the cross, which must always chill the blood and bring a tear to the eye: "My God, My God why have you forsaken me?"

Holmes was silent for a time and I could see that he was deeply moved.   He continued quietly, "To protest against God, to wrestle with the angel, is that impiety?   I think not.   It is only in deepest anguish that our own state emerges for us as it is. The frippery and frolic of our constant efforts to hide from death fall away and we are left naked to our inevitable fate.   What is the view of the Book of Ecclesiastes then but that of a somber disillusioned Job? Ecclesiastes is the book of the weary sensualist as opposed to the man of piety. Each type of man ends, as far as this world goes, at the same fate. Alike they lie in ashes. The men of virtue and of vice all alike dissolve

224

into their constituent elements after death, but the man of God, believing that God cares, protests at this injustice and cries for rescue and vindication. Does God come? Does He come, Watson? Or, is that cry the last blind utterance of the poor vain beasts that we are?"

He was silent again and a great mist of vapors from his pipe filled the darkened corner of the room where he reposed in his great armchair.

I finally broke the silence. "What do you think?"

Holmes thought before answering. "It is always a capital mistake to theorize without data and surely in these matters no final and conclusive evidence lies at hand... But in this case perhaps even evidence is irrelevant."

I answered at the time, "Then the resurrection accounts do not impress you?"

"Of course, but I wonder if you have considered them carefully. Are they mere factual accounts to be testified to in a Court room? Does that not trivialize them? Imagine any of the witnesses being cross-examined:

"Your name is Mary Magdalene is it not?"

"Yes."

"And did you on the morning in question observe a man in the garden where Jesus had been buried?"

"I did."

"I believe that in your prior deposition you stated that you at first believed the man you saw was a gardener is that right?"

"Yes."

"But you assert that upon subsequent experience you discovered that the man was in fact Jesus whom you thought had perished on the cross days before. Is that correct, Miss Magdalene?"

225

"I recognized him."

"Yes but not at once. May I suggest that in your distress and tears and bearing in mind your own desire that he return in some manner that you could have been mistaken?"

"No, I knew it was him."

"How did you know? By his clothes, voice, manner, face? Just how did you recognize him? Are you aware that your testimony Miss Magdalene will be preserved not merely in the records of this court, but will be recorded and used as sacred scripture to ground the faith of millions in the coming years? That many will suffer martyrdom rather than deny a faith based largely on your testimony here today? Now, bearing in mind this awful responsibility, do you still persist in saying that it was Jesus you saw? Well, Miss Magdalene? Well?"

Holmes smiled and I wondered if this was all a most tasteless and even blasphemous mockery on his part. I was soon to learn that it was nothing of the sort.

"Well Watson, what shall she answer to this most persistent opposing counsel in the great courtroom of the objective mind? Shall we continue our supposed drama then? Her answer might go like this:

"I believe that it was Him. I have known him for many years and his voice and manner from constant devotion was familiar to me, so familiar that I could see Jesus in that figure in the garden... but I was told not to grasp him and to try and hold him. His life was not now such that I might restore those relations of my former manner of daily contact with him. His new life must exceed my grasp so that even I, seeing him, had to have faith that what I was seeing was real. You Mr. Cross-examiner do me a great injustice in putting the burden of my personal testimony upon me alone. In subsequent ages, those who believe will have to discern as I had to discern that morning the voice, the nature, the reality of the living Jesus in the figure that I saw. They must decide for themselves whether to believe."

"Yes, but surely you were in a unique position Miss Magdalene being at the scene; it will not be so easy with others. They will have to believe without seeing."

"But don't you see, considering the majesty of what an actual resurrection to a new life would mean and being just as anxious as I that it really and truly be Jesus whom I saw, these future ones are in the same relative position as I was compared to the event itself that morning. Was it the same Jesus or was he forever changed as are we each day by what He had gone through? He had burst not only the bonds of death but all of my previous conceptions so that it was not I who could grasp and hold Him but He who must now grasp and hold me? The new and extended Christ now present intimately and sacramentally to all, meets each of us in our own individual garden as did I that morning. Each one will care infinitely that it be Jesus because his own fate after death is at stake as was mine. Surely my own weak testimony cannot be the sole basis for such a complete commitment as they must make of all that they are because they could always doubt me and any records of my testimony. Holy Scripture is not so much dispassionate evidence as it is a sign of recognition of the inner experience of the Church reflecting upon the life that exists within it. If they wish to believe then, it must be a choice that they make on their own and with their whole being. It is the only proper proportionate response to the important and essential possibility involved in the choice. The incarnation is now complete and God has identified Himself with our state and exists within us but more we now exist within Him."

"Then you are saying, Miss Magdalene...?"

"That faith is a choice not a certainty and one not based on anything that I may say here today but based instead upon our own inner need for salvation from our intolerable present state of desolation. Each soul must cry out as Jesus did: 'My God, My God, why have you forsaken me?'"

Holmes smiled, "Our little imaginative tale ends here Watson. You will no doubt see that I have made the very argument made by the Danish Philosopher Soren Kierkegaard in his, 'Concluding Unscientific Postscript to the Philosophical Fragments,' which is that

227

truth is subjectivity. Let me merely state here that I believe that no amount of documentation or original source material would ever be adequate or immune from doubt. In this case we must appeal not to ancient but to contemporary history. The proof that Jesus was who He said He was is found in the ongoing life of the people who live that faith and their collective witness to that fact. The proof is in the Church which is the bearer of the Holy Spirit. Before that Church we poor suppliants bring our doubts and our fears and even our sins and there we find Jesus Christ in whom we believe. We believe not out of our weighing of evidence but out of our need and we can trust the structural implications of that need. Once make that primal need felt and faith becomes the only appropriate response to our human situation. There you have the book of Job in a nutshell. Job submits because he has no other viable choice and the voice he hears is, if not God's, at least his own conscience upbraiding him for calling God to answer as if in a court of law and not in his own heart."

I was duly impressed at the time by this most extraordinary recital. But I needed to speak one last concern. "Why demand so much of us though? Why is our condition so painful and lacking in certainty? Why if this is the only way to find God again is God Himself forced to undertake such extremities? But most of all Holmes what of your first question: Why did the perfect God ever create anything at all? Yet if faith in the actual resurrection must proceed without the comfort of absolute historical certainty, then surely we go too far in speculating on the motives of God prior to creation. But have you any answers to these questions?"

Holmes was now in even deeper obscurity as he smoked in the darkened room, but his incisive voice pierced the gloom of our chambers.

"The answer is in Genesis my dear fellow where it says that in each succeeding day God looked upon the results of his labors and found that they were very good. The point surely is not why God created anything but rather that having created something he pronounced that it was good. The primal unity and goodness of God was thus not compromised by creation but enhanced if we may say so by creation. God delighted in his creation. He was well pleased. And surely that

228

should be enough for us. And as to evil ... well that was a subsequent event... The rational mind may probe the simplicity of goodness for it finally makes sense, but evil? No, evil my dear fellow makes no sense, before its face we may experience only dismay. Yet evil is a subject of experience while perfect goodness in its ultimate manifestation must remain within the realm of faith alone. We must turn then from the multitudinous faces of evil to seek the loving face of God. Our cry must be one with that of Jesus: 'My God, My God, why have you forsaken me?'"

"The cry of despair of Jesus from the cross, you mean?" I answered.

"On the contrary, it was not a cry of despair. Read the Psalms! Are they not one and all a great affirmation of the love of God? That last outcry of Jesus from the cross was in fact a quotation from one of the first lines of a psalm that is one of the purest manifestations of faith. Jesus felt all of our anguish but he also posed the solution to it from the cross itself. Faith my dear Watson, the faith of the man Jesus even in the darkest of all hours... you see, our individual dilemma and that of all mankind was met by Jesus in that hour of supreme personal and collective darkness. From that hour and in that affirmation redemption comes."

I have never forgotten that early extraordinary scene in Baker Street and in its light the later writings of my companion in his journal thus far encountered and his extraordinary theological quest made ultimate sense...

Our train's circuitous route home was not chosen by accident. Holmes was anxious to avoid any possibility that we had been followed after our strange sea adventure. We had each slipped aboard the train which with its many stops seemed least likely to return us to our ultimate destination. By the time that we reached Exeter though we felt secure enough to disembark and settle in for the night at a comfortable inn not far from the university that Holmes appeared to know well.

We had succeeded beyond all odds in saving England from the incursion of the threat posed by the dreaded Asian disease that might have wrought untold harm, but what of the man, Baron Maupertius,

229

who had come so close to destroying the nation. The adventure ahead of us was surely far more dangerous than our initial encounter with his agents had been. The man who invades the cobra's den must not expect to withdraw without a struggle. Could we count upon the assistance of Professor Moriarity in what lay before us? Could a mind such as his reverse itself so readily? If a kingdom that is divided against itself cannot stand, then how might radical evil lose with alacrity one its former chief agents? Or is radical evil careless of its representatives, holding them in contempt, knowing that the ranks of evildoers are readily reinforced with new recruits? Is there a logic to evil or is evil chaotic by nature?

These were the questions that now beset me as we took the train northwards that morning that would pass through Coombe Tracey. Holmes as always kept his own counsel as to what lay ahead for us both until it was clear in his own mind. Until then I could only be patient and wait.

The train began at last to move out from the confines of the station into the fog and mist beyond which the future was as impenetrable as my own fears and apprehensions...

To be continued...

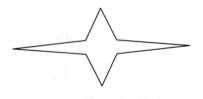

Volume One

Containing Books 1 - 3

The Confessions of Sherlock Holmes

Copyright 2014

by

Thomas Mengert, Esq.

———————

Note to the reader:

It is the intent of this writer to strengthen authentic faith rather than to undermine it by introducing difficulties that may have not hitherto entered the mind of my readers but the demands of this work include giving the furthest possible latitude to my villains to express contrary views to Catholic teaching. Nor may even Holmes claim to present an authoritative embodiment of the teaching authority and dogmas of the Church – therefore any position that any character may advocate in this work that is not in accord with Orthodox views should be read as mere hypothetical positions for the dramatic purposes of a literary work which are to be valued insofar as they confirm or illuminate the teaching of the official Magisterium and should be abandoned if they vary from that teaching in any way. Particular care should be exercised that any positions herein be abandoned if they contradict any of the strictures of the Encyclical Letter of Pope Pius X entitled Lamentabili Sane given in Rome on July 3, 1907.

Summary of the Seven Volumes
The Confessions of Sherlock Holmes

In this twin narrative the lovers of Sherlock Holmes will hear from both Holmes and Watson – from Holmes in his journals kept between 1891 and 1897 – from Watson in his ultimate account of the philosophy of Sherlock Holmes begun in 1914 and finished in 1917 during the years of the Great War to end all wars.

This is the ultimate Holmes adventure - one of over 800,000 words consisting of sixteen books plus a prologue and epilogue - now being published in seven volumes.

Volume 1

Holmes at last tells Watson the true story of what occurred between Holmes and Professor Moriarity at the Reichenbach Falls and explains that not only is Moriarity still alive but he is about to lend his aid to help Holmes and Watson to foil a daring and outrageous plot to destroy the British Empire.

Volume 2

Holmes and Watson meet their greatest foe yet in the person of the evil Dutch financier, Baron Maupertius who, to cover his plot, has had two men murdered: the Banker Abel Crosby and Cardinal Tosca of the Vatican. We also meet again Sir Henry Baskerville and learn of the kidnapping of his wife the beautiful Lady Beryl Garcia.

Volume 3

Holmes gives his account of his visit to Africa and France after leaving Tibet and Mecca. His guide on this epic hiatus which occurs between 1891 and 1894 is none other than

Professor Moriarity's second in command, Colonel Sebastian Moran!

Volume 4

In this volume the truth is finally told about Holmes' relationship with "The Woman" Irene Adler Norton of dubious and questionable memory. Holmes travels to Monte Carlo and then on to Rome where he meets the reigning Pope. At last we learn of Holmes' experiments with the coal-tar derivatives which promise to save Holmes from his life threatening disease of tuberculosis. We also meet Holmes other brother, Lord Sherringford Holmes!

Volume 5

In volume five Holmes and Professor Moriarity resolve the great issues that have long stood between them in an epic battle of wits to resolve once and for all the problem of evil and the nature of God.

Volume 6

In order to defeat Baron Maupertius, Holmes and Watson travel to America where they meet Theodore Roosevelt, President McKinley, and the great Speaker of the House of Representatives, Thomas Brackett Reed. They must convince the Americans to build the Panama Canal!

Volume 7

After leaving Washington, D.C. Holmes and Watson travel to San Francisco by way of Wounded Knee in the Dakotas. While staying at Cliff House they meet Adolph Sutro the Mayor of San Francisco and the builder of the famed Sutro Tunnel on the Nevada Comstock silver lode. This concludes their epic adventure before returning by ship to England.